THREADS of CHANGE

THREADS of CHANGE
A Quilting Story
Part 1

Jodi Barrows

Moody Publishers

CHICAGO

Edited by Sandra Bricker
Interior design: Ragont Design
Author photo: Holly Paulson / Sillyheads Photography
Cover design: LeVan Fisher Design
Cover photography: Steve Gardner, Pixelworks Studio and
                   Vilnis Lauzurns, Shutterstock

Library of Congress Cataloging-in-Publication Data

Barrows, Jodi.
Threads of change : a quilting story. Part 1 / Jodi Barrows.
   p. cm.
ISBN 978-0-8024-0937-9
1. Domestic fiction. I. Title.
PS3602.A83735T57 2013
813'.6--dc23
                      2013014970

This is a work of fiction. Names, characters, places, and incidents either are the
product of the author's imagination or are used fictitiously, and any resemblance
to actual persons, living or dead, businesses, companies, events, or locales is entirely coincidental.

We hope you enjoy this book from River North Fiction by Moody Publishers.
Our goal is to provide high-quality, thought-provoking books and products that
connect truth to your real needs and challenges. For more information on other
books and products written and produced from a biblical perspective, go to
www.moodypublishers.com or write to:

River North Fiction
Imprint of Moody Publishers
820 N. LaSalle Boulevard
Chicago, IL 60610

1 3 5 7 9 10 8 6 4 2

Printed in the United States of America

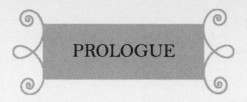

PROLOGUE

LECOMPTE, LOUISIANA
SPRING 1856

Elizabeth stepped out onto the wooden porch surrounding her home and surveyed the budding spring color peeking through tree branches. Evening had turned to night and her much loved family had all gone to bed. She stood near the steps and leaned against a pillar as flickers of lightning collided with the night sky. A storm brewed in the distance and she could smell the imminent rain.

This porch had always been her favorite thinking spot. She had spent many evenings watching the approaching storms. Tonight, she moved deeper into her thoughts, letting the sprinkle of rain relax her. She loved this place like a family member. How could she go off and leave it, never to return? If she believed her grandfather, she could leave it now under her own terms or lose it later in the conflict of a civil war. She trusted this man who had raised her, but it hurt so badly inside. So many changes to yield to, none of which she liked.

A sudden boom of thunder shook her from her thoughts, and the lightning lit up the property before her. Her grandfather's timber mill sat along the edge of the river among the ageless, majestic oak trees. Those mighty giants growing along with a few magnolia trees created a path to the house with its pointy, gabled roofline and wraparound porch.

Elizabeth inhaled long and hard in an effort to breathe in her surroundings. She wanted her home to seep deeper into her soul. This spirited Southern woman didn't want to forget any detail of her beloved Louisiana home.

The almost-full moon drifted behind the storm clouds as they blanketed the timber mill. A raccoon clicked his forest call and the cool wind of the storm called out goosebumps on Elizabeth. She tightened her arms as if to hold herself together. A single tear slid down her cheek and stopped under her chin like a raindrop on the brink of a rooftop. Her thoughts drifted back over the years, moving like thick threads through memories of the timber mill and what it meant to her family.

Generations ago, her great-grandfather settled on this land. He had brought his bride here, and Elizabeth's Grandpa Lucas was born in this very house. Grandpa Lucas married and raised his daughters and one son at this timber mill. Elizabeth was just six years old, her sister Megan just two, when they came to live at this big white house. The Riverton Timber Mill had been passed down through the generations.

To sell out and move on is unthinkable.

Elizabeth's fingers worked slowly to release her long blonde hair from its thick braid. The dampness of the night curled a few locks framing the smooth features of her face. Tears stung her dark blue eyes as she watched the raindrops hop around on the steps before running together and forming a puddle under the magnolia tree. She shifted back from the pillar and leaned on the porch railing. Memorizing every part of this home, she reached out to touch a thick waxy leaf on the tree, admiring the beautiful blossoms that had opened to the size of dinner plates. The fragrance radiated over the porch, filling the night air with its calming power.

Tears fell freely as the reality of leaving Riverton set in, but the storm covered her sobs. She hated for anyone to see her weakness. For a moment, the moon peeked out from between the clouds, as if to say it saw her tears. She batted at them and hid them on her apron. The rain began to move on, but Elizabeth continued to brood at the rumbling night sky.

In the quiet darkness of the kitchen, behind the screen door, she caught a glimpse of Grandpa Lucas as he looked out at Elizabeth and bowed his head to pray.

CHAPTER 1

Aprils in Lecompte, Louisiana, were spectacular, especially after a spring rain. New life was bursting forth with the world full of rainbow colors and delightful fragrances. The days could be long and lingering and the mugginess heavy, but it was all worth it in the beautiful countryside.

Liz sat across from her grandfather in the comfortable parlor. The essence of gardenias and magnolias floated through the open window and filled the room with their sweet scents. The curtains fluttered and hung on the breeze.

She always felt secure and calm with her grandfather. Even at his advanced age, he still seemed strong as an ox. He stood tall, with a thick chest and a heart of gold. His thick gray hair and whiskered chin gave him a ruggedly handsome look.

With a smile that reflected the wisdom of many years, Grandpa Lucas took his work-worn hands and patted her small ones.

"So our decision has been made?"

It was a statement as much as a question. He looked at his granddaughter, and she remained silent. Liz had made her decision the night before while standing on the white porch as the rain poured down. But could she live up to it now? She knew her attitude would set the mood for all the other women. This plan had been in the making for quite some time and wasn't new to any of them. But now, as the time grew closer and closer, she felt unsure. She had just lost her husband, Caleb, and now would be leaving her home too.

"Liz, I firmly believe this is the right thing to do. We will look back and be pleased with our decision."

Lucas Mailly had always treated the women in his family with respect and allowed them to voice their opinions. He encouraged their education and urged them to become leaders among their peers. He would never have forced any of this change on them.

Liz spoke softly and looked at his loving hands covering hers. "So do I. I'm ready to start planning and packing," she said as she smiled at her grandfather, reassuring him with her choice. "We can be ready in a few weeks."

Lucas stood up and faced the fireplace, his back to her. His hand went to the painting of his Claire up on the mantel and quickly moved to his face, making a rough sound on his cheek as an unexpected tear slid over the whiskers. This decision to leave, now upon them quickly, hit him unexpectedly.

Although he had turned away from her, Liz noticed as he wiped away the unwelcome tear, not meant to be seen by her. She blinked back a tear of her own and took a quick breath to steady herself. Trying to think of something to break the silence, she cheerfully said, "I got another letter from Abby and Emma yesterday. They received our letter and are coming with us! But their cousin Sadie won't be traveling with us. Sounds like her father told her no."

Liz knew that Grandpa Lucas Mailly had never been fond of the man who married his daughter. The Wilkes family owned a large plantation in Mississippi with many slaves. They had an arrogant nature about them and Lucas always felt they abused the women too. Katherine, his youngest daughter, had become a different woman after she married John and moved away to the Wilkes brothers' plantation. He didn't seem too surprised about Sadie not coming, and Liz knew he hadn't been quite sure how his other two granddaughters could get away with leaving, but he'd been excited nevertheless with their decision to go.

Her grandfather had explained that he wanted to protect his family from the growing unrest in the South, and he felt it better to sell his timber mill now than to lose it in a skirmish. His son-in-law wouldn't listen to him about selling out the Mississippi plantation and he called him a "crazy man."

"Well, it's just as well that Sadie isn't coming. You may not realize it, Liz, but not all females are like you and your sister. Sadie could hold you back, even be a problem. Your cousins are not as strong as you and your sister."

Liz blushed and answered, "It will be fine, Grandpa. I don't want you to worry over it. Abby and Emma will be just fine with it all."

She had grown accustomed to his praise and encouragement, well aware that women were treated differently in other families, and in the world in general.

Abby and Emma had confided in her and Megan about their father's ways. They were going West, with or without their father's blessings. But he was finished with the two rebellious daughters and more than ready to wash his hands of them. If their Grandpa Lucas wanted them, so be it.

Lucas paused, and Liz recognized the weighing of his words. "Liz, I know these last few months have been difficult. Caleb was a good man and a good husband. He was just like a son to me. And Luke isn't little any more. He has grown into a fine young man." Lucas covered his mouth and whiskers with his hand, holding his chin.

Liz spoke up. "Yes, this brings a thought to me. I've been thinking that Luke needs to stay here at the mill to work and go to school and . . . if Caleb is found . . ."

"Sweetheart," Lucas interrupted, "you know Caleb is gone. He won't be found. We all saw the accident at the mill. You've got to accept that he is not going to find his way back here." His hands rested on her shoulders as he lovingly but firmly spoke. "We have to move on. This thinking isn't good, Liz. I know you know that."

His eyes searched hers for a positive reaction. She blinked and shrugged. "It's just easier."

With a sense of urgency she stepped aside, brushed her skirt, and straightened her shoulders. She wouldn't let her emotions get the best of her. For almost a year, she had been a weeping widow. The timber mill accident never strayed far from her mind and she hated the sense of losing herself to the horrible nightmare. She'd been drifting for months, and she wanted to take control of her life again. Her mind and heart demanded something else; selling the mill and making a move seemed to provide that. Luke had grown up so much over the past months and had grown even closer to his namesake, Grandpa Lucas.

The process of planning the move nudged the sadness away. Liz wanted and needed a new beginning, and the lurking trouble in the South was just the push to get her started.

Her dear cousins coming along would make it fun as they embarked on this adventure together, all of them starting a new chapter. New fortunes were ready to be made, the developing western territories ripe for the picking. The tremors of unrest in the South shook louder and longer, and they made her Grandpa Lucas even antsier to get his plan into action.

"Are you sure about Luke going west with us? It could be quite dangerous. I would feel so much calmer if he were here, safe with you. Who will see after you?" Liz gave a sneaky smile, trying to coax him to her way of thinking. She wanted the only two men in her life safe, away from the uncertainty before her.

"I can't leave the mill and property until the sale is final. It could be months before I catch up to you." He swayed back and forth as he pondered Liz's request.

"Luke misses his dad, and he's so content with you."

He stepped closer to her. "Sweetheart, keeping Luke here won't stop him from getting hurt, and it won't bring Caleb back. I know it's easier to just think of him as being away, but . . . " His loving blue eyes embraced her tightly. "You know if he were alive he would have come back to us. The war is coming, we have a buyer for the mill, and it is a wise decision to go west. It's not going to get any better for the South. With each election, the western expansion licks at the heels of the unrest. I've never had slaves at the mill, so some of it has eluded us, but nevertheless, we will get caught up in it."

"Sorry. These senseless tears, I'm so tired of them," Liz admitted, pulling a lace hanky from her pocket to wipe her eyes. Grandpa Lucas stepped back and ran his hand across a wet spot on her cheek as Liz noticed Luke standing in the doorway. She would never forget what Caleb looked like as long as she had her son.

Her grandfather followed Liz's gaze to the doorway where Luke stood straight as an arrow, his messy sun-streaked hair falling over his eyes.

Luke glared at Lucas as he pleaded, "Tell me you won't let that happen, Grandpa. Tell me!"

Liz searched her memory for the part of the conversation that had angered her son. "You promised. You both said I was going west with the wagons!"

Grandpa Lucas's expression told Liz he would handle the situation. "Yes, we are still considering all of the possibilities that lie ahead, Luke. The plans are still in the works. We know what you want and will consider that along with everything else." He patted Luke's shoulder as he walked through the doorway, finalizing the conversation.

"Good," Luke huffed, his face flushed. "I thought I might have to go joining up with those Yankees!"

Lucas never turned around as he let out a big belly laugh, grabbed Luke by the suspenders, and pulled him out the door with him.

Liz watched the two of them from the window as they continued to tease each other. She laughed. "Joinin' the union?"

As they disappeared, she sank into a parlor chair. The sweet fragrance of flowers drifted across the room, reminding her to water them. Her eyes landed on the green Irish chain quilt she had made for Caleb as a surprise anniversary gift. That quilt—and her son—had been the only things to get her out of bed each morning after Caleb died. She had made it for their thirteenth wedding anniversary, and somehow the fabric squares held all of the joy and excitement of her married life. The quilt represented a celebration of their future together, her grief for the loss of her husband woven into every stitch .

Liz closed her eyes and dropped her head to the back of the chair. In an instant, she wafted back to the day that had changed her life.

The gray and gloomy day in May of 1855 had begun with clouds swirling. The rain left everything waterlogged and cold. It was the sort of day where something feels bound to happen; the sort of day where life's brittleness is prodded from its sleeping place and made to crawl to the surface and roar for a while, out in the open.

The air didn't feel quite right, and Liz recalled thinking that the rain seemed too . . . wet. She sat in the parlor, working on her most recent quilting project, the one she'd named CALEB'S CHOICE, when Luke crashed into the house, calling, "Mom, Mom, come quick!"

"What is it?"

"It's Dad. He's fallen into the logs."

The saturated grass looked limp and lifeless as she rushed to the mill, her mind racing as the wind blew fiercely against her progress. Trees bent. Leaves clung. Horrible thoughts and possibilities pulsed like the intense rain against her face.

"A horse to slide, a dock to fall," she'd said to herself as she approached the mill and waterway.

As always, they'd fallen behind on the timber orders. Grandpa Lucas and Caleb worked long and hard every day, never demanding more from their workers than they themselves were willing to give.

Rain-soaked and muddy, she stood there with her hair pressed to her head. She watched the mill workers standing in silence with faces completely baffled and afraid.

"He's gone, Liz. We couldn't reach him," Grandpa Lucas had confessed.

"I'm sorry, Liz; I couldn't get to him in time," Thomas, Caleb's best friend, had cried in disbelief.

Their words still shot through her like the heavy bullets from a steel pistol. She'd looked away and fallen to the ground. No one revealed how long it had been between that moment and the one where she awoke in her own bed. Maybe days had passed. She recalled that the sun had broken through, leaving the property dry and the grass a brilliant green. She'd glanced down to find Luke asleep across the end of the bed. Her sister Megan sat in a chair that hugged the side of the bed as she threaded a needle with embroidery floss.

The clopping of horses' hooves jolted Liz back to the present, her hands still shaking and damp with perspiration. She peered through the parlor window. Workers from the mill unloaded wooden crates and old cloths for packing.

On the other side of the parlor, Caleb's completed quilt rested over the back of a small chair. She walked over to it and brought it close to her face, hoping to smell Caleb on the quilt, even though he had never used it. She ran her hand over the sewn patches of tans, reds, and greens that represented their namesake.

Caleb would have loved this quilt, she thought.

Each piece and every stitch had come to memorialize his life with her. And now that completed quilt announced the final chapter of their book as well.

CHAPTER 2

Luke had turned twelve, and Liz would reach her thirty-second birthday that summer. She'd been a widow for almost a full year. Several Southern gentlemen had made their courting desires known to Grandpa Lucas. He'd even tried to convince her to see Doc Gaither. He was handsome and agreeable enough, she supposed, but Liz loved Caleb. She missed his smile, and the two freckles on his ear.

Across the hall, the bustle of Megan's treadle machine brought Liz to the doorway. She watched as Megan sewed pieces on the new treadle. Petite, with dark and shiny straight hair, Megan had hazy green eyes, big and intent, their gaze revealing her passionate nature; playful and happy. She pedaled the machine hard, her shoulders even with the movement of the machine, her hair swaying this way and that as she pushed through the quilt top of vibrant creams, reds, and blues.

Darkness had begun to roll in, and Liz knew she'd have to light the lamp for the evening. She didn't like Megan to work by lamplight. With so much shifting and motion, she feared the lamp might fall and start a fire. Megan slowed the motion of the treadle wheel and looked up at her.

"I think Luke will probably go with us when we leave for Texas," Liz said.

"What happened? I thought you were against it," Megan commented.

"I told him that Grandpa and I would consider it. But now that I think of it, we could use him."

"I've thought so all along, really."

Megan adjusted the fabric under the needle of her treadle. She had taken to the new machine immediately. Learning the difference in hand piecing and treadle sewing hadn't troubled her one bit.

"What happened a little while ago with Luke?" she asked.

"He overheard us discussing whether he would go with us or not. He got mad and said he would join the Union Army if we forbade him to come."

They shared a giggle at Luke's idea.

"I know it is safer for him here, Liz, but I do think it would be better if he went with us. He can even go to school there." Megan brightened suddenly. "Oh, Liz! I didn't tell you. I got a letter today from Pastor Parker and his wife."

"You did? I must've been sleeping. Did you read it?"

"Yes, I did. By fall, they'll have the church prepared for holding classes, and they want Abby to teach there!"

"Oh, Meggie, that's wonderful."

"Yes, they're preparing a classroom in an extra room of the church. I can't wait to tell her."

"She will be delighted. Did they say when to expect them?"

"Their stage should arrive late Thursday afternoon."

"I must say, Meggie, I'm growing rather excited about our journey."

"Me, too."

"I wonder if Abby and Emma are as well."

"Oh, they must be!"

A wagon jangled as it rolled away from the house, dust trailing just behind. Liz watched as two lanterns dangled from the side posts of the wagon, realizing she must have dozed for longer than she'd expected.

"Where are the Lukes off to?" Megan asked.

"Grandpa wanted to take Luke for one final fishing trip. And they prefer to fish at night. Grandpa says that's when most of the fish are caught."

"Oh, maybe we'll have catfish for supper."

They shared a laugh without verbalizing their usual joke about whether or not there were any fish left to be caught in that pond at all.

"Is that Granny's pattern?" Liz asked, and Megan nodded.

They gazed at the cotton top, a lovely, pieced appliqué quilt with nine beautiful flower blocks. The various triangles had been meticulously stitched together so that the corners ran smooth and flat against the borders. "This is beautiful! I simply adore this pattern. Do you remember the one she made with pastel fabrics and paisley border? Granny always loved appliqué."

Liz traced her fingers over the seams and down its edges. She'd always felt that quilts were made to be touched. It was part of the process. Love poured from her fingertips, circling through the quilt and straight back into her.

"Yes, I do. It was very pretty," Megan replied.

"You've finished so quickly, Meggie. It looks wonderful. You've become quick friends with this machine."

"Thank you." Megan glowed. "I would like to have this one in its frame by morning."

"Oh! Well, I can't wait to see it quilted. I can help if you'd like."

"I imagine that Abby and Emma will want to help as well." Megan started the pedal moving again.

Megan hovered over the treadle and concentrated on the needle as Liz peered out the window at the red dusk-shadowed barn.

"Liz, do you think you will ever remarry?"

The question caught her by surprise. "I don't know. I don't want to be a widow, but I don't feel like I could right now. I just . . . want Caleb to come home. I know he won't, but I just have to hang on to that thread of hope that maybe he just might. Not seeing the accident," she said, and then paused and bit her lip. "Not seeing a body just makes me wonder or hope that he's out there somewhere, trying to find us." She shrugged her shoulder. "Silly."

Megan sighed, and Liz felt her sympathetic affection. But the matchmaker in her sister seemed always at the ready.

"Have you thought about Thomas?"

"Caleb's best friend?" She dipped her eyebrows at the thought. "Thomas, as a suitor? No, not really. Isn't he like family?"

"Yes, we already know him." She paused. "You've both lost Caleb, Liz." Megan's interest no longer remained fixed on her sewing, but on her sister.

Liz squirmed a little. "Is that what we would start a relationship with? Our grief?"

"Well, maybe it does sound silly now, but think about it." Megan paused for a moment. "I think Thomas wants to see you as more than a family friend."

"What?" Liz blushed. "Now, who is being silly?"

"Pay attention, Liz. He lingers sometimes, and he watches you constantly."

Liz did remember some longer looks from Thomas, but she'd always attributed it to his concern for her.

"I don't know, Megan. It's too soon."

"Are you going to be a widow for the rest of your life? You're past the required six months of mourning."

Liz looked at her sister sharply.

"I'm sorry. I didn't mean to hurt your feelings. Just think about it, Liz." Teasing her sister into a smile, Megan added, "Thomas is a catch, you know, and our lovely cousins will be here in a few days."

❊ ❊ ❊

Liz placed Caleb's quilt at the foot of her bed, and it dipped down and touched the wooden floor. She smoothed it with her hand, fixing the wrinkles she had made from sleeping the night before.

She glanced at the empty side of the bed and contemplated what Megan suggested about Thomas.

Perhaps I should speak with him, she thought. *I wouldn't want him to get the wrong idea.*

The sound of horses brought Liz to the front porch, and Megan arrived at the same time. They looked out over the railing as six wooden wagons met in the yard and in front of the barn. The mill workers unloaded empty crates and boxes of sawdust from the mill.

The late afternoon felt quite muggy from the previous night's rain. Springtime in Louisiana always brought with it a hot spell. The daytime air remained damp and heavy. Today, however, seemed especially humid. Liz ran her hand across her neck. The back of her dress stuck to her shoulders.

"Miss Elizabeth. Miss Megan. Good afternoon," Thomas said in full stride as he approached the steps.

"Good afternoon," they said politely.

"We're unloading your packing crates," Thomas said.

"Thank you. We are ready to start packing," Megan said, inspecting the crates from a distance.

"Yes, we also brought the sawdust to pack your breakables for the trip."

"Thank you. That was thoughtful," Liz replied, and she suddenly found herself looking at Thomas in a way she never had before.

Thomas's muscles rippled under his snug shirt, and he held a quiet confidence that boosted his attractiveness. The neutral-colored trousers fell over his boot tops.

Liz suddenly realized she was looking him over from head to toe, and she scolded herself, afraid her thoughts might show up on her blushing face. "It was just as easy to bring the wagons, too. Everything is ready."

"When will more of the horses arrive?" Megan asked.

"Most likely, in a few days."

Grandpa Lucas motioned to Megan from the side of one of the wagons. She gave a polite gesture to Thomas and hastily walked down the stairs to meet him. They exchanged whispers and looked over to the couple standing in silence under the porch. Try as she might, Liz couldn't avoid their scrutiny.

Grandpa Lucas wanted nothing more than for Liz to be happy, she knew that. And he had always been quite partial to Thomas. More than twenty years ago, his wife Claire and their young son had died, and her grandfather had never remarried.

It's different for a man though, she thought.

Grandpa Lucas had the mill and the farm and two granddaughters to look after. His Claire could never be replaced, although he had never really looked. Not too long ago, however, Liz and Megan told him about a widow his age who lived just outside of town. The woman had made it known that she was interested in Lucas, but he seemed insulted by the mere thought of it. Afterward, he stopped going to any of the church socials that she attended.

"Nonsense!" he had called it.

"Thomas," Liz said, all of a sudden uncomfortable standing next to him alone. "I suppose I should let you know something."

Thomas focused his gaze and listened anxiously. His silent attention somehow made her uneasy though, and she quickly lost her words. She had never felt this way with Thomas before.

"Oh," she mumbled.

He seemed to sense her nervousness, and he moved closer.

Liz took a sudden small step backward to avoid him. Her foot searched for a stair behind her. A board creaked under the weight of her foot and startled her. She tried to adjust her footing, but her balance shifted on the top step. Somehow, she lost control of her feet and her hands and arms rummaged desperately for a post, a column, anything to steady herself.

I'm going to fall. The words dashed through her mind.

And flat on her fanny she fell!

As she hit the ground, a burst of laughter erupted from the yard. Everyone had seen the whole embarrassing ordeal. She looked up at Thomas, and he and the mill workers burst with laughter. After a moment, all she could do was join them. She was sick of crying, after all.

"Nothing to see here, nothing to see," Thomas said, waving his arms at everyone and trying to be funny while removing the attention from Liz.

"Ahh, are you all right?" Grandpa Lucas asked, rushing over to help her stand.

"Yes, yes. I'm fine. Just wounded my pride. I don't know what is wrong with me."

"Lizzie," Megan teased. "Did someone move the porch?"

Another small burst of laughter erupted among the bystanders. Liz smiled and tried to act busy dusting the ground off her dress. She had needed a good laugh and she really wasn't hurt.

The timber mill workers, pleased with the disturbance that had interrupted their work, walked back to the wagons with smiles and recaps of the incident with a "*Didyousee*," and an "*Andthenshe*" before they all laughed.

"Are you okay?" Thomas asked now with everyone gone.

"Yes, I'm fine."

"Good, I didn't mean to cause that . . . if I did."

"Would you like some currant tea?" Liz asked with a tilt of her head, clearly letting Thomas know she was changing the topic.

"Please, I'm quite thirsty." He smiled back at her.

"Okay, I'll bring it to you on the porch."

When she returned from the kitchen, the front yard bustled again with mill workers and wagons, unloading and preparing to leave for the day. Liz and Thomas sat on the porch sipping currant tea, both of them seemingly somehow pleased by being separated from it all. Liz felt mischievous for it, like they should be working but weren't.

※　※　※

Luke sat hunched over the porch steps with the catfish fillets he had recently caught and cleaned. They awaited breading before Liz cooked them, and the barn cats hovered about, awaiting their chance to have a taste of the leftovers.

"Would you like to stay for dinner?" Liz inquired. "We're having catfish."

"I can see that. Catfish sounds delicious." Thomas sent Luke a pleasing smile.

"Great then, I think Grandpa would like to discuss some things about the trip with you." Liz gathered her thoughts, preparing to change the subject. "I want you to know I've really appreciated all that you've done for us, for Luke and the mill and everything."

"I've enjoyed working for your grandfather. He's a good man." Liz's hands wrapped tightly around her tea glass. "I'm going to put the marker on the hill for Caleb in the morning. Would you like to come with me?"

Liz hadn't wanted an empty casket for Caleb, or a memorial service. Anytime it had been mentioned, she firmly shut it down. But now that they planned to leave, she felt the time had come to do so.

"It would honor me," Thomas said, and he seemed surprised at Liz putting a finality to Caleb's death.

Before either could speak again, Megan appeared from the house.

"Li-zee," Megan interrupted from inside as she stepped out onto the porch with cornmeal on her hands. "Oh, sorry! I didn't know you were out here, Thomas," she said. "Well, dinner will be ready soon. But could you give me a hand, Liz? I need your help with something." She winked.

"Yes, I'll be right in," Liz said, wondering what her sister was up to now.

"Thomas, are you staying for dinner?" Grandpa Lucas asked merrily as he approached the front steps.

Liz intervened, "Yes, he is."

"Good then, we've got so much catfish we could never eat it all."

"Mom, is Thomas staying for dinner tonight?" Luke asked excitedly.

"Yes, honey, he's staying for dinner." Liz wondered if anyone at all had paid attention to what had been happening on the porch.

Liz walked into the house with Luke straggling just behind with the catfish in hand. Thomas and Grandpa Lucas lingered on the front porch, looking out at the dusky sky. The sun dipped down below the trees, just beginning to settle for the night, and magnificent pinks, reds, and oranges smeared the blue sky through the clouds and final beams of sunlight. The locusts sang their low whine from tree to tree.

※　※　※

"What an incredible sunset," Lucas suggested while chewing the stem of his tobacco-less pipe. Thomas recalled him saying that the general store happened to be out of his brand, and he hated Lyon tobaccos.

"It is especially incredible tonight, isn't it?"

"Mm-hmm," Grandpa Lucas said, in a form of masculine agreement.

A long silence lingered, but Thomas figured silence was quite the norm for men standing on a porch together. They were just more comfortable with the idea of silence. It wasn't at all awkward.

"Well," Lucas said, breaking the silence. "I have been thinking some, and I must say that I don't feel completely at ease with sending my granddaughters alone on this trip. I just don't like the idea." He paused for a moment. "I've made plans for them to have an escort part of the way, with the Rangers from Texas, but I'm still not eased by this."

"I can understand that. I think it's normal, sir."

"The reason I'm telling you this, Thomas, is because I would like for you to go along with them and be their escort."

Thomas paused for a moment, thinking about what to say. "And this would make you at ease . . . if I went along with them?"

Lucas chuckled and pulled out his pipe to examine it. He had a contagious laugh, and Thomas couldn't help but laugh along with him. Though, he wasn't sure what about.

"Thomas, I don't think anything would ease my mind completely, but it would help to know you were there."

Thomas understood the old man's feelings.

"But I also know the ladies, and Luke too, would want for you to go rather than any of the other millworkers."

"I see."

"So, what do you say? You can think about it some if you'd like . . ."

"I'll do it then, sir." Thomas blurted out his answer with excitement, offering his hand to Lucas. They shook hands firmly.

"Dinner is ready!" Megan called from the door. Even though she had a comb in her hair, it swung with every feisty movement.

"Wonderful, I'm hungry," Lucas said, placing his hand around the back of Thomas's shoulder. "Let's go eat. We can discuss the details later."

※　　※　　※

Dawn had a hard time breaking through the fog the next morning. Liz could barely see the corner of the barn from the house with its red outline poking out through the muddled mistiness. The fog had a way of filtering out any distant noises until they drew near so, when Thomas's wagon showed up in the yard, the sudden jolt of the horse announced his arrival.

A large wooden marker and two shovels lay in the wagon bed, along with about ten feet of rope. Liz didn't know the purpose of the rope; but it was always in the wagon.

"Good morning!" Thomas called as he stepped down. "How are you?"

"Good morning. I'm fine; a little tired, however," Liz admitted. She hadn't slept well the night before.

Liz had decided to put the marker on the "bodiless" grave. She'd never wanted to before, but she felt she needed to do it before they left their home behind. Caleb's marker would rest on the hill where Claire and other family members had been buried. Her husband needed to be remembered.

Thomas brushed something from the horse as he said, "Sure is foggy. Are you sure you want to do this today?"

"Yes, we need to," she replied, looking around as though she might manage a glimpse through the fog.

Thomas helped Liz up into the wagon and they went on their way toward the hill where the family gravesite sat. On the way, the little lives that thrived only at night scurried around, not yet aware that morning had arrived, the sun to follow soon. A dull green bullfrog waited in a scummy waterhole, croaking out its prayer for catching some breakfast before daylight blew his cover, and little field mice scampered about gathering seeds of their own. The birds hadn't yet warmed up for the chirps that would announce the day.

On a clearer day, the mill might have been seen next to the river when traveling along the main road. Standing on the slope behind it under the cover of fog were small cabins where some of the millworkers stayed; at least the ones that didn't live out in Lecompte or Meeker, just a few minutes from the mill. The barn and stable where the horses, chickens, and Belle, the very old cow who had outlived two coats of milk paint on the barn, all lived, stood farther up the path and closer to the house.

Liz and Thomas rode along in silence until they reached the small graveyard, Thomas jumped down and immediately helped her down from the wagon. He grabbed the larger shovel and began digging a hole in which to place the marker. Liz watched from the sideline, first trying to lean against the wooden wheel. She quickly gave up and decided to pick some wildflowers to tie on the cross instead.

Thomas carried the wooden marker from the back of the wagon to the grassy area, inspecting the coat of paint along the way. He had constructed the large pine cross months ago at Luke's request, and he'd carefully applied a couple coats of white paint. Liz's heart squeezed slightly as Thomas grabbed a square marker for the base of the cross and set it into place.

To a true friend;
We will miss you.
To a father who fathered honorably;
You won't be forgotten.
To a husband who loved faithfully;
Your memory will never fade from our hearts.

Thomas carefully packed dirt all the way around its base and then secured the square marker to the bottom of the cross before standing back to examine his work.

Liz thought he probably felt obligated to say something, so he decided to recite the words from the epitaph that he had painted on the marker. Afterward, silence shrouded them again. They both just stood there, looking down at the newly placed marker, each of them remembering Caleb in their own way. It felt so lonely to Liz without Caleb that she thought she might scream. Fighting back the urge to cry, Liz placed the flowers on the ground and walked back to the wagon, ready to be done with this. When she glanced back at him, Thomas still knelt silently beside the marker. And he was crying.

She knew Thomas still held a heavy burden for Caleb's death. Liz knew he had risked his life jumping into the rushing water to try and rescue Caleb, and she felt she could never repay him for it. Caleb's childhood friend had been willing to give his life in order to save her husband.

After a moment, Thomas stood up, cleared his throat, and placed his shovel in the rear of the wagon.

"Thank you, Thomas," Liz said, "for everything you've done. I can never tell you how grateful I am."

Thomas nodded his head without really looking at her.

They slowly loaded up again and were on their way, both glancing back at the memorial as they rode past. Silence followed them, and neither noticed when the morning fog finally lifted. By the time they got home, the sun shone brightly, not a single cloud to be found in the sky.

CHAPTER 3

Liz imagined the stagecoach bouncing recklessly along the rocky, rutted road that led the way to a whole new life for her cousins. She pictured Abby and Emma trying for two solid days to sit upright in the leather seats, and she knew Emma would have given up long before Abby. After endlessly pricking her fingers as she stitched, Emma would have folded up her work and placed it back into her sewing pouch while Abby stared at the same two pages of her book for miles upon miles.

Abby, the schoolteacher, sat tall in her seat—in Liz's imagination anyway—looking almost as fresh as the day they left. Emma, on the other hand, likely felt all five days of wear. Dirty, tired, and longing to arrive at their destination.

Part of Abby's decision to go west with her grandfather had been Emma's rebellious disposition. Tensions had been so heavy back at home that Liz wondered if Emma had even told her father goodbye. Abby had written that she hoped Emma might come into her own during their adventure.

Abby, calm, composed, and patient, had always seemed to occupy the flip side of Emma's coin. She never blurted out any words for which she had to later apologize or try to take back; Emma, on the other hand, seemed to explode at times. She often slammed doors and spilled out things she didn't really mean. They were so different in every way, from looks to attitudes to dreams.

Liz and Megan stood anxiously, fidgeting about in their puffy dresses, both of them burgeoning with anticipation, wiggling much more than two grown ladies should. Liz felt a little silly for it, but she couldn't help herself. Grandpa Lucas had dropped them off at the general store earlier, then parked the wagon nearby.

"I see the stage," Megan called out with girlish excitement. Liz jumped a little as Megan squeezed her hand a little too hard.

Liz pulled back slightly. "Megan!"

"Oh, sorry."

"There it is! I see it now!" Liz said, pointing as the stage pulled to a stop.

She caught sight of Abby and Emma looking out the stagecoach window, and Megan sprung into action as she rushed to the stage. Liz scurried close behind, both of them holding up the edges of their dresses so they wouldn't trip as they hurried. The stagecoach door opened and the Wilkes sisters stepped down to the dirt road, dust still swirling about. Their Sunday dresses looked slightly wrinkled, but the hats pinned on their heads sat perched straight and proper. With tired smiles, the girls greeted the others with joyous hugs.

"You look wonderful." Liz spoke first, her arm around Abby. "But I'm sure you're both exhausted from your travels."

The commotion from the women drew the attention of bystanders. Some smiled, and a few gentlemen tipped their hats as the four women bustled up the steps. As the ladies chatted and hugged for the third or fourth time, Grandpa Lucas and Chet, one of the millworkers, grabbed the trunks and carpet bags, loading them into the wagon. Each man moved back and forth, taking several loads. When they finally finished, the two men exchanged big smiles.

"How many granddaughters are we picking up?" Chet asked.

Grandpa Lucas looked at the loaded wagon and shook his head. Finally, he slapped Chet on the back and said, "See ya in a while."

Lucas's four granddaughters held up traffic on the boardwalk, all of them chattering at once, but all of them keeping up with every

conversation. Abby and Emma both kissed their grandfather and
thanked him.

Emma looked deeply at her grandfather, as if she wanted to etch
every detail about him in her mind. Liz smiled as she watched them.
Grandpa Lucas still looked spry for a man of his age; the repayment for
a lifetime's uncompromising work, she supposed. He had many years
ahead of him, simply because he refused to quit. Even now, he still put
out nearly the same amount of work as he did in his prime.

Liz loved the twinkle in his eyes and his big smile. Lucas Mailly was
a man of risk and reached for what he wanted. It was contagious and Liz
wanted it, too.

"You ladies go on down to the bakery and take your time. When
you're ready, Chet and I will drive you home."

Liz chatted happily with her sister and cousins as they strolled down
the sidewalk to Granny Smith's Tea Room and Bakery. Abby and Emma
looked about the town of Lecompte and seemed intrigued by it. The
wheels of passing wagons crunched over the small rocks covering the
street. Horses were tied to most every hitching post. They stomped their
hooves and swished their tails, snickering and snorting in the hope of
attracting attention and receiving a treat. A brown horse with random
white spots made eye contact with Liz, watching her as the girls strolled
along. He let out a stern huff and stamped his hoof.

Emma stopped and rubbed the horse's velvet nose. She had always
loved horses. Liz recalled Isaac, the stable hand at her cousins' plantation,
teaching them how smart horses were and how they never forgot a person's kindness; or lack thereof. Emma winked at the horse and hurried
to catch up with the others. She looped her arm through Liz's as they
stopped in front of a large glass shop window.

⁂ ⁂ ⁂

Chet strolled down the wooden sidewalk up ahead of them, the
nailed planks beneath his feet creaking as he walked. Liz caught him
watching after the rustle of their four long skirts as they swished toward
the tearoom. He stepped off the boardwalk and pulled out his handker-

chief, folding it carefully and then dipping the end of it into the horse trough. He wiped his face and neck and put the damp cloth into his back pocket. As the girls headed into the tearoom, Liz watched Chet head toward the saloon down the street. Chet, born a Texan, had moved to Louisiana at twenty-two, and Liz remembered hearing him say that he'd stumbled upon Lecompte for "no particular reason," and a few weeks later he met Lucas and went to work at the mill. Chet had been respected and paid well, but Grandpa Lucas had said the man had desperately wanted to go back to Texas—he said it was in his blood.

✕　✕　✕

The sweet and enticing fragrance inside the tearoom made Liz remember how hungry she was. She imagined Emma and Abby were half starved by now.

Emma rubbed her leg and commented that it felt sore from the trip. "For two days," she explained, "it hit the side of the stage until now it's tender and bruised."

Liz noticed the little half-moons that hung under her cousins' eyes, and she smiled as she thought that they paraded their fatigue around like a little girl in a fancy dress. They likely felt horrible, mostly from the poor sleeping conditions, and the half hour of excitement since their arrival had disguised their tiredness. But now, as normalcy set in, their exhaustion looked unmistakable.

The four of them sat down at a white linen-covered table. They ordered dessert and tea and the cousins took turns relating everything that had happened to them since they had last exchanged letters. They were brought up on all of the latest news, including most of the plans for their journey west. They talked about the future and recent quilting projects, wagons, flowers, men, lacy hats, and hairstyles.

At a break in the conversation, Abby pulled off her thin gloves and looked over at Liz. Abby seemed overwhelmed by the heat. "Abby, I think it's time to start home."

Chet cautiously entered the tearoom just then as the ladies finished the last of the crumbly pastries. He walked with the confidence that comes from a shot of whiskey, and he touched his hat with a greeting as he reached the table.

"Hello, Chet," Liz said cheerfully. "What perfect timing. We were about to leave."

Chet smiled as his chocolate brown eyes went to each female. He looked handsome in his brown cowboy hat and green cotton shirt. His dark blond hair hung loosely under his hat, and his boots were dark and slightly dusty from constant wear.

"I'd like for you to meet my cousins, Chet. This is Abby," she said. "And this is Emma, her younger sister."

"Ma'am, ma'am," he said, tipping the brim of his hat twice, greeting each of them.

"Nice to meet you," they both said, almost in unison.

"Nice to meet you, also." Chet shifted his weight to his other hip, causing his belt buckle to shine in the afternoon sun. "Well, I'll be out front with the wagon when you ladies are ready to leave."

"Thank you, Chet," Liz said. "We'll be right along."

He smiled toward Emma, and gave her an extra tip of his hat as he headed out the door. Emma smiled back, her cheeks blushing red.

"Oh!" Megan teased. "I think Chet is sweet on you, Emma."

"No . . . really? You think so?"

"Yes, really."

"Maybe so, Emma," Liz teased. "I saw the way he looked at you."

Emma looked dazed and slightly embarrassed. "Who is Chet again?"

Megan giggled. "He works at the mill. You'll see him again later, I'm sure."

Liz quickly paid with the money that Lucas had given her, and they walked out to meet the men at the wagon.

⁂ ⁂ ⁂

Like each one before it, Lucas rose first that morning and started the coffee and the first skillet of bacon.

"The smell of bacon is better than any alarm," he'd often told Thomas just about the time the girls trotted down the stairs to the table, sleepy-eyed and ready to eat. The same trick had come to work on Luke as well.

After Claire had passed away, Megan started making the biscuits, and Liz oversaw the eggs and the general needs of getting everyone fed. Caleb and Thomas had started joining the family for breakfast each day even before Caleb married into the Mailly family. Lucas ran the family timber mill straight from his morning breakfast table.

Thomas supposed that Liz and Megan had both learned the timber business while pouring coffee and flipping bacon. Liz said once that she believed more things in life are caught rather than taught, and that was certainly the case as the family trade passed down from generation to generation. Gathering around that breakfast table for the organization of the day's responsibilities had become a Mailly family tradition.

A bright, warm sun greeted the family on this morning. The clear blue sky boasted a few puffy clouds floating about. No breeze fluttered the curtains on the open window, and when the sunlight crossed the front porch and peeked through the windows, Thomas usually followed. He tried never to show up late for his first cup of coffee!

He moseyed through the back door and greeted Lucas. Luke sat across from him, eating in complete silence. As usual, Thomas grabbed the coffee cup, poured the strong black liquid, and joined the silent breakfast table. He knew that the morning conversation would begin once Lucas completed his reading.

Lucas's Bible sat open to the book of Nehemiah. He looked up and greeted Thomas as he poured more coffee into the old man's cup.

"I don't recall ever reading that book in the Bible," Thomas commented.

Lucas swallowed his coffee and set the cup back down half full. "One of my favorites. I've read it often."

"Oh," Thomas replied. "Why?"

"An old man does his best work," he chuckled, "and he doesn't hesitate to tell a group of women how to help."

Luke spoke for the first time that morning. "Tell me the story, Grandpa."

Thomas leaned one arm on the table and prepared to listen to what Lucas would say.

"Well, Nehemiah had a big vision. He felt led by God to build back the city walls of Jerusalem. He made a plan, oversaw the work, financed it, and he prayed a lot. This story tells me to dream big, stay focused, get to work, refuse to give up, and always include God in every step along the way."

"What else?" Luke asked.

Lucas looked at his audience and continued. "He had every reason to give up his dream. He didn't think about the obstacles but looked toward the goal. The workers got tired and overwhelmed, and the town's people were negative; some even wanted to kill him. He included the women in the plan, as well as the children, and together they accomplished the goal."

"Hmm," Thomas said as he leaned back in his chair. "I like this man. Sounds like I need to read this book for myself."

"That's what we have, Grandpa. We have a big goal to go west, and with lots of women!" Luke's voice grew louder at the end.

Thomas and Lucas laughed out loud.

"Speaking of the women, aren't they late coming down today?" Thomas asked. Usually breakfast was in full swing by now.

"I heard them up half the night talking and laughing like little schoolgirls. Guess coffee and bacon is gonna be it this morning. We can cut some bread from the loaf. Butter and blackberry jam will fix it right up."

Thomas stood to get the bread and a knife. Luke got the jam and a spoon from the basket. About that time, they heard Lucas's four granddaughters on the stairs. Megan and Abby appeared in the kitchen first, with Liz and Emma just a few steps behind.

Abby, the tallest and thinnest of the four women, wore her brown hair pinned securely at the back of her head. She definitely had the poise of a schoolteacher, Thomas thought.

"I see the Mailly breakfast ritual is as it should be," Abby said as she greeted her grandfather with a kiss to the cheek. "The smell of bacon is the best way to wake up. I had forgotten." Thomas figured Emma might be too young to remember much but the love and warmth of the home. She smiled and greeted her Grandpa Lucas with a kiss as well.

"You men give up on breakfast this morning?" Liz asked as she put the teapot on the burner and stirred the flame under it. "Oh," she continued, "Thomas, do you remember my cousins, Abby and Emma Wilkes?"

Thomas stood and greeted the Mississippi cousins. "Yes, it's been awhile, ladies."

"Sit down, girls," Lucas commanded. "There is plenty of bacon and bread. Get your tea ready and let's talk a few things over. Get everyone up to speed around here."

The Wilkes sisters watched their grandpa as he spoke, with their plates in front of them full of bacon and bread.

"I'm pleased Abby and Emma are joining us," he continued. "I wish your parents shared our views. As you all know, I firmly believe the Southern states will withdraw from the Union soon. With the presidential election before us, the time is upon us. I have a buyer for the timber mill."

Every face focused on Lucas, and not a bite had been taken. The seriousness of selling the family mill and the unrest in the South as well as an extended journey west seemed to weigh upon each person, with both excitement and apprehension.

"It seems all our plans are falling into place, Lucas," Thomas said. "After talking with Chet and the stage driver, I think it will take five or six weeks to get to Fort Worth."

"Yes," Lucas continued, and he looked directly at Abby and Emma, "from our letters, I assume you know the military is leaving the fort abandoned. A freight system and mercantile is badly needed there. That area has seen growth with ranches and a few farmers, and I see it as the business opportunity we are looking for. They are expecting us and quite excited about it all. Fort Worth has the ability and desire to grow into a proper community."

The teapot on the stove started to whistle, and Liz got up to make the hot tea for the women. Coffee wasn't their morning choice, Thomas observed.

Emma started to eat, watching Abby as she asked, "I heard the cavalry is moving west to fight the Comanches. Does this mean we won't have any problems with Indians? That's been my greatest concern of our move."

"Most likely we won't see any, but they are still out there. We could get worried about it, but I choose to just be smart with our choices. We won't provoke them if we see them, and we'll stay together." Lucas's expression darkened as he added, "I repeat, always stay together. I have also been in contact with a small group of Texas Rangers. I've made arrangements for them to meet up with your wagon train at the border. They will continue on with you to the fort."

Abby felt a little better and took in a deep breath.

As each family member prepared their breakfast plates at the Mailly table, they seemed to fall into their own thoughts of the adventure before them, and Thomas was no exception.

Liz interrupted his thoughts as she verbalized a list of the tasks she needed to complete and how many days she needed to accomplish her list.

"Dishes and glass cups will be packed in the sawdust, hopefully keeping them in one piece over the bumpy wagon trail ahead," she said to no one in particular. "We'll need one wagon alone for Megan's fabric and new sewing machine. There are trunks to pack, food to prepare, and all of the barn supplies need to find a place."

She looked as if her mind had set to swirling without a pencil in front of her to organize it. She smoothed out the skirt of her blue cotton dress with its crocheted collar as if she might hop up and tackle all six wagons at that very moment.

Young Luke seemed more troubled by the looming civil war than about what he might pack to take the journey. Like his namesake, Luke dreamed of open territory, fresh and green, someplace untouched and unchanged, where bison roamed and stallions galloped; a place in the West where adventure saturated every day and Indians settled on mountaintops and deep in the valleys. Thomas smiled, realizing Luke wasn't frightened by any of it.

Lucas lifted an eyebrow at Thomas. "I'll have to get gold for the sale of the mill. Any other currency is just too unstable with a civil war so close to exploding."

After all, it was essentially war from which they fled, which, according to Lucas's assessments, would devastate the mill's operation. He had a keen understanding of the politics of the day from the many newspapers he regularly read.

Thomas knew it just about broke the old man's heart to sell the timber mill, his only way of life. On the last fishing trip they'd taken with Luke, Lucas had told them, "This is what life is all about. Take a risk, see if you can fly. Regardless of the outcome or what may develop, it is better to try than always wonder."

"'We've almost finished all of the blackberry jam," Megan commented as Abby reached for it.

"I know," Liz said, surprised.

"We should grow our own blackberries again," Megan said, "when we get to Texas."

"Do you think they'll grow in Texas?" Emma asked.

"Surely they will grow," Megan said, and she turned to Liz. "Don't you think so?"

"I don't know for certain," Liz replied, "but I can't imagine breakfast without blackberry jam."

The women all looked down at the generous layer of jam that covered each slice of warm bread. Thomas smiled at Luke as they watched and listened to the jam conversation between them.

"Too bad we'll miss the last berry-picking season in Lecompte," Liz lamented.

"We have six wagons, full of supplies to drive," Lucas interrupted them. "So I've hired John and Blue from the mill to help drive the two extra teams. Chet is from Texas and knows the area well. He will ride scout for us."

Thomas gulped down the last of his coffee as Lucas continued. "I'll be there as soon as the sale of the mill is finalized. The new owners need to be comfortable before I can leave. I feel this is the respectable manner to address the new owners. Also, the land contract in Pineville will need to be finalized for the purpose of logging rights. I will be along as soon as I can. We'll start packing today. It will be a lot of work to fit it all in, but we can do it."

Luke squirmed in his chair. The excitement seemed to amount to more than he could handle.

"Well, let's get started," Megan agreed.

"I thought Emma and Megan could start here in the kitchen," Liz began. "Only leave the bare minimum. Grandpa will have most of his meals at the mill with the other men. The sawdust and wooden crates are stacked in the breezeway. Pack the breakables in the sawdust and nail each lid down well. Also, think about what we will need for the next few days. We can pack those items right before we leave. We want to take as much as we can on this trip. Grandpa will only bring what he has to, because all of his wagons will be freight."

Thomas watched Emma and Megan swish out the door to the breezeway, and he smiled at the way Liz had taken charge.

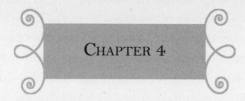

CHAPTER 4

As Emma gathered several of the crates from the porch, Megan struggled with a heavy bag of sawdust. She tugged with frustration on the sturdy burlap, but it wouldn't budge. She stepped away from the bag and placed her hands tightly against her hips, her hair damp at the temples from the morning sun, which beamed straight through the open porch.

Emma tapped her on the shoulder with a giggle as Liz and Abby headed to the cellar to retrieve the canned goods. The door creaked open and dusty sunrays ran ahead of Abby down the stairs. The dark place filled with light as she gathered her skirt and entered the coolness. Cobwebs hung carelessly and hit Abby in the face.

"Ewww," she cringed, blinking as she tried to adjust to the new surroundings.

Wooden shelves were on all sides, bulging with stone crocks and canned goods. The pantry brimmed with peaches, dried apples, tomatoes, and several sacks of onions and potatoes.

"You Maillys are excellent gardeners," Abby told Liz. "And equally blessed in your canning skills."

Abby squealed when she found a stockpile of the special jam that had caused such a stir at breakfast.

"We won't have to worry about a berry patch in Texas for a while, after all. Look what I found!"

Even though it was the end of the season, the cellar was full. Liz and

Megan had prepared their harvest well.

"You and Megan have grown so confident since I saw you last," Abby said as they loaded crates with canned fruits and jam. "I admire your independence you've achieved in spite of . . . everything."

Liz knew Abby had aspired to attain such independence as a teacher, but she might now have matured enough to know that kind of thing came from poise and confidence and not from vocation.

Abby began to sort the abundance into categories. The shelf closest to the stairs would be for Grandpa Lucas, and she placed a sack of coffee beans and an extra jar of peaches next to the other items that Liz had requested she set aside for him. As Liz surveyed the shelves, it looked like more than her grandfather would need, especially if he were to take his meals at the mill with the other workers. But she decided to let Abby work on her own while she gathered a few things to tide them over the next few days. She lined up the butter crock, a small block of cheese, jam, and another crock that held salt.

Abby seemed impressed with Liz's organizational skills. "There will certainly be plenty of food for the trip," she observed, "and an amount sufficient to start our new home. I have to hand it to you, Elizabeth. You're really prepared to make this journey."

Liz left Abby to finish sorting while she headed upstairs to check on the progress of John and Blue. They were struggling to lift some heavy, pre-packed boxes into the freight wagons. "Miss Elizabeth, we can never get all of this in these wagons." John wiped the trickle that dripped down his face, taking one glove off as he tried to explain the situation to the obstinate female before him.

"John, I don't wish to be difficult, but if you would just try it this way. I am certain it will fit. See, I have it all planned out here." She pushed her note paper toward John.

He took the paper and reluctantly looked it over.

"Is everything all right?" Abby asked as she joined them.

"Yes," Liz firmly stated, "as soon as he completes it my way."

They laughed gently as Liz noticed that John had begun arranging the boxes her way, and she quietly delighted in the fact that they looked like they might fit into their predestined locations.

A short while later, Liz and Abby approached the kitchen area, and laughter could be heard from the two inside.

"What is so funny, dear sister?" Abby asked Emma.

Coming up for air, Emma stumbled with her words. Megan came to her aid and said, "She was telling me about the school picnic and the gift you received."

"Oh, I don't want to even think about little Samuel and the snake!" Abby waved her hands and changed the topic. "I've worked up such an appetite in that cellar with all of that food. I must eat something! And by the way, Liz, you and Megan have really outdone yourselves. The cellar is packed with jar after jar. Emma, you would not believe it. Here is the most beautiful jar of pickles I have ever seen. Did you ever enter these in the county fair?"

"Yes, we did and we gained several new enemies throughout the county," Megan teased. "Grandma Claire always had the purple ribbon until we came along. Lonnie Gluffer said his wife was right glad we're leaving. She just might have a chance at it now."

"Oh my, then! These must be worth a lovely fortune." Abby held the jar high and admired it as the light caressed the shiny glass. Secret spices and seeds floated in and around the perfect slices of little cucumbers.

Casual boot steps sounded on the front porch to announce Thomas's arrival for lunch.

"I've just been chatting with John and Blue out front," he declared from the breezeway. "It appears that Miss Elizabeth has a celestial list from which they're not allowed to deviate. Do I have that right?"

"And?" Liz remarked.

"And nothin', I s'pose," he said with a grin. "I saw Caleb wind up on the losing end of that argument many a time."

He removed his hat and walked into the kitchen. "Looks like the family pickle secret is about to be shared. Should I come back?"

"Of course not, come in," Megan said, smiling at him. "We were about to have some lunch. Won't you join us?"

"Thank you, but I have a lot to do today. Liz, can I see you on the porch for a moment?" Thomas held the door open for Liz and she followed him outside.

"Thomas, if this is about John . . . I can't imagine the problem," she stated firmly. "It's quite simple. The crates were not fitting in the wagon as I had planned and it was because he wanted to do it his way. We have a lot to pack and it will not all fit if such things are not considered. I even had the crates made a certain size so that we would not waste one lovely inch of room in the wagons. If they do not place them as I have recorded on the sheet of paper, it simply won't work. I did it to save them time and trouble."

"I think they'd have figured it out, Liz, if you had let them."

"But why should they waste time figuring this out when I already have?" she asked, not really seeking a response. "They would then tell me I couldn't take all the items and that is unacceptable. These crates are life or death." She paused, seething at the expression on his face. "I'll tell you what, Thomas, I'd load all this myself if it weren't so heavy."

Liz felt her blood begin to boil, infuriated that Thomas had obviously attributed her words to a silly woman's drama. Their life might well depend on what she made room for and where she chose to store it, in fact. Megan was to start her dress shop in Fort Worth, and she had to have her supplies, as well as the inventory for the mercantile. This was no easy task that her grandfather had given her.

"Let's not pretend. The real problem is that I told him what to do and he wouldn't have it."

Liz stared at Thomas, but he didn't respond.

"Am I not right? Are the crates fitting?" Liz held her ground like an animal defending her young, her lace-up boots pressed firmly against the porch.

She watched him as Thomas looked over to the two freight wagons. The crates appeared to fit in their places, with no wasted space; surely he could see that. He looked back to the covered porch, probably estimating the space for the remaining freight.

"All right then. I will have a word with the boys."

Thomas turned and walked down the steps, and Liz headed back to the kitchen.

Men! she silently exclaimed.

✳   ✳   ✳

Thomas stood by the wagons and examined the final boxes to be loaded.

"You came out well on that one," Blue groaned as he lifted one of the crates into the wagon.

Thomas remained silent.

"What does she have in this one?" Blue complained as he wiped the sweat from his face and neck with his red bandana. "I might need a hand here, fellas."

"No! This one? It can't be that heavy. It says Megan's fabric on the side," John answered back, confused.

"Well, it's rather heavy I'm telling you."

Thomas looked to the boxes on the porch that still awaited placement in the wagon. On the side of each box, in bold lettering, was written: MEGAN'S FABRIC—FREIGHT WAGON 2

Thomas swung his leg over the back of his horse. He had rather enjoyed the little joust with Liz. It would be his life if any of it were left behind.

"Boys, don't forget any of these," Thomas reminded the men as he rode away laughing. "It's apparently life or death."

✳   ✳   ✳

The days passed quickly and the wagons began to groan as they adjusted to their new weight. Everything had been loaded except for Megan's treadle machine. A special area had been created for it with ties to hold it in place and keep it from moving around on the trail. The work had taken less time than Liz had anticipated, and she felt relieved that they would leave on time.

The ladies would take a break all afternoon to finish their personal agendas and rest some. If time permitted, they planned to quilt around the old frame. Otherwise, they would get an early start and quilt the next day.

Liz and Abby sat in their rockers on the porch. Megan stood by the treadle machine, while Emma sat in a straight-back chair with quilt blocks in her lap. All of the square patch units had been completed, and she meticulously pieced the triangle units that would go on the sides. Two triangle pieces were sewn to a red square, which created a large triangle unit that was then sewn to the nine-patch. The fabric remained consistent throughout the quilt, except for the center squares which varied in shades of red and green. Liz noted that Emma seemed at her best with a needle and fabric in her hand; calm and at ease with the world. They rocked and waited in utter silence for the men to load the treadle.

Abby broke into Liz's thoughts.

"I have something for everyone. Being the schoolteacher that I am, I thought we should record our trip west." She reached into her apron pocket and took out a little journal for each one of them. "I have already started mine. In fact, I've been keeping one since I went away to teach school. We should do it for ourselves, but for history, too."

Abby handed a small pencil to each one just as she had no doubt done a thousand times in her classroom. Abby was a natural teacher—encouraging, patient, and persistent. "Write whatever you wish. It's your story."

"How exciting!" Megan cried, always the first to respond to something new. "I've never kept a diary before."

"Abby, what a lovely idea. I would have never thought of it myself," Liz agreed.

Emma placed her book in her sewing bag at the side of her chair. She quickly picked up her needle again and got back to her stitching. "Thank you," she said indifferently.

"Oh, come now, Emma. It will be fun!" Megan begged her cousin.

All the ladies except Megan rocked in silence and waited for the men to arrive and provide the muscle needed to load the treadle. She paced around the machine like a mother hen.

CHAPTER 5

T he ladies completed their morning routine in record time and hastily made their way into the sewing room. It had one large window and a small closet that had been turned into a bookshelf, and the wooden floors still looked new, as though they had somehow escaped the passage of time.

A large yellow cat slowly pranced across the floor in front of Emma and rubbed against her leg.

"Where have you been hiding?" Emma said, reaching down to pet the plump, yellow ball of fur.

"That's Samson," Liz said. "He's very old."

"Oh. Well, aren't you the most charming old fellow," she said in a baby voice. "Where have you been hiding?"

Liz had grown very anxious to quilt. The last few days had been filled with loading and work, with no time left for quilting. Now, they gathered around the quilt frame with their sewing baskets and started at once.

Abby licked the eye of her needle and pressed the heavy cotton thread into it. "I can't wait to get started on this quilt."

They all watched, observing Abby's technique.

"I thought you licked the thread, not the needle," Megan said, "to help thread it quickly."

"Well, you can, I suppose. But a friend of Mother's always said to do it this way."

Abby smiled as each of her fellow seamstresses eagerly tried the new hint. One by one, they placed the eye of the needle between their lips to moisten the opening and then pointed the tip of the thread into the eye of the needles, threading them the first time with no trouble.

"Isn't that wonderful!" Megan exclaimed.

The quilt top on which they worked wasn't especially big. Megan had called it a lap size because it just covered a person when seated.

"I like this smaller size," Emma told them. "I think you could even hang it on the wall, like a picture."

Liz chuckled over the idea of hanging a quilt on the all. Its only purpose would be a source of beauty, a wall decoration, which seemed like a rather astonishing idea.

The quilt, layered with cotton batting in the middle, would be covered at the back with a length of muslin. Stretched tightly in the wooden frame, it might finish up quickly as a smaller piece of appliqué art; and of course because four talented hands flew across it.

Each of their needles had been threaded with a knot at the end of the thread, except for Liz's. She never used a knot; instead, she used a double backstitch each time she started a line of stitches. The eye of the needle allowed the thread to move through it without hindrance as she worked each stitch into the quilt.

The needle pushed into the middle layer of the batting and pulled through tightly, popping the knot into the batting and between the layers of the quilt sandwich. An accomplished quilter would never allow a knot to show on either side of the quilt, and Liz knew that each seamstress at this particular quilt frame could be considered an expert with the needle. Abby and Emma had been taught the art of the needle by their mother, Katherine, the youngest daughter of Lucas Mailly. Elizabeth and Megan were taught by their grandmother, Claire. Like the pieces of the quilt that they'd fit together so carefully, the women of their family were sewn expertly together by the stitches of their shared love for the art of quilting.

The women in the community were always excited to go to a quilt gathering, sometimes called a "quilt'n" or "a quilting bee." One of their projects could be finished rather quickly with so many hands at work, and sewing secrets were passed around as readily as community news and activities—not to be confused with local gossip, of course, a behavior which the church gatherings frowned upon.

"I will certainly miss our little group of quilting friends," Megan said to Liz, as if she'd read her sister's thoughts. Turning to Abby and Emma, she added, "We have a lovely group of friends here in Lecompte! I hope we'll have one in our new home, too."

Row after row, the thimbled fingers loaded stitches into the appliquéd, flower-patterned quilt. The ladies rolled it several times as the work progressed from the pattern that their grandmother Claire had designed myriad years ago. Liz concentrated on her stitches, twelve to the inch to be exact.

Two gray kittens played with old Samson's tail, which had a mind of its own. They swatted and jumped at it as another kitten curled around Abby's leg under the quilt frame and rolled itself into her skirt, making it look like a gossamer puddle on the floor.

Liz was finally at the end of her thread when Emma and Megan went off to retrieve some lunch. She slid the needle under the top layer of fabric and secured a backstitch to the cotton batting. She pulled out her stork embroidery scissors and neatly clipped the thread before placing her needle into the edge of the spool.

"We certainly have accomplished a lot this morning," she said, looking over the quilt. Her fingers smoothed over the tiny stitches she had just placed. "It's coming along nicely," she said, mostly to herself.

The playful kitten suddenly jumped into her lap, and she jumped. "Cally, you silly thing, I sure will miss you." She stroked the soft fur and held the kitten to her face.

Liz felt Abby's eyes on her. "Abby, I am so glad you are here. It has been far too long. I was beyond excitement to hear that you and Emma were willing to make the move. I'm sorry your cousin Sadie wasn't able to come, too."

Abby reached for Liz's hand across the quilt and smiled. "Grandpa is so certain about this political unrest, it is frightful, Liz."

"I know." Liz gently squeezed Abby's fingers. "Let's not worry ourselves though. Grandpa seems certain of this move, and I have faith in him."

"Yes, I do as well. But that doesn't mean that I won't worry."

"Well, let's not dwell on things we can't change."

Abby nodded in agreement.

"Are you excited about your new teaching engagement?" Liz asked her. "Pastor Parker seems so nice, and his wife Anna does too."

"Yes, I am. Excited and worried all at once." Abby expelled a deep breath. "I do not know where to begin. I have to be careful to not scare myself into running back to my Mississippi classroom."

"We'll take it one day at a time." Liz comforted her with soft words and a pat on her hand. "Together."

"Liz, I'm very curious about Texas, and I do not feel that I know much about it. What can you tell me?" Abby pressed. "Settle my nerves."

Liz sighed before she began. "I understand the weather is actually quite similar to here, hot and such. Only less trees and rain, which might not be too terrible! Our area has trees and a river; the Trinity River, to be more specific. Sounds like home almost, doesn't it? Except they say it's ranch country. It has cattle grazing land and open prairie. Cattle with great long horns roam about all over. Grandpa and Thomas are always talking on the porch about this ranching. Thomas told me that a person could round up as many of these longhorns as they wish, brand them, and they're yours!"

Abby smiled.

"The idea of a ranch is very exciting to them. Luke is taken with the idea of being a cowboy, but Grandpa Lucas forgets how advanced he is in years now. He never quits, and Thomas seems to forget that Grandpa isn't a young man anymore, too. Thomas has just stepped into the shoes Caleb wore in Grandpa's life, and Luke's too."

Liz paused realizing what she had just said.

"Well, what about you, Liz? Has he stepped into those shoes for you?"

"I haven't thought about it exactly like that."

Liz looked to Abby with tears in her eyes again. She tried to blink them back. "I still feel married, except that I get lonely. My heart hurts, but I want to feel better. And," she paused, "if forgetting Caleb is what I have to do to get better, then I don't see that I can do it. I will never be able to do that."

"I have not been here long, my dear cousin, but I can see that Thomas adores you. He doesn't have to court you. He is already here. He is already in this family. And he is a gentleman. I think he's waiting for you to make room in your heart for him. He won't be assertive, Liz. My only advice is to not wait too long for happiness to find you."

Megan and Emma appeared with sandwiches and lemonade on a tray, and Abby reached for her drink.

"We have much work ahead of us," Liz told them. "Though we've already accomplished so much, there is even more once we reach Texas."

She looked to the others for support.

Emma leaned forward, propping her elbows on the edge of the quilt frame with her chin in her hands. "I am growing more excited each day. I can barely manage the anticipation. And though it's exciting, a part of me feels frightful too. I only wish Grandpa was coming with us now, not later."

Megan munched something crunchy and prepared to speak.

"At first, I also felt frightful, and though it may come again, I have confidence in us. We may be women, but we can do this, I've no doubt. It's an opportunity, and as such it will be wonderful!"

The ladies were amused at Megan's outlook.

"Besides," she said, "I've become a wonderful shot!" She raised her hand to look like a revolver and pretended to blow smoke from its barrel.

They all laughed at Megan as she sat down, still in an excited state of mind as she continued. "I am most excited at the prospect of having a dress shop. Just wait until you see that new treadle sewing machine work.

We ordered it from Chicago, you know; I paid for it myself. The dresses will simply fly off the machine."

She finally stopped for air, carefully sipping her lemonade as Liz smiled, affirming her sister's words.

"It will be a hard life for a while. I don't know how far the water is. We might have to carry it. We might even have to live in our wagons. It certainly won't be as comfortable as we have it here." Emma's eyes opened wide and round as saucers as she listened to Liz speak. "We will experience firsthand how our grandmothers lived," she told them. "We'll get to know what their daily lives were like."

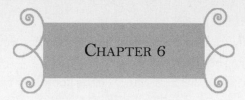

CHAPTER 6

Liz sat on her front porch mending the binding on Grandpa Lucas's favorite quilt, which he himself had named Southern Skies for the long, thin blue and red star points. The background had been constructed from tan scraps, and he'd told Liz that the stars were as big and beautiful as the stars in the Louisiana night sky.

Lucas loved to sit on the porch as much as Liz did. When she was a little girl, he told her the story of the geese flying south for the winter, and the way the birds knew when to fly north or south. He said the birds supported and encouraged each other in the journey. The bird in the lead had the hardest job because he had to break the wind currents for the others behind him; thus, each bird behind the front one had an easier time flying. The flock always flew in the V formation, her grandfather had taught her; the last held the resting or coasting spot. They squawked as they flew over the Mailly property, and Grandpa Lucas said the birds voiced their support and encouragement to each other, praising the lead bird for its leadership.

"When a goose is injured and needs to leave the group," her grandfather said, "they send down several to aid him in his recovery. They can join up with any flock again when the injured bird is ready and able to fly."

Grandpa Lucas had always said that people needed to be like these creatures: praising the leaders, encouraging others, and working hard.

When Liz made Grandpa's quilt, she put twelve flying geese in each block. She told him that it made her think of the time they spent on the porch together, and his lessons about life.

Liz would miss this porch, but it calmed her knowing that her family would go with her, and they could build a new one.

She felt so tired. She'd endured some busy, laborious days preparing for the trip west. Liz looked at the six wagons standing packed with goods. The structures looked like they might give birth at any time; they stood waiting as a metaphor for the new life now upon Liz and her family.

Her family had already retired, all of them as tired as Liz, but she hadn't been able to sleep. She'd spent many nights out on the porch lately, this one her last. In the morning, she would leave the Mailly home. She would leave Riverton.

Liz prayerfully pondered God's promises. She asked for wisdom, guidance, health, and safety. She asked for strength and endurance. She thanked Him for Thomas, willing to travel such a long way with them, and for Chet, who knew Texas as his home, for agreeing to act as their scout.

Liz sat rocking, comforted in knowing that the Texas Rangers would help guide them in the more dangerous areas. Grandpa Lucas had thought of everything.

"Please God," she requested one more time. "Protection, special protection."

"A penny for your thoughts?" her grandfather asked from the doorway with his pipe in hand.

Liz looked his way. "I just finished mending your favorite quilt."

"Thank you, Liz. You know how much I love those Southern Skies."

He stepped forward, leaning on a post of the porch as he lit his pipe. She looked down at the flying geese on the quilt.

"These birds are amazing, the way God created their nature . . ." She looked up to her grandfather and smiled. "How do you know they are squawking encouragement to each other? Maybe they're just cranky."

Smoke went up from his pipe, and he crossed one leg over the ankle of the other. His eyes twinkled through the darkness, and he chuckled. "I choose to believe in the good and positive, Liz. Besides, a little bird told me." His eyebrows teased with a wiggle.

She stood up, placed the quilt in the rocker and went to her grandfather. With her arms around him, she said, "I miss you already." Her voice cracked, and she looked out over his shoulder and blinked back a burn from her eyes. "I'm a little melancholy about leaving my home, but I am ready to go. In the morning, I will be ready. Why aren't you in bed?" she asked him.

"I was waiting on my quilt," he chuckled. "Can't sleep without it, you know."

She picked it up and placed it in his arms.

"I love you."

"I love you too, Liz. I will see you soon, real soon. When the birds fly south."

Liz looked back at her Grandpa on the night porch and chiseled the picture into her heart.

She never wanted to lose such memories.

※　※　※

Liz must have fallen asleep the very moment her head hit the pillow. She didn't even remember getting into bed or saying her nightly prayer.

Liz rolled over in the darkness to face the window, her hair in her eyes. She brushed it aside. "Is it almost morning yet?" she whispered to herself.

She arose and went to the window, peeking out. "No sun yet."

While she'd slept, the moon had slid across the sky, now showing from a position opposite of where she had last seen it. The stars shone over the house and the six wagons waited in the yard; waiting for their dusty day ahead, when they would be useful and satisfied.

Excitement squeezed her insides. She slipped back into her warm bed and tried to sleep, knowing she might regret not having a full night's rest when weariness caught up to her out on the trail.

A pink ray of sunlight sliced through Liz's morning curtains and splashed against her face and pillow. Within just a few short moments, she was in the kitchen preparing a small breakfast and packing a lunch they all might eat along the journey. She wrapped a piece of bread and cheese in a small cloth for everyone and then placed each of them into a larger cloth sack that held two green apples and a tin cup. She made a sack for each person and planned to place the sacks under the wagon benches for later.

Cheese might prove a real luxury for lunch along the trail on their first day. Afterward, high temperatures would surely spoil such treats. From then on, they would have to eat dried meats, breads, and beans. Hopefully, the men could kill something for dinner each night. The jars of preserved fruit and other items from the cellar, packed neatly away in the sawdust, would serve them for special occasions or hard times on the trail. The four chickens she planned to bring along would hopefully produce eggs for their nourishment.

Grandpa Lucas had already risen, and Liz saw him out there inspecting the wagons once again, reassuring himself of their trailworthiness. In one wagon, he placed several extra wooden wheels and other materials that might be useful if the originals were damaged during the journey. Liz knew how surprisingly easy a wheel could break; sometimes the spokes caught and stripped the insides away. Or, as happened more often than any other scenario, the bolts could wiggle off and lose hold of the wheel, sending the wagon down in a dusty crash. Grandpa Lucas had seen this many times before, and Liz knew he wanted to ensure they would have enough materials in the instance that it happened along the trail.

The group gathered in the kitchen and quickly ate breakfast. Afterward, they collected all the essentials that could not be packed the night before and placed them in the appropriate wagons. Most of the millworkers waited in the yard next to the wagons, noticeably intrigued that Lucas Mailly had actually allowed his four granddaughters to embark on such a voyage west. Alone! It was a rare occurrence for any woman or group of women to have such an opportunity. Liz supposed that, in essence, it positioned a stepping-stone in their small community, and she hoped that stepping-stone might be utilized by other women in the months and years to come; used again and again.

Luke placed his mother's chickens into her wagon, and Liz surveyed their placement, adjusting the wooden cages as she saw fit. Luke smiled at his mom and gave her a hug.

"They could drop off," she defended. "It's not going to be trails like we are accustomed to. These trails are much shakier and not used so often."

"Are you set?" he asked her.

Liz's eyes widened and she smiled. "Yes, I suppose I am all set."

"Good! I can't wait to get out of here! I wonder how far we'll make it today."

Liz smiled at Luke's excitement. "Where's Bear?"

"Grandpa has him," he said, motioning toward his grandfather and Thomas. "Bear! Come boy!" Luke whistled.

The fluffy-haired black ball ran toward them, stopping just in time to keep from colliding with Liz. Luke patted the dog's sides and rubbed his head with two hands.

"Are you all set, boy?" The dog grew more and more excited with Luke's encouraging words, and he began to bark. "Good boy," Luke assured him.

The wagons had been lined up according to Grandpa Lucas's instructions and stood patiently with drivers now onboard. Liz's grandfather decided that the best manner to travel would be in pairs, two wagons traveling side-by-side and two wagons traveling behind and so forth. This allowed each person a partner who could assist them if necessary. The wagons had been arranged accordingly, and Grandpa Lucas appeared satisfied to have the matter settled in his favor. Thomas took the lead out front, the leader for the wagon train. He also agreed that this method of travel was a good idea in case one of the ladies needed help with the reins. Behind his wagon, Liz and Megan teamed up, then Abby and Emma, Luke and Blue, and John as a single at the back. Chet planned to ride on horseback. Thomas's saddle horse had been tied to the side of his lead wagon, and Grandpa Lucas insisted that they take a few extra horses along, leaving them fresh in case they were needed to scout ahead or search for water, so they'd tied them to the back of John's wagon.

"It looks like we're rough and ready!" Luke exclaimed, and he wrapped his arm around his mother's shoulders. The current of excitement emanating from him felt palpable. "We're off to start a whole new life."

Liz took one last look over her shoulder before she nodded.

A whole new life.

She wondered for a moment whether she'd truly let go of the old one.

※　※　※

Lucas had given all of his granddaughters a final hug, and Thomas noticed Liz's pretty eyes well up with emotion as she turned away. Lucas saluted the men with a handshake and a few words of advice, and he asked everyone to join him as he said a prayer for them before they left. He asked God to keep His hand over the group and guide them in safety and health. He asked special wisdom and grace for Thomas as the trail leader, and for the overall protection of each person, calling them by name.

"Amen," everyone said together as he finished his prayer.

Lucas raised his hand to Liz. "Will those chickens be a bother?"

"They won't," Liz quipped. "They know how much I love chicken soup."

"Thomas!"

"Yes, sir?"

"Take my women to Texas!"

"I will, sir!" he replied with a firm nod.

The millworkers that stood watching erupted into applause, clapping and hollering at the wagons, waving their hands and shouting their goodbyes.

Thomas slapped the reins and shouted at his horses to start them off. The wagons pulled out of the yard while all of the millworkers and Lucas stood by, watching and waving. Thomas looked back as he rounded the curve and caught a glimpse of Liz as she watched the house and her beloved porch grow smaller and smaller. He imagined how she felt, like she might never see it again. When he couldn't see Lucas anymore, Thomas looked out at the river until it disappeared as well. His heart lurched a bit for Liz as she said goodbye to everything she knew, including Caleb, putting it all behind her and boldly ran forward into The Great Unknown.

⁂ ⁂ ⁂

When they reached the edge of the Mailly property. Liz looked over to Megan, who could hardly stay seated over the wagon bench as her petite gloved hands drove the team of horses.

Liz smiled at her sister. She had always admired Megan's love for life. It was in the small things, the day-to-day matters, that she found the oddest satisfaction for living. The special way she held the stem of a flower bulb before placing it carefully into its allotted square hole, or the way she threaded a needle and secured a perfect knot, even the way she cleaned the house.

"We're leaving! I can't believe this," Megan exclaimed to Liz, trying to talk over the horses. "We're actually leaving Riverton! Did you ever dream?"

Liz bit her lip and tried to smile back at her sister. She hadn't, actually. She'd never once dreamed of leaving Riverton or the timber mill. That lone tear found its way to her chin again, and she quickly looked back as she went around the final bend in the road. She caught sight of her grandfather on the porch with his hand held high, still waving.

No, she'd never dreamed of leaving it all behind one day.

CHAPTER 7

The hot sun perched boldly, straight overhead. The group had made surprisingly good distance for the time they had been on the trail, which pleased Thomas.

Chet rode over the crest of a small hill and slowed his horse to the speed of Thomas's wagon, and Thomas motioned toward the region to the right side of them. Chet's head dodged in the direction after it.

"What's up? How does it look over there?" Thomas asked.

"Still like Louisiana," Chet joked.

"Go back and make sure the others are doing fine. If we can find water, I'd like to stop for the horses."

"I'll tell them."

Chet pushed back and rode back a short way to where Liz and Megan's wagons were driving.

"Hello," Thomas heard him call out, slowing his horse to their speed.

After Chet had confirmed that each wagon was doing fine, he rode on to relay the news to Thomas.

"Good," Thomas said. "Did you tell them that we would stop soon?"

"Yes, I did. They supposed the sooner the better."

"They need to stop?"

"I reckon everyone would like a break soon."

"Very well. See if you can scout a place for water."

"We've been traveling parallel to a large creek. Almost six feet across I'd say."

"Really?"

"For about three miles."

"Can you lead the way?"

Chet dipped his head and nodded. "It's only a short way. Follow me!"

The wagons tracked off to the right side with Chet leading the way. Up ahead, Thomas spotted a thick group of low trees; just beyond them, a rocky area and a flowing creek—almost six feet across, just as Chet had said.

The wagons came to a halt before reaching the area of thick growth that bordered the creek at a wide perch where the horses could enjoy the shade and drink water. The ladies quickly unloaded and headed upstream a bit to wash and enjoy the fresh water.

Blue, John, and Lucas walked to the creek, downstream from the women, and filled several buckets from which the horses could drink. Chet and Thomas stayed behind with the wagons and horses.

"Everything is going well," Chet said as Thomas took a long drink from his canteen and then pushed the cork lid over the opening.

"So far," he said flatly. "It's not what's up ahead that concerns me. It's what is traveling behind us."

Chet glanced over his shoulder. "Behind us? What do you mean?"

"The women," Thomas said, wiping his mouth.

Chet looked concerned. "Why? What did Lucas say about the women?"

"To watch out for them."

"We've only just gotten started."

"Anything could go wrong when half your wagon train is women!" Thomas joked, but a sense of serious concern washed over him and he shook his head. "What I mean is that we're still close to Pineville and the ladies don't seem anxious just yet, but they're women. They could easily change their minds. And really, I have no wish to turn around to Pineville for their sake."

Chet cut in. "Do you really think they would turn back?"

"We should keep a close eye on that for a few days." Thomas propped his arm on the wagon. "A man never knows what a woman might do, and they've left everything they know behind them."

Chet reached into his vest pocket and brought out a small bottle of homemade sour mash. He took a short swig and extended the bottle for Thomas.

"Just what I need," Thomas said, and he took a long gulp. "Thank you."

Chet put the bottle back inside his vest.

"I'd like to camp close to water tonight," Thomas said. "See if you can find out how long this stream carries. The place where it breaks off in the other direction is where we'll camp."

"You'd like for me to go now?"

Thomas nodded. "Keep your pistol handy," he warned.

"Very well," Chet said, loosening the ropes to his horse and immediately climbing onto the saddle.

"See if you can find something for dinner, too."

Chet tipped his hat to Thomas.

"Yah!" Chet commanded, kicking his spurs at the horse. He disappeared almost instantly through the thick brush.

Thomas waited like a mother hen as the ladies went about their business, not realizing for a minute or so that he'd been holding his breath.

Blue walked up from the creek and must have seen the consternation on his face. Slapping him on the back, he told him, "Relax, cowboy. Everything's fine!"

"You're right," he said, slightly startled as he removed his hat. "Lucas will kill me three times over if I don't keep his granddaughters in one piece."

"Everything will be fine. They aren't children."

"Yes, they're women!" Thomas laughed. "Did the horses get water?"

"Yeah," Blue replied with a chuckle. "I'm going to look over the wagons another time. I think the middle one is rattling too much for our own good. Then we only have to wait for Chet and the women to return."

Thomas stood up and stretched.

"But you should rest some," Blue said. "The sun is out strong today."

Thomas quickly found a place in the shade and sat down with his back leaning against a large tree. Blue busied himself looking over the wagons and inspecting them for cracks around the wheels. He'd helped Lucas build most of them, and Thomas felt confident in his familiarity with their assembly.

Thomas tilted his hat over his eyes and dozed off almost immediately after sitting down. He hadn't planned to sleep, but the late afternoon sun was enticing; even the strongest of men grew tired from its intensity and vigor.

✳ ✳ ✳

The ladies chatted relentlessly as they walked their way upstream. Their legs had grown tired and cramped, and Liz felt thankful for the opportunity to stretch. As Megan squatted beside the water and nursed her hands in its coolness, she realized the reins had done their worst on her sister's uncalloused hands. "Hurry, Megan! You can do that later," Emma squealed. "I've got to go badly!"

"Why wouldn't Thomas allow us to stop?" Abby chimed in. "'Just drive on, just drive,' he says."

The women laughed at her impersonation of Thomas. She even acted out the hand gestures, just as Thomas did when he gave directions or talked seriously about something.

"Gracious," Megan added, "we've been driving for such a time, my hands have become raw from the reins."

"Megan's right, Liz," Abby suddenly said. "You must talk with Thomas about this."

Emma nodded in agreement.

"Riding so hard on our first day out," Megan joined in as she gathered up her skirts, "can't be good for us. It can't be healthy!"

"Why am I the one who has to tell Thomas we need a break?" Liz protested.

"Well, you are the oldest, of course," Megan said, as if it should be understood.

Abby agreed. "If anyone were to talk with him, it should be you."

"I will speak with him."

"Lizzie," Abby said, as she looked at her hands and wiggled her fingers. "Look at my hands! Are yours so swollen?"

"Good heavens, dear lady!" Liz said, holding her cousin's red and swollen hands. "Megan's are faintly red, but nothing like yours."

"You don't need to hold the reins so stiffly," Megan said. "Only tug when the horses need to be commanded."

"I must have held them too tightly without realizing it."

"Let's fill our canteens down here," Liz told them, watching her steps as she made her way down to the water.

The others followed her down to the creek, and they all washed their hands and chatted for a time.

"We should get back to the wagons," Liz said, looking up at the sun. "We left a while ago."

The ladies finished washing and made their way up from the creek, following their own trail of trodden weeds and grass that they'd blazed on their way to the water.

The women strolled leisurely back to the wagons to find the men with their hats over their eyes, napping and obviously in no rush at all to start the wagons rolling again. The ladies giggled and, after a brief moment of whispering discussion, decided to wake them.

Thomas looked up, his eyes half squinted from sleep. "Wha-what is it? Has Chet returned already?"

"No," Liz said, smiling at his sleepiness.

John awoke and leaned forward, listening from underneath one of the wagons, and Blue groaned as he sat upright from against a thick tree trunk.

"What if . . . he's been bitten by a snake?" Emma speculated.

"Ladies, please," John said. "You're only scaring yourselves. He hasn't been gone long. There's nothing to worry about."

John looked to Thomas, somewhat confused over the situation.

"Well, what are we going to do about this," Emma demanded. "What if he's not back by nightfall?"

"What would you like us to do?" Thomas asked calmly.

"Well," Emma said. "I would only hope that you wouldn't be so passive if I were the one out there and had been gone for this long."

"Emma." Liz looked at Thomas and stepped in. "Let's not worry about it just yet. We must hope that everything is fine and he will return soon. We can't worry like this every time Chet leaves to scout out our trail."

"Can't we go look for him?" Emma pressed.

Thomas pushed up to his feet and grabbed hold of the horse's ropes and loosed them from the tree. "I will go and search for him."

"Where will you go?" Emma questioned.

"I'll follow the river a short way," he said, and then he paused. "And I'll come back a different route."

Blue and John stepped closer to Thomas's horse as Luke listened in silence, half asleep.

"Is all this really necessary?" he asked, rubbing his eyes. "Do you want one of us to go with you?"

"No, it's best that you stay here. I need you to stay with the women and keep them calm," he said, pulling himself onto the horse. "I will be back soon. Do not come looking for me."

Thomas left on horseback immediately and rushed through the thick area, disappearing at once.

"I just know something is wrong!" Emma exclaimed. "I knew he had been gone for far too long! What will we do without a scout! We can't . . ."

"Emma, please!" Liz said. "It's not certain that anything is wrong at all. Thomas will find Chet, if he needs to be found at all, and they will return soon."

"Yes, exactly," Abby said before turning suddenly to Blue for reassurance.

Liz swallowed her own worry, only pausing to look after Thomas's trail for a moment. Nightfall would come soon. The sun had already dipped low in the sky and the heat of the day had passed. The silent calm that covered her seemed to wind its way through the rest of the group. No one seemed sure what to do or say.

John looked up from the small log on which he perched. "Well . . ." he said slightly muffled, "let's get supper on and make ready for nightfall."

"We have plenty of food to eat," Abby said.

"Yes," Liz jumped in. "It's only the first day. We've plenty to eat. Besides," she said seriously, "I would suspect that we should have things in order when Chet and Thomas return."

John stood up quickly and placed his hat over his head. "Blue and I will tend to the horses and wagons. Luke, help the ladies collect wood for a fire."

Luke nodded his head and immediately set out on the search.

※　※　※

The forest was heavy with underbrush. It seemed like a deep ocean that someone could fall into and easily disappear.

Thomas waded through the brush, looking for signs that Chet might have left behind. He figured Chet should be easy to follow since he hadn't been gone for long, and he hadn't been trying to hide his tracks. But something still gnawed at Thomas's insides.

He peered into a small clearing and blinked hard.

That can't be . . .

Chet's painted pony stood before him, riderless. The calm horse casually munched on a green bush, one bridle rein dragging the rocky water's edge.

The horse looked up, chewing, and shook his head as if to say hello. He whinnied at Thomas and quickly returned to his supper. Thomas rode up close, swung one leg over his mare and slid down. He patted the pony and checked for signs that would tell him how Chet might have displaced his mount. He found no blood from the horse, or from the rider. The saddlebag and bedroll were intact and showed no signs of a struggle. Everything seemed as safe and normal as a church picnic.

Thomas scouted the area for a trail or clue about Chet's whereabouts. His eyes skimmed the water and, as he walked to the far edge of the clearing, something caught his ear.

It had grown quite dusky-dark now, difficult to see through the shadows. But there lay Chet, his head by the edge of a sharp rock with dried blood coating both his hairline and the rock near Chet's head.

"Chet," Thomas said softly. "What happened? You all right?"

Chet moaned again and half opened his eyes for a second.

"I knew," Chet struggled to say each word, "you would come. The women made you."

Thomas cleaned the cut and washed the blood away with cool water. He gave Chet a drink of water from his canteen. The head injury didn't appear to be very serious, but Thomas wrapped his friend's head with a long rag and pulled it tight before he tethered the horses to a tree line and unsaddled them for the night.

"Your head isn't bleeding very badly, but it's too dark to ride back tonight. We will have to camp here until morning."

The forest surrounded them on all sides, making it difficult to set up a camp. Thomas cleared the leaf-strewn ground for their bedrolls and quickly built a small fire.

Thomas wondered what might have happened to Chet and his pony. It seemed unusual to him how Chet, an excellent rider who worked so well with his horse, had been overcome in such a way. Like all Texas cowboys, Chet took great pride in that horse of his. He'd spent a great amount of time training his mount exactly as he had wanted. Thomas ran his hand down the leg of the filly again and lifted her foot.

What had made him fall? Thomas asked himself again

When he couldn't find the answer, he concentrated on how to make Chet more comfortable for the night. Each time he tried to move him, Chet moaned in pain. He went over each bone for breaks, but all seemed well. Just one nasty cut on the head.

He wished he were back at the wagons with a needle and thread nearby. Emma always had her quilt bag of supplies close to her. With his head resting on his own saddle, Thomas's eyes began to drop as he drifted to sleep. He almost tuned out the slight but heavy footsteps that padded close to the small clearing.

Startled, he opened one eye and both ears. He couldn't see anything, but the horses appeared to sense the danger as they tossed their manes. Thomas slowly moved his hand to the side of his leg where he'd strapped his gun. He slipped it gently from its holster, waiting. The horses settled slightly, but Thomas felt as though something or someone watched him. He did not know how or why Chet was thrown from his saddle, but the whole situation seemed amiss, and his sense of duty to Lucas's grand-daughters throttled him around the throat.

A few moments passed before Thomas sat up and stirred the fire. He placed more wood on the burning coals. He intended to keep the fire high tonight. He glanced over at Chet who slept soundly.

One slight crack of wood sent Thomas's hand lunging for his gun again, and he rested it on the grip as he surveyed their surroundings.

✳ ✳ ✳

Bear sat silently next to Luke at the campfire while John and Blue talked about the turn of events from the day and considered their options for the morning, and Liz sat with Emma, chatting softly. With his head resting on his crossed front paws, Bear's eyes followed each of the men as they talked.

Suddenly, the dog's nostrils flared as he picked up an unusual scent. His nose twitched, trying to get more of the smell. Immediately, the dog rose and hastily bounded into the darkness.

"What is it, boy?" Luke asked, looking through the undercarriage of the wagons and wheels. He tried to adjust his eyes to the blackness of the night after staring at the campfire for so long. Bear, up on all fours, had alerted to something. He let out a low growl. Liz had been around the dog enough to know that he meant business. His throat puffed and his black lips curled, exposing black gums and long pointed teeth. The deep growl continued and grew more intense. He now had the attention of Blue and John, guns in hand.

Liz's thoughts flew to Abby and Megan, already retired for the night.

"Luke, get your mother and her cousin into the wagons," Blue said sharply.

"Yes," Luke answered, and he flew to his feet. As his eyes searched the darkness, he grabbed Liz by the elbow and softly commanded, "Let's go. Into the wagon."

Liz went into full Mother Hen, nudging Emma along like a baby chick toward the nearest wagon.

"Liz," Emma squealed.

"Shhh. Let's do as they've asked and get inside."

"What is it?" she heard Luke ask the men.

"I don't know," Blue said, "but the back of my neck is crawling."

"I don't like it at all," John said quietly, his finger tapping the trigger of his revolver.

Bear's gaze never left the small gap in the trees. He prowled toward it and let out a fierce growl that Liz didn't know her son's dog could make.

Suddenly, a white form emerged: Megan, in her nightgown, panting and looking around frantically, her face white as a ghost.

"Megan! What are you doing out here?" Blue swore, irritated and relieved as he lowered his gun. "Are you alone?"

John let out a breath and bent over to his knees. Bear ran to the opening Megan had flown through, his throat still rumbling.

"Come here, boy," Luke pressed, but Bear didn't move.

"What was that? Did you see it?" Megan panted, trying to catch her breath.

"We didn't see anything. We only heard it," Blue said. "Or heard you. I'm not sure."

"Well, what did you see?" John asked impatiently.

"Megan, you know not to go out alone," Blue told her, and Liz let out a heavy sigh.

"What's going on?" Emma whispered. "What is it?"

Shushing her, Liz urged, "Let's wait for them to call us out."

"It was big with glowing eyes," Megan exclaimed, and Liz's eyes widened. "It moved so quickly. Did you hear it? I haven't a clue what it was, but it could have gotten me! It's still out there," she cried. "Where's Liz?"

"There," Luke said, pointing them out, and Liz drew back the tarp just in time for Megan to fly through it.

CHAPTER 8

"Am I alive or dead?" Chet asked, his eyes still shut but his hand pressing against his head.

"Morning, cowboy, you still with me?" Thomas asked.

"If I'm dead, surely my head wouldn't hurt so badly. I must be alive then. What happened?" Chet asked.

"I was hoping you would give me the details," Thomas said, concerned at Chet's confusion.

"Where's my pony? Is my girl fine?" he asked.

Thomas had found some coffee in Chet's saddlebags and built a small fire to heat some water. He poured a cup of coffee and walked over to his friend.

"She is fine. I checked her over last night and this morning, looking for a few answers. I tried to get her to tell me what happened," he said with a grin, "but she wouldn't talk."

Chet took the coffee Thomas offered and rested on one elbow. After taking a sip, he cringed.

"Plenty hot, but not too good. I'd forgotten how bad your coffee is."

Thomas watched Chet. He didn't look badly wounded. "Do you think you can ride today?"

"I think so. How deep is the cut?"

The open gash on his head still oozed, and the blood had matted at his hairline.

"We need to get you to Miss Emma's sewing bag. She can put in a real neat stitch for you," Thomas teased him. "After breakfast, I figure I'll ride back to the camp and alert the others to where you are. We can bring the wagons through this way and settle you back on one until you're keen to ride."

Chet managed a small nod and carefully sipped his coffee.

"So, what made a cowboy like you get thrown from his best filly?"

"Well," Chet cleared his throat and sat up to speak, "we were riding along the creek when she got spooked for no reason that I could tell. We were in this clearing and were trapped with only one way out. I heard a growl that appeared to be close." Chet grew more excited as he spoke. "Immediately!" He clapped his hands together. "I looked up and could see a huge black panther about to lunge at us. Just then, Tessie bolted!" Chet stopped and thought for a moment. "And that was the last thing I remember. I thought we were supper!"

"A panther?" Thomas questioned.

"Yes, sir, I know it was."

"You didn't have any idea that this cat was after you? I've seen a few before, but they usually aren't so aggressive."

"Yah," Chet answered. "Tessie didn't even have much warning. Usually, she can smell danger and warn me when something's near."

They both sipped their coffee. "Where did you find her?" Chet asked.

"Not too far from you right now. I could tell she'd been run hard, but she was calm when I rode close up on her."

Chet lay back to rest his head on the saddle and closed his eyes. "Ride on back to camp. I will be fine here."

Thomas loosed his mare from the lanky oak tree that he'd fought all night for sleeping space. He checked his saddle and prepared to ride back to camp.

"Rest a bit more. I'll be back with the wagons well by noon."

✳   ✳   ✳

At the breakfast campfire, Megan recounted her story for Abby, who had slept through the whole ordeal.

"What it was exactly," Megan said, "I'm not sure. But it was big, dark, and quick as lightning. That was the part that was so strange and frightening to me. It would have easily torn me to pieces!" She shook when she'd gone over it again.

"Megan, I am upset with your judgment. You should never go out alone like that, and you did not tell any of us!" Liz scolded her sister.

"You know I always have to go at least one more time in the night, and I didn't want to disturb anyone. I thought all of you were already asleep."

"It's only the second day, and we've already lost Thomas and Chet, and you go out at night all by yourself? How could you do something like that? I just don't understand. What if you didn't come back? And then, what would we do this morning with three people missing? We already don't know what to do now!"

Megan didn't say anything.

"Well?" Liz demanded an explanation.

"I'm sorry, Liz. You're right." Megan lowered her head. "I shouldn't have done that."

Blue approached the ladies from his wagon, pulling up his droopy pants along the way. He managed a groggy greeting for the women. "G'mornin.'"

"Good morning," they replied flatly.

He rinsed a tin cup and prepared to make coffee.

"Where is Luke?" Liz directed to Blue.

"Still sleeping."

Liz stood seriously and put her hands on her hips. "What should we do this morning? Do we stay here and continue to wait, or do we go search for them?"

Blue looked up at her and grimaced.

"I don't think we should search for them," Abby said.

"I don't either," Emma agreed.

Liz noticed the corner of Blue's mouth as it quirked. "I don't think that would be wise either. We stay and wait. That's all we can do. If they come back and we're not here—"

Just then, over the hill that blocked their campsite from the river, they all seemed to notice at the same time as someone approached on horseback.

"Who is it? Is it Chet?" Emma asked.

"No," Liz exclaimed. "It's Thomas!"

Thomas pulled back on the reins and the horse came to an abrupt stop as the group of them swiftly approached.

"Everything's fine," he said, slightly out of breath. "Chet is all right. He fell from his horse and injured his head, but he's going to be just fine."

"Oh! Thank God!" Liz exclaimed. "Thank God!"

"Yes, his horse got spooked and threw him. He hit his head and was knocked out entirely. I found him just as he came to. It was too dark for us to ride back to camp."

"What spooked his horse?" Megan asked.

"He wasn't sure."

"Where is Chet now?"

"He's waiting for us by the creek."

"Gracious, Thomas," Liz said pensively, "we were so worried. We didn't know what we would do this morning."

"Everything is fine now," Thomas reassured her over the thumping of her heart. "Let's pack up. Chet's a-waiting."

As Thomas dismounted and joined in the process of packing up, Liz noticed him look up and she followed his gaze. The southern sky had quickly turned greenish and dark.

It took some time to hitch up six teams of horses and wagons. Finally, they rolled out of camp, Thomas in the lead wagon once again. He had instructed them that they would travel in a single wagon row because of the narrow path he'd encountered along the small river, and they followed along the creek until it forked south. To the southwest, darkness and fast-moving rain clouds would block the sun out completely soon.

Thomas slowed the lead wagon to an abrupt halt and jumped down. He loosened his horse and walked back to the others.

"Thomas," Blue called out over the whipping wind, "those clouds are moving fast."

He took off his hat and looked up to the dark sky.

"I've been watching them as we rode," Blue said. "I thought they would move north, away from us."

"Everyone stay in the wagons," Thomas called out. He looked directly at Liz when he added, "Chet is down through the brush. I'll go get him."

Liz nodded and called out to him, loudly above the whipping wind. "Be careful, Thomas!" Her concern for him stoked an ember or two in the center of his chest.

Thomas rode down a steep hill and into the brush. The trees grew thicker the closer he got to the creek. Before he reached the bottom of the hill, he already felt raindrops on his neck. His horse shivered from an unexpected south wind.

"Whew! That's cold, Bootsie!" His horse grunted. "Keep going, we're almost there."

Bootsie plowed her way through the thick bushes. Small branches scraped across Thomas's face as he tried to shield himself with his arm. A narrow area of smooth stones and rocks bordered the skinny river and made it less thick with growth. Just as Thomas reached the area, he saw Chet's horse and bag.

"Chet," he called out from atop his own horse.

He spotted Chet eating a dried piece of meat, seated on a fallen tree. "Chet, we've got to get going! A storm is coming in."

The long rag Chet had worn across his head now protruded from his back pocket.

"How do you feel?" asked Thomas.

"I can ride."

Chet hurried to place his cup and food into Tessie's saddlebag and hastily hopped into the saddle.

※　※　※

The flaps on Liz's bonnet pressed against her face. A fierce gust of wind caught her attention and compelled her to look up. The huge dark storm had already pressed upon them.

We should take cover, she thought.

As a young child, Liz had been taught how to read the weather and how to distinguish a severe storm from a mere rainstorm, and she wondered how this one had crept up on her. She had educated Luke with all she'd learned about the weather and they'd always pulled together to prepare for such circumstances. She felt a little frustrated over allowing the storm to catch her off guard.

Dead limbs hung carelessly over Blue's horses at the back of the wagon train. A strong flurry of wind blew across the trees and suddenly, with a big crack, one of them collapsed to the ground in one swift movement. As they hit the ground, Blue's horses spooked from the commotion and immediately took off at a full run with Blue yanking back on the reins. As Emma and Abby screamed, Blue shouted at the horses as he tried to gain control, but couldn't seem to manage it.

As the horses and wagon sprinted to safety, the back wheel clipped the side of Luke's wagon, sparking discord among the animals. Still hitched to their wagons, the horses ran off in a panic. The rain pelted stronger and lightning flashed. Luke and Blue, still on their wagons, struggled to gain control.

Lightning illuminated the dark sky, revealing a snaking twister that reached toward the ground with smoky fingers. Liz gasped as she watched the tornado fly over the trees, her own heart spinning with fear as it approached the ground.

Cold rain splashed her before it whirred around her and pelted faster with each frantic breath she took. It became difficult to see as the rain and wind whipped her hair and bonnet. Panic began to swell inside her.

"Twister!" Liz called to the frantic group as Blue and Luke steered their wagons back toward them. "Take cover! It's coming our way! We need to find a low spot! Get to shelter!"

Blue pointed toward a ravine just a short ways from them. The teams of horses seemed as eager as the drivers to find safety, and they moved without prompting.

It surprised Liz to find how easy it was to get the wagons to the ravine, and they made it there quickly. The horses became jittery over the hailstones that bounced on their targets.

The men had nothing to which to tie the teams, and Liz felt frightened that the horses might spook and run again. Abby, Emma, and Megan had found their way to safety, and Luke stood away from the shelter holding his team while John, Blue, Luke, and Liz each did their best to keep two teams calm during the worst of it.

Hail pounded across Liz's shoulders as she tried to protect herself next to the animals and, at the same time, hold onto the reins to keep the horses calm. Her bonnet flew up, and she found herself soaked to the skin and shivering almost immediately. She nestled in closer to one of her horses and tucked her head under the soft velvet line of its neck. She wondered who actually comforted whom. The wind whipped her dress around her legs in a tight embrace and, when she glanced out to see how Luke fared, her bonnet flew back from her head and a hailstone pelted her on the mouth. Her lips felt numb from the cold and she tasted blood.

Liz hung her head down under the protection of her horse while sobs escaped from her, almost before she even realized she was crying. She continued to weep as the rain mixed with her tears. She could not keep the sensation away. With the storm came a feeling of hopelessness, and the rain that hit her face beat memories of the Riverton Mill and the day she became the widow of Caleb Bromont straight out of her. What had happened to the good luck that her Irish chain anniversary quilt was supposed to bring?

Thoughts of Caleb summoned fear and dread for their son, and Liz shoved the wet hair from her face as she looked for Luke. The storm still raged, but his two teams did well. The hail had passed quickly; hopefully, the threat of the twister, too. "Liz," Abby called. "Hurry, come inside. The thunder is almost gone now. The horses will be fine."

Abby had the strings untied from the wagon cover and held them tightly as the wind whipped about to keep it from invading her almost-dry habitat.

Liz gave a word of encouragement to the animals and pulled her black boots from the mud and streams of water that flooded past her ankles. Her saturated dress had lost all its absorbing power. The water flowed past her hemline. She felt bone tired as she waded her way toward Abby, her dress weighing more than she did. She nearly missed the wooden foothold on the wagon bed and, as she climbed up to comfort, her heel caught the edge of her skirt and ripped it at the waist. Her hand then slipped off the top edge of the wagon and she fell, hitting her cheek bone on the wooden sideboard.

Abby heard the whack of Liz's face against the wagon. "Oh my, Liz! Are you hurt?" she cried.

Liz climbed into the wagon, falling into a state of exhaustion with mud, blood, and tears burning over her cut and swollen face. Abby, seeing her cousin's distress, quickly went to work.

"Megan and Emma are in the wagon over there." She motioned to the back corner of the wagon as she cared for Liz's cut cheek, and she pulled out some dry things for her cousin. She turned around to grab the cords of the wagon cover and peeked out quickly before pulling them tight again and dropping the big flap from the top. She pulled another string around a toggle nailed to the wagon's side.

"Luke just climbed up in his wagon, and the men are headed to theirs. Hopefully, the worst is over. Oh, Liz, you are drenched and bleeding. I hope you don't catch your death of a cold. Hurry and dry off."

Liz pulled the remnant of her dress from her body. As she swept her hair up in the empty flour sack, Abby saw her battered shoulder where the hailstones had bruised her skin. Liz jumped as the cotton sack touched her tender shoulders.

"I feel beaten, inside and out. I don't know which is worse," she told Abby. Then, in an effort to reassure herself, she asked, "Luke's in his wagon?"

"Yes."

"I hope he has his pinwheel quilt where he can use it."

Liz had quilted Luke's quilt with wool batting from Mrs. Dongreen's flock of sheep. Liz thought she made the best wool batting. However, she could only afford one length a year.

"It will help keep Luke dry. It is the best for humid climates, though. Oh . . . I must be delirious, rambling on like this, dear Abby." Liz popped her head into the surprisingly dry and welcome nightgown.

The rain continued to come down in sheets all night long. Liz felt so exhausted that, once again, she fell asleep nearly the moment her head hit her pillow. She pulled Abby's soft worn quilt up to her battered shoulder and snuggled into its comfort and warmth. As she drifted off to sleep, she wondered if Caleb would arrive in the morning and take them safely to their new home in the west. Somewhere in her sleepy thoughts came the realization that Caleb would never rescue her again. She was on her own.

CHAPTER 9

The rumbling storm continued to drop massive amounts of rain all night long. Thomas and Chet found an area under a stand of trees to stay as dry as possible in such conditions, the cover still insufficient. They were both icy cold and wet to the core. Thomas kept a close eye on the creek. He did not want to be caught in a flash flood on top of everything else.

"Thomas? Do you think any of the big paw prints we found will still be around in the morning?"

"I don't see how in this storm."

"I've seen 'em before," Chet told him. "But those tracks . . . they'd have to come from a large cat, what the Indians call puma. They pull their claws in when they walk. Dogs and coyotes—even bobcats—leave a claw mark when they walk. These panthers can get pretty big. I once saw four-inch pad tracks on a black one. It stalked us for two days over in east Texas. Killed one of our horses just for sport, then didn't take one bite from him. It was evil, just plain evil."

Thomas looked over to Chet, water streaming off the brim of his hat and onto his poncho, which he had retrieved from his saddlebags before his horse ran. "What else do you know about these panthers?"

"Puma cats have front paws that are larger than the back. When they walk, their rear paws step into the print of the front one, causing overlap of the paw prints. They walk clean, straight lines, distinct with three lobes at the heel of the pad and two at the top, with four toes. Those tracks we saw today are puma prints, for sure. It has to be a black panther, and the size is the biggest I've ever seen or heard of. That's what spooked Tessie, I'm sure of it. I scouted with an old Indian. He told of a legend about a black puma. It was an evil spirit to his people. Would stalk his people and bring bad luck. As long as it prowled about, destruction was close at hand."

Thomas wasn't sure he believed in evil spirits or legends with curses, but he knew one thing for sure: Luck didn't seem to be on his side at the moment. Thunder boomed overhead, and the rain slowed to a heavy drizzle. He glanced toward the stream once more and noted its rising and rapid movement. His immediate concern, however, focused on where his horse had run off to, and whether or not she remained safe from the puma.

"Where do you reckon the women are?" Chet asked.

"I hope just up the hill a short ways. I saw plenty of trees for them to take cover. We'll know which way to head to look after them in the morning once I find my mare. I hope the men got the teams tied up good in all this thunder."

"If we get an early start, we can be there before they have time to get too anxious," Chet said.

"Well," Thomas said, "let's hope our bad luck was washed away in this weather." He decided to catch a wink or two until the storm passed and they could meet up with the wagons. The sun would be up in an hour and the rain was falling like a gentle shower. The ravine they camped in looked like a prime candidate for flooding in this type of gully-washer.

※　※　※

Liz had realized that the water had begun to rise in the night as the storm raged on, but it looked as if it had also been working against the top-soil around the wheels of Blue's wagon all night long. Finally, the wagon began to groan and shift as the ground gave way beneath, and she figured the lurching had awoken Blue as she heard him call out for help.

"John! John!" Blue cried in the darkness, "Wake up! Get them all up! Hurry! Flash flood!"

Liz fought the sleep from her eyes as Blue shouted, "Stay where you are, ladies!"

His team of horses sprang into action, dragging his wagon up to higher ground. The women, all awake now, clambered about to reach their own wagons without touching the rain soaked ground.

For several minutes, driver and team worked hard pulling the wagons from the clay ruts. Finally, Liz realized all the wagons but one had reached higher ground. The wagon Thomas had driven was now driverless, with no one to direct it to safety. With the open rushing water current threatening to break it to pieces, the horses struggled against it, barely able to keep it from being swept away. Liz noticed that one of the wheels had been caught by a stump.

No! No, not that wagon!

They would have to act fast in order to keep the team and wagon from being lost, not to mention all of the precious cargo inside.

Liz had no time to think, and she sprang into action, darting across a branch that had fallen, creating a makeshift bridge. If she could just make it to that rock up ahead, she could jump into the drifted wagon seat.

"John! Blue!" she called. "Hurry to the wheel. As soon as I grab the reins, break the branch and release the wheel."

Their faces betrayed their quick flashes of thought. No time to tell her to let it go. They had to help her.

Blue trudged into the water and held onto the wagon as he worked his way around to the tree branch lodged into the spokes.

"Ready," Liz called out, encouraging the horses to pull with all their might.

Four horses pulled, two men pushed, four on dry land prayed.

Suddenly, with a mighty groan, the wagon broke free and the horses scrambled to dry land. John and Blue held on to the back of the wagon as they lumbered through the remnant of rushing waters grabbing their ankles.

"Well, good morning everyone," John said with mock cheer once they had reached drier ground. "I see we are off to a good start already today."

They all groaned, and Liz leaned back against the bench and sighed.

"At least we won't have to wash up for breakfast," John added with a chuckle.

Blue looked down at himself dripping in muddy water and suddenly noticed his ripped shirt. Wiggling his finger around the tear, he remarked, "Miss Liz, what do you have in that wagon? It is as heavy as gold bricks. What did Thomas pack?"

Liz gasped sharply. Blue had no way of knowing that the wagon, in fact, contained all of her grandfather's gold; information that, at the instructions of Grandpa Lucas, only had been shared with her and Thomas.

Once Liz had gathered her wits about her, she lurched. "Where's Luke? Is he all right?"

"Right over here," Luke piped up, and Liz sighed in relief yet again. "Both me and Bear made it through unharmed."

"Well . . . thank the Lord. How about everyone else? Do we have any injuries?"

When everyone—except Thomas and Chet, of course—had been accounted for, Liz collapsed against the bench seat once more.

John walked away to prepare the wagons, placing his arm around Luke's shoulders.

"That is one special lady, that mother of yours. I was feeling pain from those hailstones last night and was ready to give up when I looked around and saw her out there with the men. Soaked and beat up, but never giving up. Now she pulls a wagon from a watery grave in her nightgown. If Thomas doesn't hurry back, I might have to ask her to marry me!"

Liz flinched. Did he think she couldn't hear?

Marry John! she thought. *Not very likely.*

John slapped Luke on the back and withdrew to his wagon. "Pulled a wagon from a flash flood in her nightdress," he mumbled, shaking his head in disbelief.

They had a lot to do before they would be ready to leave. The teams needed to be unharnessed and rubbed down after wearing wet riggings all night. The wagons would need to be checked for wear and examined for any damage suffered at the flight of the wild horses. Each wagon needed to be dried out correctly.

While the men went about the business of tending to the teams, Liz spent time feeding the chickens. They surprised her with a couple of waiting eggs, both miraculously unbroken. Luke made sure his special quilt was dry and folded in his wagon while Bear, excited to get out and run, frolicked around them.

"I think I'll let him run with the wagons once we get going," Luke commented. "He really needs some exercise after the night we've had."

Liz agreed that it might be a good idea for a bit. Soon, they would be ready to continue on the trail, but her thoughts of Thomas and Chet flooded her with concern. She felt sure that, if they continued on in their direction, Thomas and Chet would eventually meet up with them. She hoped so, anyway. What else could they do?

Liz stood before the group and informed them of her plan, explaining that Thomas and Chet were sure to catch up with them but, all things considered, they should make haste.

Blue nodded firmly, and John agreed. "It sounds like a good plan."

"We follow the sun west," Blue declared. "And we start our third day with the worst sleep yet."

Everyone laughed, and Megan squeezed Liz's hand as they headed for their wagon. On her way, Liz stopped to check on Abby and Emma.

"How about it, you two?" she asked. She'd never heard the two of them so quiet.

"We're with you," Emma said with a weary nod. "You lead, we follow."

※　　※　　※

It took most of the morning for Chet and Thomas to locate Bootsie, but by noontime, they'd set out toward the big group of trees where they'd all been together last. They searched for signs that might tell them where everyone was, but couldn't find anything. The wagons weren't where they left them, and so much mud made it impossible to make out any tracks. The storm had washed away any sign that might have been useful, and the campsite sat empty.

"I think we should ride southwest and see if we can pick up a trail," Thomas said from his pawing horse. "They wouldn't have headed back to Lecompte."

Thomas had thought about the group during the storm, and he especially wondered how the women had fared. He had no idea how bad it had been or where they were. As he made his way up a steep hill, he spotted where a small twister had gone through, leaving a clearing in the trees. Those that remained had been pulled up and twisted like weeds in a garden, and the loose ground looked like a stampede had stomped through.

※　※　※

Liz suddenly thought of the little journal Abby had given her. What better time to start writing in it than after such an adventure? She wanted to put the first days into words if she could, considering the hardships they had encountered. Perhaps her grandchildren would read it someday, hardly able to believe the escapades she and the others had experienced on their way across the country toward a new life.

Her hand went to her cheekbone, and she touched her wound before picking up her little pencil and beginning to write. She neatly titled the entry: *May 1856, Elizabeth Bromont's Journey to Fort Worth, Texas.*

She smiled at Megan as she gathered her thoughts.

Several days on the trail. We have made a small stopover. The ground is fresh from the rain. The scenery appears to be the same as Grandfather's beloved Riverton home. The trees and wildflowers are sweet and untouched. We are faring better as the days go along. Luke and his dog, Bear, are good help and they are enjoying the trip, even with the mishaps. For him, I suppose the challenges simply add to the adventure.

Bear cornered a rabbit for supper and our group is happy to have fresh meat. It will be a lovely treat. With all that we have encountered, our meals have lacked the nourishment to which we're accustomed.

This afternoon, the sky clouded up again, reminding us all of the days before when the fierce rain nearly took our wagon and team of horses. I prayed and therein it passed by. Megan is excited that her prized treadle machine weathered the storm sans any undoing. I, too, am excited we've made it thus far, and, for the most part, in one piece. Megan remains confident and contented about life, but I wish Emma could consider such outlooks. Megan is elated at the thought of cooking our rabbit stew for the night. She also has made plans to make some biscuits, a lovely treat on such a journey if she can manage it in these conditions. Megan mentioned that, on her account, we should not withhold any consideration we might have to travel all the way to California. For me though, if I can make it to Texas, I suppose I will never leave.

DAY 4:

I consider us to be faring and managing well. To sleep on the ground is our greatest discomfort, and I find myself dreaming of a soft bed quite often. We are dry though, and that continues to be a great luxury. Throughout the day's travel, we become very weary from the intense turbulence of the wagon's ride. At night, we are content only to be still, for the wagons shake us beyond belief.

Blue's team of oxen smell so bad in the day's heat. After today, we've agreed that it would be best for him to drive at the rear of the train from here on out.

At night, we have been required to cook over an open fire. It is different in many ways, though I am already growing more accustomed to it. It is amazing how such tasks can quickly become routine.

I consider it a peculiarity the way the men have allowed me to lead the group and manage even the smallest considerations. Many times throughout the day, I have considered our direction west and have rightly hoped that we are going the correct angle, south and west. Thomas and Chet have now been gone two complete days. I do not allow myself or the others to dwell on this.

Blue and John are faring well with the repairs that our wagons might require. Bless them, they are trying to keep us safe. Each evening when we make camp, Blue goes to each wagon and checks it over for any damages that might have occurred throughout the day. He pushes and pulls on all facets of the wagons, making certain that every inch is favorable. I find it strange that they rarely speak to us women. I think they feel a certain responsibility to Grandpa Lucas and, perchance, they are already concerned about his opinion of the trouble we've encountered.

Blue does well rigging the harnesses so that each of us women can handle the wagons. He has taken both of the oxen teams and follows behind us as we make our way. Of course, he eventually catches up to us after we stop for camp each evening. I have decided it is wise to push long each day. The sooner we can reach the edge of Texas, the sooner we will meet with the Rangers.

John takes care of the teams well. One harness is rubbing badly and we've had to make some salve from the root of a stickery bush. I decided to try it on the injuries to my face. It helped the soreness and seems to be healing faster, though it stains my face purple and the others laughed at me.

John and Blue have brought whiskey. Blue allowed me to pour some in my coffee, and it helps me to sleep better. I was not as sore and tender when I awoke.

DAY 5:

The weather has been hot. Now and then, we get a cloud, which gives us a short spell of relief, but it seems to make the air more thick. I want nothing more than to find a place where we could swim and rest for an entire afternoon. Our clothes are so damp they stick to us. I would like to change clothes but don't want to until we find a place to rest and bathe. I am still wearing my torn dress from the storm. I did a quick repair on the waist. I know that I must look a fright with my injuries and my dress torn and my purple stained face.

Megan said she would fix my dress better than new for me. She has been so worried over the trouble I've had. I am so glad we had no broken bones. Blue said if it would rain, we could all take a shower. Megan and

Emma keep us on our toes, the rascals.

We are all sore from the shaking of the wagons and the team handling. Though I haven't looked at the condition of our freight, I am glad that we had the sawdust for packing. I will put a little of John's whiskey in all of our coffee tonight. We all need to sleep well at least once this week.

DAY 6:

About mid-morning, we found the perfect place to bathe and take a short swim. I halted the wagons and told the team this ought to be our day of repair and rest. They all agreed. Camp was made after only a few hours of travel time. We did repairs on the wagons and we washed clothes and repaired them as well. The rest and cleanliness was good for our souls.

After supper, Blue and John pulled out some instruments and we enjoyed some music and sang our favorite hymns. Music always makes the mood lighter somehow, and it somehow forged a more friendly relationship between us and the men. We even had a dance or two, though I know many forbid it.

We pulled out our quilting and stitched during the late afternoon and before supper. Emma cheered up a great deal after we sewed. I asked her if she had tried to stitch in her wagon as we traveled. She said that she had and that it hurt too much. She showed me her sore fingers. She laughed and said that it hadn't worked on the stagecoach to Lecompte either.

It was a wonderful day. Megan said the landscape had begun to change as we passed through different land.

As I went to the wagon to sleep tonight, I asked John what he thought about Thomas and Chet still missing. He reassured me that they would be along soon and not to worry. I'm choosing to believe him.

DAY 7:

I was surprised this morning as we came upon Fort Polk. We stopped and got a few supplies and had a nice visit with some of the officers' wives. They prepared a magnificent lunch for us and it did our souls well to have such food and hospitality. We surely were not ready to go when the captain gave the call to load up. All of us had made friends quickly, even Luke and Bear. The young troops were interested in our unusual group and quickly saddled up to escort us to the border where our Rangers are supposed to be waiting. They said we ought to be there by evening.

I was upset when I learned we had angled too far south and now would have to go north to our location in Texas. We have lost time by our troubles and losing our direction. The lieutenant assured me that the storm had disrupted the path we were to be on and we would have had to come south anyway. Truth? I'm not sure of it, but it made me feel better. I also decided that Thomas and Chet are fine and that they must be worried sick over us and wondering where we are. I hope they have not gone back to Grandpa Lucas as I would hate for him to worry so over us when we are well.

It was a good thing also that we cleaned up yesterday. We would have died for the fort ladies and soldiers to see us in such disarray as we were. Captain Sewell was concerned over my injuries and had the doctor take a look at my head. He scolded me and said a lady had no business taking such risks out on the trail. I didn't tell him how much I enjoyed taking part in leading our group.

He said to keep putting the salve that we made for the horses on my face, even though it turns one's skin purple. Captain Sewell also advised us on the route to take north after we cross over the line, and he said he would put word out to Thomas and Chet as to our whereabouts. He said the Indians have been quiet lately, but that we will go through a certain territory where we should stay most alerted.

Mrs. Sewell had a new baby girl that we all fell in love with. I think all of us were thinking about our own mothering feelings and wondering if we would have our own children in the future. I don't know why Caleb and I never had more. Luke came so quickly that I assumed I would have plenty. Abby and Megan certainly are old enough to have a houseful of their own by now. It is, in fact, quite unusual for all of us to be single and Luke the only child. I never thought of it in such a way until just recently.

We made the Texas line by dark and the army made camp with us. They drew us a map and gave us the landmarks for which we should stand watch as we move farther west.

DAY 8:

This morning it was rather difficult to see the troop ride away. I slept well in light of my not having one of John's special coffee mixtures. My body feels stronger and my injuries are all but healed.

Megan always has admirers, and our visit at the fort was no exception. She certainly is pleasant to them in general, but she never seems to have an interest in anyone specific.

As we continue, we are to go along the Angelina River and through the forest. As I saw all of the lumber from the trees, I began to wonder if Grandpa ought to leave the lumbering business. Timber is plentiful in this land.

It seems like ages since we were back home. Captain Sewell's wife showed us a number of her patterns, and I have just now realized that I forgot to write them down. She had many beautiful quilts that we all loved, my favorite being a star with a blue center and points. It had a small burst of triangles around it. It will be the first one I attempt after I settle in my new home. As always, we traded some cloth with her. She had some of the blue from the star and, being the lady that she is, simply gave it to me. I promised to inform her on my progress.

She had more quilts than I had ever before seen, almost all of which were stacked and neatly folded. She rarely uses many of them. I suppose that she has a lot of empty time on her hands while residing there. Another one I liked a great deal had a wreath with points. It was very unusual in its design. Each circle had a bluish hue to it. It appears to be an organized scrap quilt. It seems difficult to fashion, however. Upon curiosity, I counted over seventy pieces in each block. It had many curved pieces. One day, perhaps I can work up the courage to make it.

DAY 9:

Today, while searching Thomas's wagon for some supplies that John and Blue required, I came upon a large wooden box with a lovely log cabin quilt inside. I took it out to admire its wonderful construction. The blocks were unique: four log cabin blocks sewn together with fire red triangles around the outside edges. When I spread it out for closer inspection, a letter fell open at my feet. I saw it was from his mother before I realized how intrusive I'd been, and I quickly folded it back into the quilt.

CHAPTER 10

Thomas had spent nine days searching for Elizabeth Bromont and the others, perplexed as to how they could have disappeared. He talked to many folks along the trail after the storm and no one had heard of this group of women and six wagons. If they'd met with trouble or harm's way, such news would have certainly traveled fast. He didn't want Lucas to get wind of this—or more importantly, any outlaws—so he maintained caution in his investigations, mostly listening for conversation that might lead him to his cluster of females.

He sat in a tipped-back chair outside the saloon as two men in military uniform started up the steps.

"And you're certain that the wagon train was all single women?" the light-haired man with fuzzy eyebrows asked.

"Yes," the tall one said, stooping his head to enter the door of the saloon. "I was there when they stopped at Fort Polk with Captain Sewell and his wife."

Finally, word of the women! Thomas nearly knocked his chair over as he popped up from it, his glances darting around for Chet. When he didn't find him, Thomas entered the saloon and walked straight over to the men in blue and ordered three drinks.

"Gentlemen, did I hear right that you saw a wagon train of women?"

The two soldiers cautiously looked at Thomas, Chet now standing next to them. Thomas noticed the hesitation in the light-haired man's countenance.

"Let me introduce myself," he said warmly. "I am Thomas Bratcher. My friend and I are employed by Lucas Mailly to lead his wagon train and freight to Fort Worth. In the storm last week," Thomas paused, feeling the embarrassment of losing his group, "we lost track of our charges."

"As I remember," the man said cautiously, "it seems they had come across some trouble. They appeared to be managing just fine."

"Was anyone hurt?" Thomas asked.

"The lady that was leading them, but only a few scrapes. One nasty one to the head."

"The others," his companion stated, "seemed just fine. But they're headed right for Indian country now." He reached for his whiskey. "What's wrong with that pa of theirs?"

"How badly was she hurt?" Thomas asked.

"She was banged up all right. Captain Sewell sent her to the doc."

"Tell me. Please, where was she hurt?"

"Her eye was purple and she had a gash down her check. As well as her lip, it was cut."

Thomas poured himself another whiskey, "And what direction were they headed?"

"The captain gave them a map and some men of ours rode with them to the edge of Texas."

"Please. Can you tell me where they left them and where they told them to go?" Thomas implored.

"Our men left Fort Polk and were going west to the Sabine Forest. I suppose that's where they camped, but that's all I know."

"Well then, men, thank you for your help."

Thomas stood to shake their hands.

"Good luck," the blond man said, "and thanks for the drink."

Thomas and Chet both gulped down their whiskey and headed out the door.

Once outside, Chet turned to Thomas. "I think we should cut across to the north of the Sabine. I know a place we can cross the river and find a spot to meet them, close to where the Rangers should be. There's a stage station close to the Crockett Forest and Nacogdoches. Maybe if we push it, we can do it in a five-day ride."

"How long do you think it will take them?" Thomas asked.

"I'd say at least six," Chet replied.

✕ ✕ ✕

Liz shook the reins of her team and looked out from beneath her bonnet, searching for a place to make camp. She watched Bear as he playfully ran along with the wagons. Bear had quickly learned the routine of each day, and no one had to worry about his whereabouts as he galloped into the thicket of trees and happily reappeared a mile or so later. When he didn't return soon enough for Luke, Liz's son whistled and the dog came running.

One night when camp was made and everyone had settled, Bear flew out from the thick trees with an angry raccoon chasing him. "Blue, do you see him? Hurry! Over there," Liz called.

Bear barked and tormented the masked creature as it hissed at the dog and rose to its back legs.

"Luke, stay back," his mother commanded from the wagon seat. "Let John scare him off!"

John stalked around the wagon with his gun, firing two shots into the air. The raccoon hurried off with Bear at his heels. Luke whistled for a good minute or two before the dog finally turned for home base.

"That was funny seeing that raccoon chasing Bear like that," John said.

"I guess so," Liz replied. "I was afraid it would be a crazy one and cause us harm. And that is all we need, another sack of trouble."

The day turned out to be sun-filled, only a few clouds overhead. The heavy green branches on the trees insisted upon shading them, and the picturesque deep, thick grass rippled in the breeze. The rain of the past few days had painted the area with such rich color that Liz felt a deep sense of happiness as the sun warmed her face, penetrating her brain like a mild drug.

Megan jumped from her wagon seat and twirled in a circle around the prairie of lush grass. "It is beautiful here!" she exclaimed. "What a gorgeous day."

Abby approached the thicket of trees. "I have never seen a place like this. I wonder if we're still in the Sabine Forest."

The meadow at the edge of the forest looked like a fairyland to Liz, and she smiled at her cousin.

"Our Mississippi home was pretty," Abby told her, "but not like Riverton, and not anything like this place called the Sabine."

They had traveled along the bottom of the Sabine Forest after the soldiers left them, and they now turned north to the Angelina River and Crockett Forest.

Liz soaked it all in. "Well, do you think our new home will continue this beauty?

"Oh, I hope so," Abby cooed.

Liz freed her chickens and let them scratch and bob around the camp while she and Emma dug out their quilting supplies. After they settled, each of the women sat in relative silence, engrossed in her own world of fabric, needle, and thread.

Emma pulled out the nine-patch squares that she had recently completed and inspected them carefully, pulling one block to the side.

"This one needs to be ripped out and restitched," she said, and she went to work on the repair to the lovely block of browns and blues.

Abby had a few dark colors in her basket and decided to work on her appliqué. Liz knew it was Abby's favorite. She cut out the small flowers and leaves, and then turned under the edges as she stitched it to the background piece. The quilt Megan had made for Granny Claire had been her inspiration. A myriad of red and brown triangle units came from Megan's quilt box, all of them precut and stacked neatly together inside a pecan box lined with velvet. A gentleman caller had given the wooden box to Megan as a gift, and she'd later lined it with the fabric and turned it into a project box. Megan had never been too keen on any of her gentleman callers. The box, however, was a keeper with its rich, pecan coloring, pewter hinges, and carved trim. Megan had created a small needle cushion inside. "Megan," Liz said, "would you like some help with all of those triangles you have in that Feathered Star? It will be a masterpiece once you've finished it."

Megan passed the box of triangles to her sister with a warm smile and, as it passed Emma, she reached out to hold it.

"Tell me about this box?" she asked as her fingers passed over the carvings.

Liz jumped in. "It's from one of Megan's callers. She received it as a gift from Mr. Matthew Coldwell. He was a buyer who came to the mill often, a master craftsman of furniture back in North Carolina, and quite handsome and wealthy. He was very intrigued with our Megan, and he carved the box himself."

Megan gave her sister a disapproving glance before she returned to her needle and thread.

"Well, what happened?" Emma asked, wanting to know more.

"He is gone and the box is here. That's all there is to it," Liz remarked.

Megan worked to move the topic along. "Sometimes it is best for a relationship to come to an end . . . even when . . . they care about each other and all appears to be well."

Liz took the box and picked out the pieces she would sew together for Megan. She smiled at her sister and asked, "Will each star be the same?"

"Well, yes and no. The center of the stars are all different eight-inch stars, and the larger feathered star will be blue, red, or green, and with black tips. I think I will make it large, with twelve feathered stars."

Megan became herself again as she spoke of her design. She accepted the box when Liz passed it back to her. As her fingers passed over the engraving on the inside of the lid, Liz sensed Megan's reminiscence of Matthew.

"I can still hear his deep voice sometimes," Megan had confided once during a late-night quilting session back at the timber mill. "I'll tell you, Lizzie, his voice could melt you all the way to your toes. I loved to hear him sing hymns in church when he was last in Lecompte. I could recognize that voice anywhere."

Megan never said so, but Liz suspected she might have just married Matthew if he'd have asked. But he never did. Not after Matthew's mother, the real first lady in his life, had accompanied him on one of his business trips. Liz didn't know the details, and Megan never wanted to talk about them. All she knew for sure was that Megan had gone for a walk with Matthew, and they met with Mrs. Coldwell on their return. The next morning, Matthew and his mother were gone, and Megan had never truly been the same. Little snatches of conversation here and there had revealed Megan's hidden—but broken—heart, and Liz didn't press. She could only pray for her sister that God would heal her heart again— and that she'd one day find true love.

The sun began to fade for the day and as the light dissipated, it became too hard to sew. Megan placed her needle in the special box and Liz caught a glimpse of her sister as she ran her finger along the engraving on the inside.

To my special Megan. All my love, always. Matthew

"I'm tired," Megan said, and she stood up and withdrew to her wagon.

❊   ❊   ❊

Three cowboys sat around the campfire, just a short distance from the Angelina River. They'd gathered several thick logs and other kindling and arranged them at the base of the fire pit, forming a teepee around some tall, dried branches, creating an intense furnace inside them that no wind or cold could pierce.

The remains of a trail supper surrounded them. The coffeepot bubbled over the fire. Each man wore traditional trail attire. A cowboy hat made of straw for shade and air circulation was deemed most necessary, and the only time it left a man's head was when it swatted the owner's leg in anger or frustration. Even with a lady present, the hat was only tipped slightly, just enough to signify polite courtesy. In such occurrences, the cowboy's hand went toward the brim to tip it in acknowledgment, usually in accord with a "Ma'am." The removal of a cowboy's hat signified the utmost sign of respect, and such a privilege was not often bestowed.

The cowboys sitting around this fire poked at its mesmerizing flame. They wore bandannas around their necks with long-sleeved shirts tucked into denim jeans. They wore ratty cowboy boots made from animal hide, and leather belts with heavy, serious buckles. All three donned leather vests with the metal star of a Texas Ranger planted firmly over their hearts.

The oldest cowboy, Tex, though not as old as Lucas Mailly, was old enough to be the father of the women for whom he searched. He wasn't a large man in stature, but in attitude and accomplishments, you couldn't find much bigger. He was a legend with the Texas Rangers and respected across the territory. Tex couldn't be sure why Lucas Mailly sent his family alone across the land; then again, why would a man leave his family at all if he had the choice. Tex's duties didn't allow him to agonize over such things. He intended to locate their wagon train and then bring them safely to the fort, accordingly. He had never met Lucas before, but he liked him. Through their correspondence, Lucas spoke of his granddaughters as a man would his sons. Tex considered it gutsy, no less, to send the women with such sizable amounts of gold. He certainly wouldn't have done it.

Tex looked over to the two Rangers with whom he had been riding all day. He had ridden with both before and he liked the way they handled themselves—professional, with integrity, like most all Rangers he'd ever known. Jackson, in his midthirties, was tall and broad with a long handlebar mustache. Jackson won most of his battles by sheer intimidation. He rode a large black stallion named Zeus that carried a lofty attitude and listened only to his commands. Even if his enemies knew Zeus as simply a gentle giant, they would certainly not want to chance it, and they rarely did.

Tex often teased Colt about his age, "still wet behind the ears." Colt was actually twenty-one, but never told anyone. He was eighteen when he started riding with the Rangers and had only ever ridden with Tex and Jackson.

The two eldest cowboys met Colt when they came upon a group of Comanches raiding a traveling group. Wagons burned and bodies lay everywhere, killed by the deadly arrows of the Plains Indians. The Comanche were fierce and superb warriors. They could release six arrows to one shot of the white man's gun.

Colt had come running out with a Colt revolver and he had an aim many could never master, a natural shot. Tex took him in and started calling him Colt, after the gun that saved them all that day, and Colt's reputation had grown bigger than life over the years. Tex was the only one who dared tease him about his age. Colt still had a bone to pick with the world, and he would not be intimidated after that wagon raid. His soft brown locks were long down his back and he kept them tied back with a leather strip. Tex couldn't miss the fact that the boy looked very similar to the Indians he stalked. Tex and Jackson never asked Colt his real name, and Colt never gave it. They also never learned where he got the Colt revolver, or how he discovered that he could shoot so well.

Tex uncorked a bottle of whiskey and brought it to his lips, taking a big swig. The bottle rested on his leg as he considered another.

"What's eatin' you?" Jackson asked his mentor.

"Ah, nothin' I can't handle."

"When do you see us finding that wagon train?" Jackson asked, and he took the bottle from his friend's knee.

"As we go north, we'll find them."

Colt stirred the fire and added another log. "Why are we sent to meet this group, anyway?" he asked. "It doesn't make sense to me. We don't guard wagons and help them across the frontier. We pull them out of trouble after they find it . . . and they always do."

Tex knew that Colt had little sympathy for wagon trains. Few, in his mind, had business going west. He guessed the boy had just seen too much in too few years.

"Women have got no business on the frontier," Colt continued.

Tex lay back on his saddle and tipped his hat forward. "Jackson, take first watch. Colt you're next." He turned his back to the fire and adjusted the bedroll under his shoulder, and he muttered, "Dang, I miss my dog."

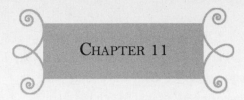

CHAPTER 11

The Mailly group had traveled several days and still not come across the Rangers, nor had they found Thomas or Chet. Liz tried to hold on to the occasional burst of optimism that all was well with them and that they would surely meet up at the fort.

The embers of the evening campfire soothed Liz, and she found it an agreeable spot for thinking. Oh, how she missed her rocking chair and access to a sturdy oil lamp for sewing or reading her Bible, but the location had little to do with meditation on Scripture. She thought about one of her favorite verses to which she had often clung since Caleb had died. She recited it softly as she stirred the fire.

"We are afflicted in every way, but not crushed; perplexed, but not despairing; persecuted, but not forsaken." She paused and took a deep breath as she looked out into the darkness of night and finished the passage. "Struck down, but not destroyed. Second Corinthians, chapter four, verses eight and nine."

Liz jerked her head toward a sudden noise just as Megan appeared from the brush.

"Megan, you could get shot sneaking around like that."

Megan laughed and sat down by her sister. "Is that a threat?" she asked, looking around in dramatic fashion. "I don't see your gun. Are you hiding it somewhere, Lizzie?"

Liz snickered. "Oh, hush now."

"I heard you reciting a memory verse before. 'Struck down, but not destroyed.' And how many times do we get up?"

"A righteous falls seven times, and rises again. Proverbs 24:16."

They smiled at one another, and Megan's hand moved to Liz's face where she touched the place where the wound had been.

"You are looking better. How do you feel?"

"I try not to think what I must look like, but I do feel better."

"You know," Megan began, "if you would ever sleep, you might never know if I'm out in the dark or not."

Liz sighed.

"Do you miss home, Liz?"

"Do you?" she asked in return.

"Not really, but I do wonder if Grandpa is worried over us and if he got word somehow about our troubles."

"He knew we would have trouble, maybe even figured we might get lost, but I'm sure he's been comforted at the thought that we had Thomas and Chet to see us through. The only way we were to be alone like this was if someone was killed."

"Poor Thomas," Megan said with a sigh. "Grandpa Lucas won't be gentle with him when he finds out. Though it was not their fault. Do you think they are alive, Lizzie, and out there looking for us?"

"Yes, I do. And most likely very upset with us for not making it easier to find us."

They both laughed.

"Why do I need a man at all in my life?" Liz proposed with a gentle smile. "I mean, if I can get us across the prairie, then I can make it on my own, don't you think so? I will have the mercantile and you can have your dress shop, Megan, and we will be just fine. Luke is almost grown, and I don't need to remarry for him. I feel like men are never there when you really need them the most." When she looked up and noticed the sadness in her sister's eyes, Liz sighed. "I have a hard heart now. I know that, but I don't want to be hurt again."

Megan stirred the fire a little and turned to face her sister. "You had a happy marriage with Caleb. Don't dishonor him by thinking bitterly about marriage. You don't mean it. We just have not met suitable men. I'm simply saying to you, don't give up on Thomas. He loves you, you know."

Before Liz could part her lips to object, Megan stood up and moved toward her. Leaning over, she gave Liz a warm embrace.

"I'm tired. I'm going to turn in. Don't stay out too long."

Liz watched after her as Megan withdrew to the wagon for the night. Liz wanted to stay and listen to the humming of the night creatures a while longer.

Deep in thought, Liz stirred the fire and didn't hear them until the approaching boot steps thumped to a stop in front of her and the fire. Startled, she looked up and gasped as she saw a man with his hat pulled down over his eyes, his long hair showing beneath it. His leather holster sported two revolvers, and he clutched a rifle in his hand with the butt of the gun leaning on his hip. Liz looked down the barrel as her heart pounded out a discordant rhythm against her dress.

"You're not too cautious," the man stated.

"And you're rather brave, walking right into my camp like this."

She straightened quickly, her thoughts scrambling for what to do. Blue and John had already retired for the night.

"What do you want, and who are you?"

"I could have killed you or—" he began.

"You might get one of us, but you would never walk the same again."

Megan's voice had come from beyond the cover of brush.

"Come out of the trees, young lady," he said, and Liz thought he sounded worried. "I don't want anyone hurt."

"You would like that," Megan snapped. "Drop your gun and step away from my sister."

The young man lowered his gun and backed away. Out of the fire's light, Liz squinted to keep her eyes on him.

"Not that far!" Megan exclaimed. "Step into the light where we can see you. Now!"

"I don't want to hurt either of you, ma'am. If I did, I could easily have killed you both by now. I've watched you all day. I know who you are. I'm a Texas Ranger come to escort you to Fort Worth." He motioned to his badge, hidden by his hair, clamped to his vest pocket.

Liz heard Megan let out a heavy sigh of relief just before Bear appeared out of nowhere, yipped out a single bark, and ran up to the Ranger with his tail wagging as if he greeted an old friend.

"Bear, you traitor!" Liz stated as she watched the two. "How does he know you?"

He laughed. "We became friends over by the ridge of rocks today. I was watching all of you and he came to me just like this."

The man lowered to one knee, patting Bear's back, and Megan stepped out from the darkness, still clutching her revolver, looking a bit insecure about letting down her guard. She came and stood by Liz, and they studied the man who stood before them.

He had as much unruly hair as the dog. Liz had never seen a man with hair that long, tied and wrapped with a leather strap on each side of his head. The texture seemed far too wavy for him to be Indian, and despite his deep tan, his skin was too light for such a heritage. His brownish green eyes twinkled slightly as he looked up at Megan.

"You have no cause to fear me," he said, still rubbing Bear's back. "Could you aim that pistol in another direction?"

"Are you alone then?" Liz asked. "We were told that a man named Tex would be our escort."

"Tex will be here. Jackson is riding with us, too. They were delayed. They'll be along late morning. You two go on to bed. Bear and I will keep guard together."

Megan and Liz exchanged questioning glances.

"What's your name?" Liz asked him.

"Colt, ma'am."

"I'm Elizabeth Bromont. And this is my sister, Megan Ronnay."

"My pleasure," he replied, straightening with a smile. "Go on and get some shut-eye, both of you. We'll head out to Fort Worth in the morning."

※ ※ ※

Thomas finished his coffee, deep in thought. He couldn't understand how he could have missed Liz and the others. He felt frustrated and embarrassed, and he couldn't seem to scratch that itch in his ear, the one that told him life was too short to waste time. The code of the West dictated doing things while you still could.

With a firm and silent nod, he determined that he would ask Liz to marry him as soon as he found her again. If they were married, he could certainly take better care of her, he decided.

"Today is the day!" Chet announced as he approached Thomas and the fresh coffee beside him.

"For what?" Thomas asked.

"I feel it in my bones. We will meet up with the wagons today. I have done all the calculations. We'll find them along the river," he declared, motioning southward.

Thomas looked off into the direction and shook his head. "I don't know, but I sure hope you're right."

Why didn't I ask her before we left? Thomas thought.

He wouldn't have lost them then; he wouldn't have felt pushed to go after Chet when he went missing. Hindsight, of course, always near perfect, reassured him of that fact.

Thomas let his memory transport him back to the porch with Liz the day the wagons arrived. He thought she might tell him something that would let him know that she could be ready and willing to move on with her life. Certainly she knew that he loved her. And he'd been hoping that their trip would be the time where she might realize that she loved him, too.

Things have not worked out in my favor, he lamented, and he shook his head.

Chet moved the dirt over the fire with his boot and looked to Thomas. "What are you fretting about?"

Thomas jumped up and stalked over to his horse, tugging on the belly strap of the saddle under his mare. "Let's get moving," he said.

They both leapt onto their mounts and headed out to find the others in the early morning light.

✳ ✳ ✳

Liz congregated the women together and they gathered up all the laundry and bathing supplies, informing the men that they would be back after a while. It would give John, Blue, and Luke a good chance to get acquainted with Colt.

The water temperature felt cool but comfortable—once she adjusted to it, anyway. Each of the women removed her dress and scrubbed it on the rocks, spreading it over a bush to dry. Liz knew the garments would dry quickly in the hot Texas sun.

"Are you sure no one is around?" Megan asked, glancing about them.

"Yes," Liz answered as she waded to her knees.

Megan and Emma looked about as the others untied their camisoles.

Liz grinned. "I'm going to wear my camisole while I swim and wash my hair. But if you want to take yours off, I'm sure you're safe in doing it."

The others boldly disrobed and washed their camisoles as well, spreading them out on the rocks to dry with their dresses before they all swam and enjoyed the cool water over their sore muscles. As she scrubbed her milky skin with the lavender soap bubbles, Liz thought back to how Grandpa Lucas had taught them how to swim one summer when they all were still very young. Lathering more of the soap between her palms, she washed her hair until it squeaked between her fingers.

"This feels so good I don't want to get out," Megan said with a sigh as she floated about. "Do you think our clothes are dry now, Lizzie?"

The other three women dried off with the heavy cloths they'd brought along, and they dressed quickly in the fresh cotton clothing.

"Oh, you were the smart ones," Liz announced. "I should have put my camisole on the rocks to dry like you all did. I'll have to wait a little longer to let mine dry. You go ahead back to camp. I'll just swim a bit more, and I think it should be dry by then."

"Leave you here alone?" Abby exclaimed.

"I'll be fine," she said as she skimmed out of her camisole and handed it off to Megan to spread out on the rocks next to her dress. "Check and see if the other Rangers have arrived. I'll be along in a few minutes."

Liz felt refreshed, happy to remain behind and swim about in the cool water for a little bit longer. She heard Abby humming an old church hymn as the group of them hiked around the bend toward camp.

CHAPTER 12

Large billowy clouds with hollow centers looked as if they'd been randomly strewn about the clear blue sky. Liz stood in the shallow water, her camisole still damp and clinging to her as she looked up at them. Water dripped from her hair as it hung down her back. The sun's rays came down in spears and bounced around the water in glistening streaks as she closed her eyes and drew in a deep, lingering breath of fresh air.

Liz opened her eyes and stood perfectly still, stunned by the presence of a young brave standing less than a yard away from her at the river's edge. Behind him, a painted pony grazed in the grass. No sound escaped from her as she sank into the water to cover her naked flesh. She felt frozen, suspended in the water, almost unable to breathe as he inched into the river.

The brave reached out toward her unexpectedly, and she gasped as his hand made contact with her face. At almost the same moment, the young Indian started at the sudden break in the silence. Footsteps thumped down the rocky path past the trees beyond the pony, and the man who emerged looked something like a large bear stumbling down the hill. On the opposite side of the river, two more Indians—until that moment, completely undetected—made their way across the water to the safety of the thick trees.

Megan reached the water ahead of the mountain of a man, and she reached for the drying cloth as she approached Liz in the water. Mildly traumatized by the experience of seeing her very first Indians, Liz's entire body trembled violently.

Megan wrapped the cloth around her and led her from the water.

"Liz, are you hurt? Look at me. Are you okay?" Megan held her sister by the shoulders. "Liz? Speak to me."

"I . . . never saw him approach. I opened my eyes and he was so close. He . . . *touched me.*"

"Did he hurt you?"

"I'm not hurt. I'm . . . frightened."

The large man reached them, and he picked up her dress from the rocks, looking away as he handed it to her. He turned his back on the women before glancing over to the wooded area where the braves disappeared.

"You scared them off, Mrs. Bromont. I think they thought you were some water goddess or something." He chuckled. "Wait till Tex hears about this. It's a good thing someone didn't get stupid and try to shoot one of them young boys. If we're lucky, they might be so shaken they won't even tell anyone."

Liz quickly regained her composure and pulled the wet hair from the back of her dress. She looked to Megan with a questioning expression. "Who is this?"

Megan quickly spoke up. "Jackson, you may turn around and meet my sister, Elizabeth Bromont."

Jackson faced her with one foot on a large rock, his Colt revolver still in hand. When he spotted her staring at the gun, he shoved it into the holster on his leg.

"Mrs. Bromont, good to meet you alive. Let's get back to camp and you can get acquainted with the others."

Megan took hold of the introductions once they returned. "Tex, I would like for you to meet my sister, Mrs. Caleb Bromont."

Liz stepped toward the aging cowboy. She liked what she saw in him. She saw both wisdom and sadness in his features, and she particularly liked his eyes. He had wrinkles at the corners when he smiled at her, and he took her hand in a hearty handshake. His spurs jingled as he took a step.

"Tex, it's good to finally catch up with you," she said. "Forgive our appearance as we were not expecting Rangers—or Indians, for that matter—today."

"Indians," Blue piped up.

"Just a couple of young braves down at the river," Jackson explained.

"Indians!" Abby cried. "Liz, are you all right?"

She nodded, and Jackson continued. "Scared her more than anything, I'd say. But they hightailed it outta there. Mrs. Bromont, this is Tex, and that young'un over there is Colt. We're Texas Rangers, here to get you all safely to Fort Worth in a few days."

"We are very grateful."

"I hear you've lost some of the others in your group," Tex spoke up.

"Yes."

"It happens more often than you might imagine that groups get split along the trail," he reassured her. "They know where you are headed, so that's good, at least. We'll keep an eye out for them."

"Thank you, Mister Tex," she said as she stumbled with his name.

"Tex is fine, Mrs. Bromont."

Elizabeth nodded to him and smiled. When she inched toward the campfire to dry and braid her hair, her sister and cousins followed.

※ ※ ※

Evening came and Liz found herself fireside nursing the evening embers, unable to sleep. Tex strolled over to join her and sat down across from her atop a log.

"Colt's on guard duty, Mrs. Bromont. You don't have to stay up."

Liz sipped her tea and nodded. "Call me Liz."

"Can't sleep, Miss Liz?" he asked.

"It seems to be a problem that I've acquired."

Tex took out a thin paper and held it gently in his left hand. He reached into his shirt pocket and produced a pouch of tobacco. He tapped a little of it onto the paper. After he'd rolled it into a thin cylinder, he ran it under his nose and inhaled its pungent aroma.

"What's it like being a lawman?" she asked him. "Do you ever wish you could just stay put somewhere?"

Tex picked up a small twig and placed it at the edge of the fire to ignite it. He used the burning twig to light the end of his cigarette. He inhaled a big breath from the tobacco and exhaled a smoke ring that floated up before he replied. "Not much difference in a lawman or an outlaw, Miss. They both stay on the move. The lawman dies with honor, and the outlaw just dies."

"I'm so anxious to get settled again. This much time on the road is more than enough for me."

Tex sat quietly and smoked his cigarette until it grew smaller. He looked at the end of it and moved his tanned fingers closer to the unlit end. "I had a family once, a good woman and four girls with golden curls, something like yours. We had a little ranch, too."

His words trailed off, and Tex remained silent for a while as Liz sat wondering about this man and his sorrow.

"I'm sorry for your loss," she stated in an effort to provide sincere comfort.

"Oh, don't feel sorry for me. It's my fault that I don't have them and the ranch. I'm an old cowboy. I've paid for my choices."

"What do you mean? I thought they were dead."

"One day, I just got on my horse and rode off, Miss Liz. I didn't mean to leave . . . I just never went back, and I never sent word. The pull of the West got to me. Once I realized I wanted to go back, it was too late. I returned to find my girls almost grown and life had moved along. Allie remarried after they felt sure I was dead. I decided to leave them with that memory."

Liz watched and listened to his story. Tex's cigarette glowed as he dragged on it, sparking pretty red ambers as it bounced from a rock at the fire's edge. His tanned, wrinkled face covered with at least two days of stubble grew serious under the shadow of his memories. He rubbed his shoulder and made a small moan. He then stretched out his legs, his boots daringly close to the flame as he drew one last puff and flicked the butt of his cigarette into the fire.

"Are you hurt? I have some ointment that might help," Liz offered the aging cowboy.

"Thank you, I'm fine. Just an old wound from breaking a stubborn mustang a few years back."

Liz looked back to the fire.

"Rain comin' in, it seems. My shoulder knows." Tex frowned at Liz as he added, "Sorry about the loss of your mister. You know for sure he is dead?"

What a strange question, she thought. But maybe not so strange considering his own life experience.

"Many of the workers witnessed the accident," she answered quietly. "You know, I'm suddenly feeling worn out. I think I'll head off to get some sleep."

"'Night, Miss Liz."

"Goodnight, Tex."

On her way toward the wagon, Liz noticed lightning in the distance. A few seconds later, a soft rumble sounded from behind the clouds.

✕　✕　✕

The moon had turned full again, and the clouds in the distance brimmed with striking power. Thomas and Chet had only stopped for a few minutes to stretch their legs and give their ponies a break, and then decided to continue on since the moon had ignited the path without the clouds blocking it.

Thomas figured a little of Chet's optimism about meeting up with the Mailly women and their wagons had begun to wear off on him when he considered it might be possible for them to see the light from a campfire if one burned off in the distance. Chet seemed certain that they had to be near. Thomas wanted to believe that as well.

As they sat atop a hill aided by the light of the reflective moon, Thomas could almost peer into the night's vastness. He reached into his saddlebag and pulled out his rain slicker when a gust blew in, and Chet looked up at the sky, pushing his cowboy hat down tighter on his head while reaching for his coat.

"It's just a few clouds. Let's keep riding," Thomas said to Chet as he surveyed the sky again.

Chet agreed and quickly mounted his pony.

They rode toward the illuminated clouds, looking for any sign of a camp beneath a sky that rumbled like a low drum. When the clouds lit up again, Thomas spotted a small trail of smoke circling up to the night sky. He looked over at Chet in the hope that his friend had seen it, too, and they both leaned forward and spurred their mares into a full gallop as the raindrops began to drop hard, like weighted metal balls.

Thomas slowed his animal as they got closer to camp, diffusing his excitement to see Liz again with a stern warning to himself about frightening her and the other women by barreling into camp. Chet took his cue and slowed his pony as well.

"Be on the lookout for a guard. We don't want to spook John or Blue as we approach."

"Good thinkin'," Chet replied.

They could see into camp now and saw John, Blue, and three others, all of them with their guns raised. They stepped down from the horses and called out as they approached the outer ring of camp.

"John! Blue!" Thomas called out from the morning darkness. "We're a-comin' in."

"It's them!" John announced.

The strangers lowered their weapons and stepped out into the open as Thomas and Chet approached them with damp rain slickers and hearty smiles.

"Who are these fellas?" Chet asked, eyeing the oldest of the three strangers.

"Texas Rangers," Blue told them.

They exchanged introductions, handshakes, and firm slaps on the back as the group welcomed each other.

"Thomas!" Luke hollered as he climbed from the wagon and ran to greet him.

Luke and his dog reached the weary travelers at the same time, nearly knocking Thomas right off his feet.

"It's good to see you, Thomas! What happened? Where have you been? We had a tornado, and Mom got herself a black eye."

John and Blue laughed over Luke's excitement and quick summary of the trip. Thomas ruffled Luke's bed hair and laid his hand over his shoulder. "It sure is good to see you, Luke."

"Thomas! Oh, gracious! Thomas, is that you?"

He looked up to find Liz, awakened by all the commotion, hurrying toward them.

"It's me, Liz. I found you!"

Liz ran into Thomas's open arms and threw her own arms around his neck and held him so tight the breath knocked out of his lungs. As Thomas wrapped her around the waist and pulled her closer to him, Liz started to cry.

"I was beginning to worry, Thomas. We didn't know where you were."

Wiping her eyes, Liz's cheeks turned dark pink as she pulled away and gave Chet a clumsy embrace.

"I can't believe you made it back to us. Are you both all right?"

"Yes, Miss Liz," Chet replied. "We're both fine, just very tired."

"Is the coffee on?" Thomas asked.

The group moved toward the fire, and Liz began to pour the coffee. As the sun rose in the east, Emma, Megan, and Abby joyfully joined the gathering to help the exchange of stories and began to piece the puzzle together on how they had lost each other for so long.

"Then the storm came and erased all the tracks and chances of us following you," Chet added at last.

"Guessing you went too far south while the others went west," Jackson surmised.

"Miss Emma, I sure wish you could have sewn me up." Chet pulled his thick, long hair away from his forehead, revealing his healing—but still wide—gash atop his forehead.

Emma stood and moved close to inspect the cut. She placed her hand on his chin to tilt his head toward the early light for a better look.

"Yes," Emma said confidently. "I believe I could have helped more with the scarring. At least it's close to your hairline. It can't be seen, really."

"What luck!" Chet said.

Emma let his hair fall back over the cut and regarded her patient thoughtfully.

"Chet, are you certain that you're well? I'm not so sure." She placed the back of her hand to his forehead again to feel for a fever.

"Nothin' wrong with me that seeing you again can't cure, Miss Emma."

As the morning sun came up, the group continued talking about all they had encountered since they had last seen each other. Thomas was a happy man as he sat next to Liz, and he noted that she seemed perfectly at ease with him. It felt good to be together. Luke sat on the other side of Thomas, and he thought that, to someone who didn't know any better, it might look like a gathering of family as Thomas sat with his arm along the back of Liz, resting on the wagon wheel.

Maybe it's a picture of things to come, he mused.

If Liz agreed to marry him, Thomas might actually get that family he'd been wishing for so long. Maybe he and Liz and Luke could settle in Fort Worth together.

Thomas couldn't help the smile that cut his face in two. It sure wasn't like him to think such optimistic thoughts all at one time.

I guess Chet really did wear off on me a bit.

"What are you grinning at?" Liz asked him in a whisper.

"Just glad we're all together again," he replied. "Like it should be."

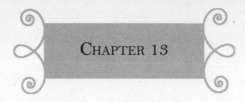

CHAPTER 13

Tex and Thomas had agreed that, with Fort Worth only a few days away, they could travel faster if the men drove the wagons. They wanted to make it through Comanche territory safely, with the women (and the gold) intact.

With the horses harnessed to their appointed wagons, Thomas doled out the assignments as to who would ride where. Colt would drive alone in the first wagon; only Thomas, Liz, and Tex knew it was full of the Mailly gold.

Because of the gold, the weight wouldn't allow any other passengers, Thomas had explained to him when he and Tex pulled the young man off to the side. Colt seemed content with the solitude and said he didn't mind driving alone. He found that women talked too much, he'd told Thomas privately, and days of constant chatter would get the best of him. Being the lead wagon, he didn't have to think about what went on in front of him or worry about what was behind. His pistol traveled right along the side of him, ready for any sign of danger. He'd checked his ammunition three times before they headed out, and he confided in Thomas that he felt proud to have the responsibility for looking after the gold.

Thomas and Liz drove the next wagon. She said she could hardly wait to watch the changing landscape roll past and think about nothing more than her future.

"What's got your face lit up like a candle?" Thomas finally asked her as they bumped along.

She would miss the garden, she told him, and wondered about planting a late one at her new home.

"I wonder what vegetables will grow in Fort Worth," she added, "and how late the season will be when we finally get around to planting. What do you think, Thomas? What shall I grow first?"

Their conversation felt easy and Thomas felt as if they had passed an invisible milestone in their relationship. He wondered when it had happened. At what point in his absence had she grown so much closer to him. Just as he began mulling that over and imagining the answer, Liz leaned over and rested her head on his shoulder.

"I'm so sleepy."

In the third wagon, Megan and Chet shared the bench seat. Chet had always been a talker, and Thomas figured he enjoyed Megan's colorful and witty point of view. Chet had once told him that Megan valued "the important things in life," and he suspected Chet's feelings for her went much deeper than a mild appreciation.

Even though it seemed like a strange mix, Abby and Tex agreed to ride together in the fourth wagon. The rough old Ranger seemingly intrigued the proper schoolteacher. Before they'd even climbed aboard the wagon and left their temporary camp behind, Tex had already engrossed Abby with story after story about the life of a Ranger in the wild, open country of Texas. From the woodlands to the prairie, he had patrolled and protected the settlers. He'd even worked with John Parker when his settlement was overtaken by the shrewd Comanches and his daughter Cynthia Ann was kidnapped. All these years later, Cynthia Ann had never been brought home and was still believed to be living among the Comanches. Abby had grabbed her sister Emma by the hand and said she thought it was the most tragic story she had ever heard. Thomas imagined Abby had spent at least a portion of the ride already looking out over the countryside and reliving the story.

"I'm glad Abby befriended Tex the way she has," Liz spoke out loud, making Thomas curious about whether she'd developed some mind-reading powers while he and Chet had been off without them. "He's intriguing, don't you think so?"

Thomas shrugged. "I guess."

"The history of this state came alive when he spoke," she told him. "The tales of adventure and despair seemed to really grasp Abby's heart, and I'll bet she's back there right now urging him to tell her more."

"If nothing else, she's learning a lot," Thomas remarked. "She could take his knowledge and pass it on to her students. History's sort of been written before Tex's very eyes. I imagine Abby is soaking it right up."

"Tex seemed to almost get a kick out of Abby's interest in the Comanches."

Thomas chuckled. "Look at you, making a love match between your young cousin and that old geezer of a Texas Ranger. You're hiding the heart of a real romantic, Elizabeth Bromont."

"Oh, I am not," she dismissed him with a giggle and the wave of her hand.

The giant Texas Ranger, Jackson, with his horse Zeus tethered to the wagon, had Emma at his side. Emma was usually a quiet one, so Thomas figured Jackson might have been somewhat bored if not for the fact that he'd heard them conversing easily before they'd ever driven away from the campsite.

Two remaining wagons picked up the rear. Luke and John were in one; Blue commanded the other, pulled by the oxen. Luke and John had agreed to take turns with their team.

※　※　※

After several days more, they connected with a well-used road taking them directly north. It had been worn down by the cavalry riding to the fort, which excited Liz to no end because it meant that they were getting close to their new home.

When the group came upon a brigade of men herding camels to the fort, the women became particularly enthused because they'd never seen these desert animals before. Liz was charmed by the humped creatures and their waddle as they rambled along. Tex told them that night over dinner under the stars that the army oftentimes used camels if they planned to travel into west Texas. They were more water-conscious than horses, though slower.

One evening, Megan convinced two soldiers to let her ride one of the camels, and she rode through both camps, balancing between the humps of the lofty animal. Neither Tex nor Thomas found it even slightly amusing, and they hiked over to the army camp to inform the officer in charge that he might want to keep a tighter leash on keeping his troops in their own camp. Liz secretly delighted over Thomas's protective nature.

As the days followed, the two groups continued in the same direction, although the Mailly train moved ahead more quickly. At the campfire one evening, Tex reported that they would be approaching the fort in the morning. Liz stood up and threw her arms around Tex and kissed his weathered cheek. Chet pulled out his bottle of homemade sour mash and passed it around the fire. Liz noticed that Tex held the bottle a little longer than the others and then he watched it as it made its way back to Chet. The women passed it along without drinking, except for Megan, who took a small taste.

"I don't know how any of us are going to sleep at all tonight, Lizzie!" Megan cried. "I'm so excited to get there I can hardly contain myself."

After a brief discussion, the group decided to wake early in the morning. The excitement of their arrival blazed through each of them like a fast-moving fire.

※　※　※

North Texas offered the newcomers a magnificent landscape. The earth rolled gently, thick with grass and majestic oak trees scattered along the small hills. The late summer sun sat high in the sky as the six expectant wagons rolled along the trail. Rainfall had obviously been plentiful that year, and the earth rejoiced in response.

In the distance, Liz noticed a small herd of buffalo mingling and grazing under a gathering of trees she couldn't identify. Each tree was shaped in a uniform half circle, its branches grown straight out from the trunk to look as if they were floating on a layer of air. Not a single twig or branch seemed the least bit out of place, and layered leaves neatly produced an abundance of shade to the earth below.

Liz couldn't stop darting her gaze from one amazing aspect to another as she admired the countryside and its unfamiliar splendor. She wanted to soak it all in—the smells, the sights, the sounds. Bumping along the open, grassy hillside, Liz felt a change occurring in her heart. Love for this western frontier had already begun growing inside her. As warm peace settled over her, she realized she felt strangely like Texas had been awaiting her arrival, and it welcomed her and her family with inviting, open arms.

Looking across the horizon that would soon be home, she inhaled a long breath and nibbled on the side of her lip. Some golden strands of hair had escaped the edges of her bonnet and the thick braid down her back. As she captured her unruly locks and tucked them away, she began to think about the man sitting on the wagon bench next to her.

Thomas Bratcher, a hard worker, always treated others with fairness and respect. Her grandfather had invested his trust in Thomas, expecting him to deliver his family safely to Texas.

And Luke . . .

Luke thought Thomas was grand!

Thomas and Caleb had been best friends since childhood. She realized she never actually knew Thomas's age. She'd always simply assumed he was the same age as her husband.

Liz leaned back on the wagon seat and let the sun warm her face. As she pushed her bonnet back, she easily remembered the day the two friends had shown up at the edge of her grandfather's property. She'd stepped through the doorway of the house and heard them talking where the pathway met the road. As Caleb and Thomas had laughed and joked with Grandpa Lucas, Liz had wondered if they had always been friends. She had certainly been curious about the handsome strangers.

Caleb Bromont was the outgoing, roguish one; and Thomas Bratcher, the thoughtful one with chiseled features. Lingering on the porch with her yellow cat, Cally, she learned that she would see the young men again, as her grandfather had just hired them.

Fresh out of school and seeking their fortune, Thomas and Caleb had stumbled upon Lucas Mailly and the Riverton Timber Mill completely by accident; although Grandpa Lucas always said there were no accidents in life. The men had left home with the intentions and high hopes of seeing the world while working along the way, and her grandfather had happened upon the two friends on the timber mill road and assumed they were there to request a job. He could have bought slaves, but had always preferred to employ his labor. After talking with the young men, he'd hired them on the spot. They had never done mill work before but, with empty pockets and emptier bellies, they accepted. Caleb told her later that it had been an easy decision with room and board as part of the bargain, and the pretty golden-haired granddaughter on the front porch, to boot. It had been only the first of their many days of good fortune.

The three men shook hands and Lucas directed them to the timber mill's bunkhouse where they would sleep as well as eat. Liz blushed as the two took turns looking back toward the big white porch where she stood watching after them.

Even though Caleb and Thomas had been best friends for many years, she never did learn an awful lot about Thomas. He was a prayerful and patient man, loyal, trustworthy, hard-working, and seemingly loved by all. He had been like a brother and a family member for years.

The thought of turning her mind around and loving Thomas as a husband felt . . . confusing. He had many traits that were like Caleb, but many that made him totally different. Yes, he was a good man, but— *could she marry him?*

"I have no idea how old you are," she blurted out without thinking, her thoughts coming alive as the wagon bumped along toward their final destination.

"What?" Thomas asked, awakened from his own private thoughts.

"Thomas, I've enjoyed these last few days with you."

He loosely held the wagon reins in his hand so that they interlaced between his fingers. A smile formed under his new mustache.

"Happy to hear it."

"But there's so much I don't know about you, even after all these years. What would you have done with your life if you and Caleb hadn't happened upon my grandfather and the timber mill that afternoon? And what kind of soap did you use all those years to make you always smell like the woods after it rains? Have you ever owned another hat besides that one? I don't remember a time when you didn't wear it."

She paused, feeling the heat of the dark red stain probably splashed across both her cheeks and the front of her neck.

"Why all of these questions?" Thomas chuckled as he glanced her way. "I knew you were quiet way too long."

Liz leaned forward until he looked at her, and she stared into his eyes, searching them to find out if he really was who she thought him to be.

"I have been your friend for many years, you know," he said, as if he'd read her thoughts like a newspaper. "What you don't know about me already probably isn't worth knowing."

※   ※   ※

That wagon ride to Texas was the longest he had ever been alone with the widow of Caleb Bromont. Thomas saw Liz's inner strength even more after she became a widow and then even more still when she ventured wholeheartedly into the dream of going west.

It seemed like as good a time as any to talk to her about their future. He swallowed the dread creeping up on him and gathered his courage before he started to speak.

"Liz, I would like to talk to you about some of our plans. Plans Lucas and I have made for the future."

Liz looked at him and arched one eyebrow. "Oh?"

Her grandfather had always treated her as an equal. Thomas knew he had included her as he devised a scenario for the future. Lucas had always valued her opinion, so she probably already knew the nuts and bolts of what had been planned.

Thomas took a breath and continued now that he had her attention.

"Lucas and I want to start a freight company to bring supplies in for the mercantile. He likely has a wagon or two on the way already," Thomas said with a chuckle as he thought of his friend. Lucas Mailly had the strength and drive of a young man and the wisdom of Solomon. Thomas respected and loved this man who was to be his new partner in the venture.

Liz looked at Thomas with her blue eyes trained on him as he spoke.

"Chet, Blue, and John will be freight drivers, if they accept. Our freight yard will be the first to bring supplies now that the military has moved on." He paused and swallowed around the lump in his throat. "I want to eventually start a ranch. I think this area has a good chance of being profitable for the cattle business. Lucas and I will be partners in that as well, along with Luke when he grows up. I feel—"

The lump arose again, and he swallowed hard before he could continue.

"The thing is, Liz, I'm already part of this family and I would like to make it official by asking you to be my wife."

Liz looked like she'd been kicked by the rear hoof of a horse as she sat there staring at him. Her eyes misted over, and he thought that her silent thoughts circled like the rotation of the wagon wheels.

Thomas gathered his courage quickly. He wouldn't let her slip away this time. He could feel her weighing his words.

"Elizabeth Bromont," he said, turning slightly on the seat toward her. "I've loved you since the first day I saw you standing on the porch when Caleb and I stumbled upon the timber mill and asked Lucas for jobs. You stepped out of the door and stood next to that pillar holding that measly cat of yours. Your hair looked like spun gold in the sun, just like it does now. I knew then you were the one for me."

Thomas ran his hand down her braid as it sparkled in the sun, and he reached over and took her hand.

"I was hypnotized by you, Liz. I waited for you to acknowledge me back then . . . and again now. Because I hesitated fifteen years ago, I lost you. I don't want that to happen now. I've wanted to court you for months, but you were still grieving over Caleb's death. It just wasn't time. He was my best friend."

Thomas straightened, released her hand, and looked at the road ahead of them.

"Liz, I want to marry you," he said without a glance back at her. "I don't want to wait any longer or run the risk of losing you again. Luke needs me and seems to love me. You will too, if you just give us a chance."

Thomas reached for her hand and held it firmly, searching her face a moment later in the hope that he'd find the answer he wanted there, almost willing the response he desired. He could see that Liz listened to his confession, seemingly amazed that he had always felt this way. She had clearly never known.

"How could I have not known this?"

CHAPTER 14

Liz felt perplexed at what she had just now learned about Thomas. He had thought things through so completely that he assumed others were already in step with him.

Liz had always wondered why Thomas never married. He'd never shown one bit of interest in any of the girls she introduced him to. Now she understood as all of this whizzed through her head.

"I never knew," she told him softly, and mostly to herself. "Did Caleb . . . Did he ever know?" she asked.

Her head swam with memories. She always thought of Thomas as family. Nothing had ever been out of place or strange during all those years, and now he confessed that he had loved her from the beginning.

"No, I don't think so. I never told him. He was my best friend! I did a good job of keeping it from everyone. Except your grandfather, of course," Thomas said as he smiled. "That man keeps track of his granddaughters like a hawk."

Thomas squeezed her hand a little and chuckled.

"Does he know your intentions now?"

She looked at him seriously, awaiting his reply.

"I don't think he would have sent me with you if he hadn't been in favor of it, Liz."

She knew that Thomas could see how deeply his proposal had shaken her. He probably wished now that he'd have waited.

"I had a brother in Caleb," he said, and she strained to hear him. "I would never have hurt him. Liz, I almost died trying to save him. I wanted to die, too, when he drowned. We had been best friends from the first day we met. I know he would approve of us together, especially if he saw the bond I've forged with Luke. I was always family to you and the boy, even when Caleb was alive."

"It must've been hard for you."

She paused and looked at Thomas through a thin veil of tears. Emotion choked her for a moment, and her thoughts and emotions tossed every which way.

Everyone had been pushing her toward Thomas in the last few weeks, telling her to move on with her life. Megan said Thomas had feelings for her. With her grandfather aging and Caleb's death, she needed Thomas.

Thomas caught her glance and instinctively bent down to kiss her. It had been more than a year since she'd been kissed, and it felt good. Warm, sweet, and gentle.

Have I grown too old to still want romance and love?

With her eyes still closed from the kiss, Thomas remained close to her face and whispered, "Liz. I know you will always love Caleb. I don't expect anything else. But he's gone and I'm here. If you can love me half as much as you loved Caleb, I will die a happy man."

When he finished, he leaned back on the wagon seat, his gaze fixed on the road ahead of them.

The wheels of the wagon continued along the grassy trail as they moved closer toward their new home. Liz watched the scenery pass, grateful that Thomas allowed her to sit quietly and absorb all he had said to her while her hand stayed gently cradled in his.

After several minutes, she carefully turned to look at him.

Is this a man I could love? she wondered as she examined the sharp line of his jaw. *Could I share my thoughts and dreams with him? Is he a forever love, or was this a business deal for him?*

She took a sharp breath, and it sparked a pain in her chest.

"Thomas, I would like to try to do that with you. I think I am ready to accept your offer of courtship with the intent to marry when the time is right. But I can't commit further than that. Is that acceptable to you?"

Thomas smiled, took her hand, kissed the back of it and replied, "Yes, that's good enough for me!"

After some time, Thomas turned toward her and said, "I don't know much about your parents or how you came to live at the timber mill. Why don't you tell me about that."

"I was only six when we went to Lecompte to live with my grandfather," she replied. Pausing to look at their entwined hands, she added, "I was so young, Thomas, and so scared. We had just lost our parents in the fire and suddenly Megan was my responsibility."

"I never knew that," Thomas commented quietly.

"My mother was pregnant then. I remember my father turning to me and saying, 'Take care of Megan.' Then he went back into the house to get Mama. I saw the fire everywhere and he disappeared into it. Just as he entered, the roof came down on them. Some people from town came when they saw the smoke and flames, and they found Megan and me huddled together in one of Granny's quilts. It was the only belonging we saved from the fire. It was too late to save the house or anyone in it."

Liz looked away just as the fresh flow of tears began to fall. She felt grateful to Thomas for listening in silence, probably imagining what it was like for two such little girls. He squeezed her hand tighter.

"The pastor put us on a stage and paid our way to Lecompte," she continued. "His wife pinned a note to my green dress that she'd made for us out of ivy-colored fabric with vines and red flowers. It had large red buttons on the bodice. Megan twisted one of her buttons off on the stage and cried. The pastor said that it was a good idea for us to look nice, that it would go in our favor to find a good home because he didn't know if an old man would want to raise two little girls."

Had Thomas begun to sniffle, or had she imagined it?

"Grandpa Lucas was in town the day the stage arrived, and he saw us get off in the street. He unpinned the note and read about the fire and the death of our parents. It seemed like days passed while we just sat on the porch in his lap. We all just cried and rocked ... two little girls curled up in their grandfather's lap. I remember Megan saying, in her cute little baby voice, 'Don't cry anymore, Pappy. We'll take care of you.' And she took the skirt of her dress and wiped his tears away."

Thomas sniffed again, and she realized that he battled his own emotions.

"Do you know what started the fire?" he asked.

"Momma's nightgown caught on fire. She was ready for the baby to come and she wasn't sleeping well. Somehow, her nightgown got in the fire and she was on fire. She was afraid and didn't know what to do. She ran through the house, making it worse. I heard her screaming and falling over things. She told me to get Megan out of the house and get Daddy from the barn. We had been sleeping and Megan wouldn't get up. As we struggled to get out, I saw her burning. The fire was everywhere."

"Liz, I'm so sorry."

Thomas choked up and grabbed Liz's hand, roughly kissing her knuckles as his tears fell to her skin.

"I'm so sorry," he repeated. "I never knew."

"I don't know that I've ever told anyone before."

"Not even Caleb?" he asked, surprised.

"No, we never spoke of it." Liz looked at Thomas, realizing how odd it sounded. "Strange. I don't know why he never asked."

✳   ✳   ✳

The wagons lumbered down the grassy path in single file. Colt drove the lead wagon and had taken over the scouting duties when they reached the Texas border.

As they pressed forward into her new home state, Liz recalled the first night she'd met Colt. He had scared her half to death, coming into the camp looking like trouble, wild and unannounced with several guns at his side and his long, unruly hair covering his badge.

Colt slowed his wagon while the others rolled up close to him. They stopped on the top of a hill where they could see far into the distance where a thick grove of trees and a few old wooden buildings came into view.

"Fort Worth," Tex shouted. "And we've made it without Indians, stampedes, or outlaws. Might be a first!"

Tex nodded his head at the two lawmen who rode with him. His curly brown hair, cropped short under his sweat-stained cowboy hat, gave way to tanned, leathery skin reflecting years of riding under the hot, Texas sun. Jackson and Colt, the other two rangers riding with him, slapped the reins and clicked their teams to move on. Thomas grinned at her as he followed suit.

Liz thought she might not have been able to handle any more misfortune, so she remained thankful that Tex and his fellow Rangers had managed to lead them into Texas without encountering the dangers Tex spoke about. The hardships they'd experienced had been difficult enough. It occurred to her that she'd discovered a full measure of perseverance that she hadn't known she possessed, and she silently thanked the Lord above that her faith continued to hold strong.

The past is behind, and now is the time to move forward, she thought with a twinge of excitement.

She felt rather proud of her ability to dive into this new adventure with such confidence. She wanted to cement all of the accomplishments of the last weeks in her mind as a living stone so that she might return to the experiences and gain strength from them as needed.

"I can do all things through Christ which strengthenth me. Philippians, chapter four, verse thirteen," she recalled aloud, reminding herself that most people quit when the battle is almost won. Perseverance is a trait most individuals never know they have until it's tested. It had been her responsibility to get the group to their new home and not disappoint her grandfather, and she hoped Grandpa Lucas would feel some gratification all his own for taking the chance and entrusting her with the task.

"That's one of my favorite passages of Scripture," Thomas commented, and she jumped back to the present. She hadn't noticed that she'd spoken the verse aloud.

"Mine, too," she replied timidly.

"You've persevered through quite an undertaking," he observed. "Done it all through Him who keeps you strong."

Liz gave him a weary smile. Looking at the grove of trees and the rundown, wooden buildings, however, her relief and joy was somewhat overwhelmed with a gray shadow of disappointment and disbelief.

"Do you suppose Grandpa Lucas knew what a tired-looking settlement Fort Worth would turn out to be?" she asked Thomas. "I fear he'll be very disappointed."

"Not much to look at from up here, is it?" he commented, and Liz shook her head and sighed.

The wagons drove into the quiet, abandoned little town, so unlike Lecompte that the difference seemed to scream at her. No hustle or bustle or business going on, and no settlers milling about. Liz felt a little confused and somewhat saddened by the thud of defeat squeezing her heart.

Was this a trick? Was Grandpa aware of what this place was like? How could they make a living here? She didn't even see a town dog!

A sudden surge of hopefulness crested, and Liz looked at Thomas. "Are you sure this is the right place? Could we have missed Fort Worth somewhere."

"No, this—"

A rider appeared suddenly from the trees and headed straight for them, whipping the reins back and forth on the flanks of his mount.

"You're here!" he exclaimed as dirt kicked up behind the pony. With a huge toothless grin, he pulled back on the leather bridle and came to a stop in front of Tex and Abby's wagon.

Liz twisted to look behind her. Luke flailed his arms at her, grinning from ear to ear, and she forced a smile to her face as she returned a wave of her own. In the foreground, she noticed Megan's dark hair, smooth skin, and sparkling green eyes providing a remarkable contrast to the somber surroundings.

Megan leaned over toward Chet and spoke something that Liz couldn't hear, and Chet let out a hearty laugh. When Megan noticed Liz looking, she lifted her chin and called out, "Looks like this place hasn't seen a human in years!"

"You must be the Mailly family," the toothless rider said to Tex. "Are you Lucas?"

"No, I'm with the Texas Rangers, accompanying the Mailly family to Fort Worth. Who's in charge here? Can you take us to them right away?"

"Yeah, they're all out at the fort. Follow me, this way."

The rider started west and continued motioning for them to follow.

"What do you call this place?" Liz called out after the rider.

He had already moved too far away to hear Liz, but Tex answered her in a baritone bellowing voice.

"This is the old outpost, the one they used before they built the fort. Did you think this was it?"

Tex and the other rangers laughed as they realized the women thought the rundown outpost was their new home. Liz let out a sigh of relief and squeezed Thomas's arm as they rode past the shabby, splintered buildings with wild vines growing through the broken windows.

"Oh, thank You, sweet Jesus," Liz muttered when the real fort appeared in their view, humming with life.

"Liz, did you really think that was where we were going to start up?" Thomas quizzed her with a chuckle.

"Yes," she replied, "and it's not amusing! I was really concerned for a moment."

She smiled when she saw a little church with white double doors and a steeple on top. A lovely young woman with long coal-black curls stood out front on the small steps, waving.

"I suppose that's Pastor Parker's wife, Anna," Liz said with childlike excitement. "Oh, Thomas, this is really happening. They're here waiting for us!"

"Of course they are."

A few townspeople began to appear from several directions to greet them, all of them friendly and anxious to help get them settled in their new home. They offered water for the horses, and Tex stood by to offer assistance to the women as they each climbed down from the wagons. The woman from the church grinned at them with animated enthusiasm.

"I'm Anna Parker. Welcome to Fort Worth. We are so excited to have you here!"

The four Mailly granddaughters gathered around Anna and introduced themselves, one by one. She gave each of them a hug as she welcomed them.

"Please don't be too overwhelmed by our excitement of your arrival. We're just anxious to get our little community up and going again. It has been quite disturbing with the fort post moving on west. You and your family represent life to our town, and we are so thankful to you," Anna gushed.

Liz knew Grandpa Lucas had said they'd be welcomed to the area, but she had not fully realized the importance of their arrival. The wide eyes and beaming smiles surrounding them told her that she and her family represented an infusion of lifeblood into the ailing town. The responsibility seemed as daunting as it was exciting.

"Let me show you around!" Anna began, and she led them in the direction of the buildings, explaining as they walked down the board sidewalks of Fort Worth, Texas. A small group of the town's people followed and listened to every word, and Liz searched the area for a glimpse of her son. When she finally spotted him, Luke suddenly appeared so much older than his years as he leaned casually against one of the wagon wheels, chatting with Blue and Colt.

"The army kept supplies in the large building. It would work well for the mercantile, I think," she said as she glanced at Liz, and then at Megan. "Megan, you're planning to open a dress shop, is that right? You may want to claim this smaller one for your purposes. I don't think either building is in much need of work."

Anna grinned tentatively, awaiting their approval. She seemed relieved when Liz returned her smile and nodded in agreement.

"There's a small living quarters above the mercantile, and the captain's house is around the curve to the left. I think you will find it most comfortable. You may do as you wish with all of these buildings. Just make yourselves right at home."

Anna paused to let her words soak in as she searched each face in hopes of their approval, looking for some indication of their thoughts.

Liz didn't want to admit that she almost felt more scared than excited. Her mercantile stood before her. She could see it with her mind's eye, visualizing burgeoning shelves with an abundance of supplies. Her imagination placed yard goods, threads, lace, and buttons in the center. On the back wall, she painted in the sugar, coffee, beans, and hardtack. Small red checked curtains appeared on the windows, and two double doors with a fresh coat of red paint swung open as a warm greeting to every customer. Over the porch, she would hang a sign reading MAILLY MERCANTILE, and beneath the sign a row of rocking chairs just waiting to be rocked!

Liz came out of her thoughts as she heard Anna's voice again.

"We would love to have all of you for supper tonight. I will have some meat and bread sent over now so you can eat a little while you start to unpack and settle in. Does that sound acceptable?"

Liz realized that Anna looked to her for an answer.

"Yes! Oh, yes. You're most gracious, Anna. Thank you."

"I am so glad to have you here safely," Anna cooed. "We've planned a good old-fashioned Texas cookout for you all, and we'll get word out for Sunday when we'll introduce you to all the lovely families of Fort Worth!"

Anna was even sweeter than Liz could have hoped she would be. Megan's eyes glistened as Liz caught sight of them, and her sister rushed over to her and squeezed her wrist.

"Oh, Lizzie, it's really happening!" she murmured. "Don't you just love her?"

Liz nodded. Anna's soft, soothing voice eased her fears, and Liz thanked her again. Anna adjusted the gold hair comb holding back her beautiful dark hair into a storm of curls that tumbled down her back. Their new friend seemed beautiful and sweet, still untouched by the hard ways of the West. Mrs. Parker seemed like she might be around Abby's age, or so Liz guessed.

"Anna, my cousin Abby is the new teacher Pastor Parker has hired."
Liz placed her hand on Abby's arm.

"Oh! In my excitement, I completely forgot about the school. I'm
sure you would like to see your classroom. Do you mind waiting for my
husband to catch up with us? He is out on a call right now," Anna said to
Abby. "But he shouldn't be long."

Abby beamed at Anna's excitement about the school. "We have
plenty to do. I can wait," she replied.

"I will send him over as soon as he returns. This is so exciting. I have
waited for a very long time to have more women here!" Anna reached
right over and gave Abby a sudden hug. When she finally released the
new schoolmarm, she noticed that the men stood at the ready to start
unloading the wagons, dusty from the Louisiana trail.

"This is Smithy," Anna said, pointing out the older man standing
across from them. "He has several men to help you fine gentlemen get
unloaded." She smiled at Liz as she added, "Just direct them to do whatever you need them to do."

Anna waved goodbye and walked back down the street toward her
home and the church that her husband pastored.

John turned to Blue with a smile and muttered, "Oh, Liz can direct
them all right."

"I heard that," she quipped, and the two of them cackled with
laughter.

A dirt road out front disappeared in both directions. On each side of
the mercantile, wooden buildings stood empty, left behind by the cavalry.
A huge pecan tree extended branches reaching twenty feet or more in
each direction across from where she stood. Two squirrels played in the
lush grassy area beneath the tree, stopping only long enough to survey
the new group of dusty arrivals before one chased the other straight up
the thick trunk.

The church and the new schoolroom were on down from the pecan
tree. On the same side of the street where Liz stood, and to the right,
stood the smithy, and next to it was a set of corrals where two mules and

a stallion with a long black mane peered out at them. The stallion pawed at the edge of the gate and shook his head. His beautiful mane shone in the sunlight but looked like it needed a little attention.

At the end of her boardwalk and to the left, the street turned toward the captain's housing that Anna had pointed out. Liz stepped to the end of the sidewalk to get a better look. A few steps more, and she gazed upon a lovely, freshly painted white house with grass and lush green trees spreading around it. Her Louisiana home had been much larger, but this one seemed to welcome passers-by and appeared manicured and—somehow—well loved. The small, flat porch sat close to the ground, surrounded with colorful flowers. A vegetable garden could be plainly seen off to one side of the house, and Liz turned to go back and tell the others of the pleasant discovery.

In her delight, she hadn't noticed that several of the others had followed. When her eyes met those of a tall man she remembered from the crowd of greeters, she immediately sensed that he, and many of the others, seemed to await her approval that Fort Worth was acceptable, and perhaps that they would be staying after all.

"Lizzie," Megan squealed, "it's charming, isn't it?"

"Did you see the vegetable garden?"

"There's a garden?" her sister exclaimed, and she hurried off toward the house.

"Mrs. Bromont," the tall, somewhat handsome stranger spoke as he stepped from the crowd toward her. "Samuel Smith, ma'am."

She hadn't been introduced to many of the strangers now milling around expectantly. She reached her hand out toward Samuel Smith, remembering her manners.

"Please excuse me, Mr. Smith. I was lost in thought and I saw the garden . . ."

She bounced from one emotion to another, visualizing her new mercantile, admiring her new home, meeting new people, and now this very handsome man before her extended his hand toward her. Liz felt herself begin to melt as he held her hand.

Samuel never took his eyes away from hers as he continued to speak. "That is certainly fine. The captain's wife liked a garden and I think she hoped you would tend to it in her absence. She did not move on with her husband."

"No?" Liz remarked, wondering why not.

"She went back east. I guess the moving about never really suited her."

"Of course, that garden she bequeathed is an unexpected treasure. I hope to thank her one day if I ever have the opportunity," Liz stated as she pulled back her hand.

"Not much chance of that, ma'am. Unless you write her a letter, I suppose."

CHAPTER 15

T homas stepped inside the building that would be the mercantile, then he quickly made his way out again. He had brought a wagonload of gold that belonged to his employer, Lucas Mailly, and while searching for a place to hide it, he scanned the area in search of a bank without finding one. Just a jail building at the end of the street, and that would not work at all! He finally decided that he could lift a section of the floorboards under the stairs in the mercantile and place the gold there for safekeeping until Lucas's arrival. He could bunk upstairs to keep an eye on it without anyone knowing.

Thomas strolled down the boarded sidewalk a few yards and surveyed the area, hoping he might spot Liz and the others. When he heard them around to the left, he walked toward their voices. What he saw produced a bitter shot of acid at the back of his throat. Who was that holding Liz's hand, smiling at her? What he disliked even more: Liz smiled back at him, seemingly in some sort of a trance.

Thomas's boots thudded heavy on the boards and kept beat with his pulse as he advanced toward them. This feeling in his gut was new to him. He'd never been a man induced to sudden anger; but there could be no mistaking it. Anger was indeed what he felt.

"Thomas, there you are." Liz turned to include him. "This is Mr. Samuel Smith."

Samuel looked at Thomas, who stared steadily back at him.

"Mr. Bromont. Nice to meet you! I was just discussing the vegetable garden left behind by the captain and his wife. Your lovely wife seems quite enthused about taking it over."

"Oh, I'm sorry, Mr. Smith," Liz corrected him, far too quickly for Thomas's liking. "I'm Elizabeth Bromont and this is Thomas Bratcher. He works for my grandfather, Lucas Mailly."

Thomas moved his glare from Samuel to Liz, and he raised an eyebrow.

Liz appeared uncomfortable under his gaze, so Thomas tried to temper it as she continued the introductions. "This is my sister Megan, and my cousins, Abby and Emma Wilkes."

Tex and the others stood close by, watching the exchange. "Well, Mrs. Bromont, maybe you could direct us and we'll get these wagons unloaded for you," Samuel offered. "Just tell us where you want things, what you might need first, and we'll be happy to help you get settled."

"Thomas," Tex spoke up. Thomas wondered if he'd sensed the tension. "Let's get your wagon unloaded first. Jackson! Colt!" he called out, and the four of them walked to the wagon holding Lucas's gold.

Thomas went to work but watched over his shoulder the entire time as they secured the gold beneath the floorboards under the stairs; keeping an eye out for two treasures: the gold, as well as his future wife.

Anna soon appeared with glasses of cool water and sandwiches piled high with meat. Thomas took two of each and went out in search of Liz.

"How about we squat at the shade tree over there," he suggested when he found her. "You must be as hungry as I am."

Thomas knew Liz never liked leaving things hanging, but this was fast even for her. She went straight to the point before they'd even headed toward the pecan tree, while Thomas still held her lunch.

"Thomas, I don't know what upset you, but you need to be pleasant to our new friends."

Thomas stood with one foot on the step above him and his back against the porch post of the mercantile.

"What upset me was Mr. Smith's hand-holding and your introduction. Is that all I am, a worker for your grandfather, Liz?"

Thomas held his sandwich without taking a bite and looked at Liz as she sat on the steps in front of the mercantile.

"I guess I'll just eat my lunch right here," he snapped.

When he looked up at her, her countenance had softened considerably.

"Thomas, I'm sorry. I was caught off guard, and I didn't mean to hurt you."

He knew he should allow her to smooth it over with one simple apology, but he didn't feel ready to let it go, and he pressed her for more. "Why didn't you tell him that we are to be married?"

"Well, I haven't had time to tell anyone yet," Liz answered quietly. "Not even my own sister!"

"What does that have to do with it?" He kept his voice low, and yanked out a bite of the sandwich before him.

Liz lowered to the step and sat beside him.

"We need to speak to my grandfather," she firmly stated. "There are rules to be followed in a circumstance like ours."

Liz took a breath and looked away for a moment, to calm her emotions, he supposed.

Before she spoke again, she heaved a deep breath and let it out in an exasperated sigh. "Thomas, so much has happened today. Please don't be angry with me. Give me a little time to adjust to the whole idea of marriage again."

"I don't know what there is to warm up to!" Thomas took another bite and looked away to the group at the wagons. "You didn't even say I was a family friend," he added. "Just an employee of your grandfather's." Calming some, he decided to take a different approach. "Liz, you have to be careful here. This is not Lecompte and we don't know who we can trust yet. Who is Samuel, anyway?"

Liz looked to the group laughing at something Mr. Smith had said.

"He knew the fort's captain and his wife. I assumed he was a friend. He was also with Anna Parker when we arrived."

"Until we know for sure, let's be on the safe side," Thomas warned. "What do we have left to do?"

"We're ready for the stock to be brought in and placed on the shelves. The building is in good shape. It just needs some sweeping out. I wish I had some glass windows to be placed in the front, like we had back home. But until we can get it, can we put two doors in the front? It will be nice to see out when the store is open."

"I think I can manage it. I will get Jackson to help."

"If you will have your personal belongings brought upstairs, I will get your things put up, and the room cleaned and arranged for you," Liz offered.

"That'll be fine."

His heart felt twisted somehow, sore inside his chest. He began wishing he hadn't spoken to Liz that way.

"Thomas, I didn't even ask if you wanted the room upstairs in the mercantile."

"I thought that would be a good idea. And I guess you want your things at the little house with the garden?" he teased.

"Yes, please," she said as she smiled.

A return to peaceful terms felt mighty good to him just then, and Thomas took her hand.

"Liz, I'm sorry I was mad. I just don't like sharing you now that I don't have to." He kissed the back of her hand and swallowed the last bite of his sandwich. Downing the water after he stood up, he tipped his hat to Liz and walked back toward the wagons for his tools.

※　※　※

Megan had been watching Liz and Thomas during lunch and didn't disturb them, but she wasted no time in approaching Liz once Thomas had headed off toward the men.

As she walked toward Liz, she passed Thomas and said, "Oh, Thomas, did Liz—"

"Yes, Megan, she said yes and we are to be married as soon as possible."

Liz almost swallowed her own tongue. Thomas never stopped walking as they passed each other, and Megan turned and watched his exit with her jaw hanging open and her green eyes wide as saucers.

Well, I guess he solved the problem of my finding time to tell my sister the news.

"Liz? Is everything all right?"

"I'm fine. Thomas and I just . . . well . . . we're . . . Oh, I don't know what we are. Confused, maybe." Shaking her head, Liz made a conscious choice to move the focus to the chores at hand. "Megan, what do you think? It's not the comforts of home, but it could be worse."

"Liz!" Megan exclaimed. "Tell me what you and Thomas were talking so seriously about. He was acting strange over there with Mr. Smith when we first arrived and now while we were eating it looked like the two of you were having a very intense conversation. Did you really agree to marry him?"

"We discussed it. But I'm tired, and it's been a long day. My emotions have been up and down. Thomas was upset with me. He said we need to be more careful in this new place."

"Lizzie!"

Megan's expression told Liz she had no intention of allowing deflection.

"Well," she hesitated. "Thomas wants to marry me."

Megan looked confounded for a moment, and she looked off after Thomas for a moment before she sighed and offered her hand to pull Liz up from the wooden step where she'd parked. "See, I told you if you showed a little interest, he would tell you how he felt. Everyone could see it but you."

Megan stopped and stared at her for a moment. "But you sure don't seem very excited."

"This morning when we were riding in the wagon, it just happened," she told her. "We discussed how deeply I loved Caleb, and Thomas said that he knew and it was fine. He is going into business with Grandpa Lucas and . . . and he said that he has loved me since he first came to the Riverton Mill all those years ago, Megan." Liz paused with disbelief as she went over it again. She had never thought about marriage for any other reason than love, and she hadn't had time to fall in love yet. "Megan, he has waited all these years for me."

Megan gave her sister a hug and told her the truth. "Thomas is a good man and he loves you more than you know. Give him a chance, Liz. I don't think you'll be sorry. It will be good, you wait and see."

Liz listened to her younger sister and wanted her to be right. She would try, really try.

"I'm going upstairs to get Thomas moved in," Liz said. "Can you sweet talk any of those men into getting the rest of our things to the house?"

Megan grinned. "Oh, I think I can manage that."

Liz continued on with her mental checklist of getting settled, pushing Thomas from her thoughts for the time being.

"Megan, the house looked fairly clean, but we need some wood chopped. And while you're at it, see if you can find out how to get the water, too."

Megan chuckled again at her sister. "You're always giving orders, Elizabeth Bromont."

"And you're so good at seeing that they're followed. Now go and flutter your eyelashes at someone, will you? It's going to be cold enough for a fire in our new home tonight."

✳   ✳   ✳

"Tex said at lunch that we should make a habit of carrying our guns, too," Megan said as they strolled down the street toward the wagons.

"Does he think we don't just because he can't see them?" Liz teased.

"Maybe," Megan said. "I like him . . . he . . . well, he's very fatherly, don't you think so?"

"I can see that."

"Liz, I don't remember our father."

Liz stopped and looked at her younger sister, stunned at the abrupt admission.

"He was a good man. He loved us a lot. He called you his wildflower.

You were a feisty little thing then, too."

Megan smiled as her sister talked, looping her arm through Liz's, enrapt.

"I will be over to the house when I finish with the upstairs." Liz gave her sister a wink as she turned to walk into her new shop and up the back staircase to Thomas's room.

At the end of the building, with easy access to a back door that went across to the main house where the Mailly women would live, stairs climbed up to a nice, open space just above the mercantile. From the windows, Thomas would have a full view of the house, and that would make Liz feel more secure.

His spacious living quarters were furnished quite nicely with a good bed, washstand, and a chest of drawers. One lamp had been left on a table with several books on the bottom shelf, and a rocking chair sat angled into the corner by the window. She dusted everything and opened the crates that had been brought up with the belongings of the man she was to marry.

It felt strange to Liz. But they were in the West now, where protocol would be set aside for necessity. Workloads were to be shared by all. She had gotten used to a variety of tasks over the weeks while managing the journey. The way west had taught her many things, and she felt pretty certain there was still plenty left to learn.

She unpacked Thomas's clothes and shook them out to air. She checked for any needed repairs and found they were all in fairly good shape. In fact, they all looked practically new. She refolded and placed them in the chest of drawers and on a few pegs that lined one wall by the washstand.

The next crate she opened contained a well-worn family Bible. She opened the cover and saw the family names written on the faded inside page. Thomas William Bratcher, the third son to Susan and William Bratcher. Liz discovered that one son had died of infection at age three. The eldest of Thomas's brothers was still living. She had met him once at the mill.

Then she saw it again, the beautiful log cabin quilt. It was unlike anything she had ever seen, with triangles surrounding the outside edges of the four cabin blocks. Liz quickly fluffed the mattress made of straw and put fresh, clean sheets on the bed. She removed the quilt from the box and smoothed it over the mattress. The colors looked stunning with brown- and cream-colored logs matching up to the deep red triangles surrounding the cabins. This pattern made a large block and Liz could hardly take her eyes away from it. As she ran her hand across it, admiring the stitches, she noticed that the letter that had been folded into the quilt had fallen to the floor. As she picked it up, a page fell open.

His mother had written, *"Thomas, we miss you so much and wish you would come closer to home, especially now that Caleb has passed. Your father and I know how close you two were and we are saddened for you. I hope you enjoy the quilt I made for you. The log cabin blocks represent your life of working with the logs at the mill and the longing for a home of your own. You will be a great father and husband when the time is right, son. The red center of each cabin is the love you have for the woman who won't or can't return it. Somehow you have kept that love alive in your heart. She must be very a special woman, Thomas."*

Liz stopped reading for a moment and gulped around a dry spot in her throat. Curious now, she read on. *"The red triangles or claws are the troubles we all have finding our own home and happiness. Thomas, please don't be upset for me speaking my mind and caring about my youngest son. Please consider coming back home. We have many fine young women who would be honored to be your wife and would make a loving home for you. I have prayed for you endlessly as I worked on this quilt. I hope you can feel your mother's love and my desire for you to be happy, and I hope this quilt brings you what you wish for the most. Love always, your Mother."*

Liz folded the letter and slipped it into the Bible and closed the worn book into the table drawer next to the bed. She sat down in the rocker across from it and mulled over what she had just read.

Thomas had loved her for years and she hadn't even known it. He had waited for her, not knowing if he would ever have a chance to express his love. She would have to be far more respectful of his feelings, even though she was not at the same point emotionally. Thomas was a good friend and she certainly didn't want to hurt him. How would she feel if this were her own son, Luke? She would want him to be happy with a family of his own. But she wasn't sure she wanted the fine women back home waiting for Thomas either.

Liz looked back at the beautiful quilt, shaking her head.

I didn't mean to read it, she thought, immediately acknowledging the partial fib.

She surveyed the room and it looked almost cozy. It would need a rug on the floor and some fresh curtains as soon as she could get to them.

Sounds were now coming from below and she started to rise from the rocking chair just as Megan appeared at the top of the stairs.

"Liz? Oh my, where did that quilt come from? Does it belong to Thomas?" Megan was as drawn to the quilt as Liz was when she pulled it from the box. She started to inspect the pattern and workmanship. "Who made this? I don't recognize the work. It's very good."

"Thomas's mother made it and gave it to him as a gift. It's lovely, isn't it?" Liz answered her sister.

"Yes, it's beautiful. I don't think I've seen a log cabin like this before."

"The red triangles." Liz paused. "I like them but they almost look like they are keeping something out."

Megan looked about the room and said, "It looks nice up here. The furniture will work well. Not quite as homey as it should be. What do you suggest, Liz?"

Liz thought Megan sized up the room and the quilt quickly. She watched as her sister continued to look around the room, taking it all in.

"I think some new curtains and a rug will work fine!"

Liz looked the room over again and tried to see Thomas living there while Megan stood at the window to inspect the view.

"His view is good of our house. The large trees in the back are really in a perfect spot, don't you think so?" she asked Liz. "We can get someone to build us a porch on the back and the house will work well. We must sleep two to a room, but they are a nice size. And the kitchen is convenient. We have a large wood-burning stove. Samuel . . . um, Mr. Smith is seeing to the wood that we need to get started."

Liz moved to the window where her sister stood.

"Well, it looks like we are fortunate with our new home," Megan continued. "To my surprise, our new house even comes with a garden. After the rain, it will need to be tended. The weeds are fully grown and the vegetables need to be picked. It seems that the lady of the home has been gone several weeks."

Liz could see the weeds from the upstairs window as they peered out. She chose to ignore Megan's slip of the tongue calling Mr. Smith by his first name, but she'd noticed. Turning from the window, she said, "I'm finished here. Are you ready to see how the doors are coming along on the storefront?"

The two sisters went down the staircase, along the back of the mercantile storeroom and through the storefront where Thomas and Jackson worked on enlarging the front entrance. Both men had smiles of admiration on their faces as they watched the women approach.

"Miss Megan, how is it coming along at the new house?" Jackson asked.

"Just fine, but we need an easier way to get water when Chet grows tired of hauling it for us. The river is so far away. Can we get a well or a pump?"

Jackson looked puzzled. "Did you go to the building in the back? They had a pump put in and made a bathhouse there. It's quite fancy. It seems the captain's wife was always ready to pack up and go back East, so the captain kept doing things to get her to stay a little longer! I think you women will enjoy the luxury of the tub. You might be willing to rent it from time to time if you got a notion to run a bathhouse."

Liz and Megan were delighted by the prospects of a real bath and eager to see it. Megan picked up her skirt and almost ran toward the house.

Liz lingered a moment longer by Thomas, looking at the new entrance. "The doorway is looking good. Do we have any red paint? The doors would be perfect painted red!"

Thomas chuckled. "You would like red just about anywhere."

She grinned at Thomas and lengthened her step to catch her sibling. She'd nearly forgotten, but she stopped and turned to say, "The upstairs is all ready for you. I will bring you a rug in a few days when I finish it."

As she left, Liz heard Jackson suggest to Thomas, "I do know where some red paint is stored. Let's finish these doors and get ready to go to Miss Anna's supper. She's a real fine cook."

As the two women came upon the little building that Jackson called a bathhouse, they found an outdoor pump to a well and a large flower garden. They admired the flowers in full bloom and picked a few to bring into the house, minus a few ants that Liz shook off.

Liz turned the wooden latch on the door and pushed it open, not sure what she would find inside. Both women dropped their mouths open when they saw a large-footed tub in one corner with drying racks for towels beside it. They spied a simple heating system that would allow plenty of hot water required for bathing. It looked like a cookstove almost, with two open areas for the wood to be placed inside and burners above that held two very large containers of water. An indoor pump allowed the water to come right into the heating buckets! Next to the stove, a basket held an extra supply of wood for heating the water.

Megan moved closer to the ornate tub and picked up one of the glass bottles on a shelf beside several others, and took off the lid. She placed it under her nose and breathed in the rich fragrance.

"Can you believe all of this? It smells just like lilacs." She took another deep sniff before offering it to Liz for a noseful.

"I'm certainly surprised. I never expected anything like it. Do you think Abby or Emma have seen this?" Liz asked.

"No, we thought it was a smokehouse and we didn't see the pump or the flowers. Let's keep it to ourselves!" Megan teased.

Liz thought for only an instant that it would be much easier if they didn't have to share with two others; however, she couldn't keep something so special all for herself.

"It would never work. They would find out and be really mad at us!" she reluctantly admitted, and she and Megan had a good laugh over it.

They left the bathhouse and went through the back door of the kitchen. Liz commented again how a porch would be perfect on the back as they entered to find Abby and Emma getting ready to unpack the kitchen supplies. They had just finished moving into their bedrooms when Megan informed them, in detail, about the claw-footed tub, complete with beautiful, fragrant smelling jars to use in the bath.

"Well, I have to see this to believe it," Abby commented and walked out the back door with her sister.

Liz took a quick survey of the house and found it all to her liking. It was really much better than she had ever hoped.

The cousins returned, chattering on about the bathhouse and how thankful they felt toward the captain who loved his wife so much and wanted to provide such comforts for her.

"Her blessing has turned into ours," Abby said. "It certainly will make it more pleasant for us, won't it?"

"I think the good captain wanted his wife to be happy," Emma said. "It's so romantic, isn't it?"

Leave it to Emma to romanticize any situation, Liz thought, and she grinned at her cousin.

"The marriage vows say for better or worse. I think you stay with them anywhere, if you really love them!" Megan returned. "She shouldn't have moved back east without him."

"It has been a busy day. What do we do next?" Abby asked as she dropped onto a straight-back chair by a wooden table large enough to seat eight.

"I think we should get out of these rags we've worn for weeks and put on something we haven't seen since packing back home."

Emma had spoken the truth about their clothing. They were in rags, Liz realized.

Abby picked up the edge of her skirt and said, "The next time I see this skirt, it better be at the end of the kitchen mop handle!"

They all laughed and Megan added, "My dress is so thin that my arms have turned brown by the sun, even through the sleeves!"

Laughter erupted again and Liz gently tugged at the well-worn waist of her dress, and it began to come apart in her very hand.

"I had to keep my apron tied on tight or my dress would have fallen off days ago." Liz held the waist up where the stitches had vanished.

"I can't believe I had this on when Thomas proposed to me."

Abby and Emma both straightened, looking to Megan for confirmation that they'd heard her right. At Megan's nod of validation, Liz's excited cousins lunged at her and encircled her with an exuberant embrace and a parade of questions.

CHAPTER 16

Anna opened her door wide and welcomed the Maillys and their escorts to her cozy home, which appeared to have many modern comforts. She wore a clean white apron over the same dark blue calico she had worn when she met them in town earlier in the day.

Along the back wall, two doors opened to a wooded area where she'd set two tables end to end. Large trees canopied the tables, creating a cool spot for eating together. A breeze came through and kept the summer evening enjoyable.

Two beautiful scrap patchwork quilts with single squares and thin triangles served as tablecloths, and crocks blooming with wildflowers decorated the centers of each table. Anna had enough benches and chairs set out to include all the people who came on the wagons, plus Smithy and Samuel Smith. Pastor Parker hadn't made it home yet, but Anna told them she expected him at any moment.

The women gathered together in the back of Anna's house where she prepared to serve cold tea in tall metal cups.

Emma approached Anna and said, "I simply can't wait any longer. I have to find out how you control all of your curls; they look so nice, and mine are just a wild mess everywhere."

Liz chuckled, noticing that Emma's curls had gotten the best of her in the humid heat.

"Oh, it's bearable with a little beeswax, and it's grand when the wind blows too. I will show you how to do it and share some of mine with you until you can get some of your own."

Liz admired the tablecloth quilts, wondering if the women in Fort Worth were avid quilters or just the kind to make them as needed. These beautiful coverings were perfectly pieced and the color pattern carefully selected. They had grown worn over time, but each still showed the love stitched into its blocks.

As she did with every quilt she came across, Liz ran her hand over the fabric and threads, hoping to soak up the story that could be told. Was a friendship strengthened as the stitches were sewn? Or was it possibly a new bride asking advice from her mother as they stitched? Or could tears have been shed over the hope for a future or the loss of one?

"Oh, good! My dear husband," Anna announced.

Liz looked up as Pastor Parker rode up to the back of the house. He was a tall man with wide shoulders, wearing a white shirt tucked into dark trousers that covered his cowboy boots. A black string tie surrounded his neck and a dark cowboy hat was planted firmly on his head. His nicely groomed mustache and warm smile made the new arrivals comfortable immediately.

He dismounted his horse and approached them with his jacket over his arm and a Bible in his hand. A leather holster on his left leg held a Colt revolver tucked down into it. He looked as if he could have been a gambler or a hired gun until the smile and worn Bible showed up. With wide steps from his long legs, he went straight to his wife and bent to give her a kiss and a one-armed hug before greeting his guests.

"It doesn't look like Lucas made this trip," Parker said as he looked over the group. "These good folks must be starved for some of your fine cooking, Anna. Let's sit and pray."

The pastor sat at the head of the table with his wife at his right side. Next to Anna were Liz and Thomas, then Luke, John, Blue, and Tex. Samuel sat at the other end of the table with Smithy, Colt, Chet, Jackson, Megan, Emma, and Abby at the end by Pastor Parker.

Parker took Anna's hand and laid his other open for Abby. "Let's give thanks," his rich, caramel voice began.

Each one followed the pastor's example and took the hand next to them. Even the rangers and millworkers followed suit. When Pastor Parker spoke, it was hard not to follow his command.

"Our faithful God, we worship you and are grateful. Thank you for our safe journeys. Thank you for our new relationships, and we ask that you would bless this fine food that my dear wife has prepared."

Parker gave Anna's hand a little squeeze. Liz and the other women at the table raised their heads slightly, watching this powerful, godly man. They had never seen or heard a preacher like this one before.

Thomas broke Liz's train of thought when he gave her hand a squeeze.

"And thank you for bringing the Mailly family to us. Bless them, oh Lord. And all of God's people said, 'Amen.'"

Amens sounded all around the table as each one lifted their head.

Thomas continued to hold Liz's hand until he had to start passing the heaping bowl of mashed potatoes and the platter overflowing with fried chicken.

Liz noticed that Megan still held Jackson's hand, her little hand swimming inside Jackson's large one. He glanced at Megan and seemed satisfied to let her hand remain right there, too.

After a moment, Megan jumped slightly, as if she'd just realized what she'd done. She slipped her hand away and giggled a little. "Sorry."

Pastor Parker started the conversation after all the food had gone around the table and justifiable praises had been given to Anna for all of her hard work preparing the meal. Luke teased his mother that her chickens had barely made it to Texas, and this gave him the idea that they would make a tasty supper! Laughter and good humored joking abounded around the table.

"Miss Abby," the pastor said, "the appointed men hired to oversee the school are here tonight at the table. Mr. Owen Smith, otherwise known as Smithy, his son Mr. Samuel Smith, and me, of course. They tell me that your wagons are unloaded and you're almost settled in."

Parker took a bite of a chicken leg and smiled at his wife with approval. Anna blushed, and Liz could see that she appreciated the way her husband rewarded her with compliments, silent or spoken.

"We want to welcome all of you to Fort Worth," Parker said to Liz. "If there is anything we can do for you now or later, please let us know. You can talk to any of us and we will do our best to accommodate you. We want you all to settle here and plant some deep Texas roots. It is a wonderful place, and we are excited you are here!"

Liz noticed Abby looking over the three governing men, and she thought her cousin appeared as surprised as she that there were only three, and that Samuel was one of them. Before, at Abby's Mississippi placement, there had been five men, all of them older men with families. She didn't know what to think about one board member being single and only a little older than Abby. But this was the West, where everything was different.

Thomas addressed Parker. "You said earlier that if you could help in any way to just ask."

"Yes," Pastor acknowledged the request. "What can I do for you, Thomas?"

Liz's heart fluttered slightly. She almost heard the words before they were spoken.

"Well, this morning I asked Liz to marry me and she said yes. We would like to be married in a few weeks after we get settled. Lucas should be here by then."

Cheers and congratulations were heard from everyone around the table. Thomas smiled at Liz, and she forced a smile back while willing the chicken in her belly to be tamed.

※　※　※

"This is such wonderful news," Anna exclaimed. "Anything I can do to help you plan the nuptials, Liz, don't hesitate to ask me. All right?"

Liz nodded, forcing a smile to work its way around her gloomy attitude.

I'm suddenly not feeling so matrimonial, she thought. *How dare he simply make an announcement of this kind without discussing it with me first!*

After everyone finished the peach cobbler made with sweet, ripe Texas peaches, the Mailly women pitched in to help with the cleanup. The men stayed seated around the table, chatting about the recent relocation of the county records that would ensure Fort Worth as the county registrar.

Tex leaned into the table and said to Pastor Parker, "So, you're saying that a group from here went to Birdville and stole the county records?"

"Yes, as I was riding back from a visit just south of here, I came across ol' man Jeb, who told me he saw several men riding back with all the records from Birdville. Now that the Maillys are here, the townsfolk think this should be the place for Tarrant County records instead of Birdville. The county seat will bring growth and life to our area, which we'll need if we are going to prosper."

Tex leaned back in his seat and looked to Jackson and Colt.

"Guess it's a good thing we're here. We'll take a day's ride out at daybreak and see what we can find out. Maybe Birdville won't put up a fuss. We'll tell them we're Texas Rangers are aware of the issue and will be handling it appropriately."

"Hopefully, it will stay calm," Jackson chimed in. "But if they do choose to make an issue, we'll be prepared."

"I think they're right about the records," Tex said. "I feel strongly they should be kept here. I'll send word back to the authorities and see where we stand legally. Do you know where the records are now?"

Parker raised his shoulders. "I'll see what I can find out in the morning."

"Good," Tex said. "See if you can get them to your house for safekeeping until we can get this straightened out."

Thomas followed Liz to the kitchen when she carried out away the last pile of dishes. "You look bone-weary, Liz," he said. "I don't think anyone would be offended if you let me see you home."

"I want to finish the cleanup, Thomas. And there's no need to see me home. I'll just see you in the morning."

No need to get into the whole wedding announcement argument in someone else's home. Especially when she felt so tired she might drop at any moment.

But Thomas hadn't been dissuaded, and he insisted upon seeing Liz to the front door of her new home. When they reached the house, he kissed her on the forehead. She leaned against his chest. He felt strong and solid. Even though she knew he wasn't Caleb, it felt good to be held at the end of a long day.

Thomas put both arms around her and said, "I love you, Liz. I can't believe I can finally say that to you. I know a lot has happened today. Get some rest and we can talk about our plans later."

Liz watched after him as Thomas strolled to the back door of the mercantile. She went into the house, found her nightgown, and returned to the bathhouse. As Liz removed her worn dress and folded it on the wooden stool by the tub, she sighed as she thought about all the garment had been through.

She stepped into the tub and let the warmth caress her skin. The water smelled like lilacs. She slipped down into it until her shoulders submerged, combing the braid from her hair with her fingers. She held her breath and slid quietly under the water, soaking every inch of her aching body, even over the top of her head.

What a wonderful feeling to surrender mind and body to the warm tub of water. She surfaced and reached for a bottle of thick, pearly soap and poured a small amount into her hand, and then coaxed luxurious lather from her hair. Afterward, she used a pitcher to rinse her hair until it felt squeaky clean and satiny soft to the touch.

After a time, her fingers began to wrinkle like a piece of dried fruit. The fluffy cotton towel just within her reach soothed her skin as she stepped out of the tub. She thought again about how pampered the captain's wife must have been to have such a fancy, expensive bath sheet to use out here in this rugged part of the country!

Liz dropped the nightgown over her head for the first time since she'd driven the wagon out of the flood. She had decided on that day that a wet nightgown was not what a lady needed to wear when driving a rain-soaked team. She would just sleep in her clothing, like it or not.

How can I write this day in my journal? she wondered as she dried her hair in the towel. *It has gone on for an eternity.*

Liz pulled the wrapper around her and tied it at the waist. Her clean, damp hair fell over her shoulders. She stepped out of the bathhouse door and looked around the yard. The sounds of the night hummed a slow song and a coyote yodeled in the distance. She paused to admire the moon that hung lazily in the big Texas sky.

"Thank You, God," she silently prayed. "You are good."

Liz cranked the handle of the back door and slipped into the kitchen. She walked toward the two bedrooms and tried to remember which one she now shared with her sister. It seemed like days rather than hours ago that she had chosen her room. Her soft and familiar quilt was a welcome sight. As she turned down her bed, her journal fell to the wood floor with a thump.

"I'll write it in the morning," she mumbled as she pulled Granny's quilt over her legs.

As she drifted off to sleep, Liz's thoughts meandered across the tradition of every new homestead receiving a star quilt for good luck. The women of the community would make one and send it in the settlers' wagon on their way to a new home.

She thought about the hardships of the wagon trail endured by so many, and now she knew what it meant to have the support and prayers of a family as you suffered through the long, tireless days.

That's what I will write in my journal tomorrow, she thought as she snuggled into the cozy quilt.

She hardly heard the whispers from the hallway as Megan, Abby, and Emma prepared for bed, and she thought she might be dreaming when Tex's low baritone voice rounded up the men and they headed to the old military bunkhouse.

Her very last thought as she drifted into a deep, dreamless sleep: *Even an army bed will be a treat for them tonight.*

Chapter 17

Thomas hadn't ridden very long before he caught a glimpse of that for which he'd set out searching that morning.

"Hello, anyone there?" he called out as he approached the peddler's wagon.

"Mr. Skelly here," someone returned through a thick Irish brogue. "Friend or foe?"

"Oh, friend for sure, Mr . . . ."

"Skelly. Just peddler Skelly," the little man sang as he appeared from behind the wagon. "What might I do ya for?"

"I wasn't sure I'd find you," Thomas said as he dismounted. "I was told you were due this morning."

"Ah, so I was, laddy. So I was," Skelly said as he adjusted his strange little suit. "Just taking a quick break, I was. I stopped at a few ranches and farms on my way to Fort Worth. Made me some nice trades, too. Is that where you're from, boy? Came from Fort Worth, did ya now?"

"Yes," Thomas replied. "Thomas Bratcher. I'm new to the area."

"Oh," he said, lifting a hopeful eyebrow, "are you a married man now, Thomas Bratcher? With a family? Do you need something for them? I have some lovely things. Yes, I do Mr. Bratcher. Would you like to see?"

Thomas smiled at the round little peddler. He had to listen carefully to understand what he was saying over his thick accent.

"Yes." Thomas paused. "Well, they'll be my family soon anyway. I'm traveling with the Maillys from Louisiana and I've recently become betrothed to—"

The peddler's eyes ignited like a torch, and he squealed with glee as he took one hop off the ground, launching into a little jig as he landed.

Thomas wondered how the peddler could get all of his weight off the ground like that and had to hide his amusement at the Irishman's dance.

"The Mailly family, you say? Imagine that! The luck o' the Irish holds true." He talked excitedly as he searched the inside of his vest pocket until he produced a letter. "I have something for them, you know. This letter is from Captain Sewell's wife back in Fort Polk and it is to be hand delivered from me personally. Can you show me the way to the ladies?"

"Yes, I can. I'm going that way now. But first I thought I might need to purchase something from you. Elizabeth Bromont is to be my wife, and I would like to buy her a special gift. Would you have anything in your wagon for my future bride?" Thomas asked with anticipation.

The peddler put his finger up as he asked, "Could your bride be the same as the fair Liz Mailly?"

"Well, yes, the very same. She is the granddaughter of Lucas Mailly and the widow of Caleb Bromont."

"You must secure the reins of that horse of yours, Mr. Bratcher, and come see what I have for you. It's your lucky day, Thomas Bratcher! Your new bride will love you even more when I show you what I have!"

"Show me," Thomas said as he quickly wrapped the reins of his horse around the wooden bar at the back of the peddler's wagon.

The little man scurried up into the back of the wagon rather quickly considering his girth, and he began moving things around inside. Finally, he appeared with a large cloth bag and began the story of the quilt inside it.

"Mrs. Sewell, the precious lady, has a new wee one and was in need of many things, and she wanted to buy a special gift for her husband, the captain. He is a lucky man to have the love of that woman . . . yes, indeed . . . and she wanted to buy the gift for him and trade for the baby things."

Mr. Skelly untied the knot at the end of the bag as he told Thomas his story. Thomas couldn't imagine what the peddler could have in that bag, or why it had him so elated, but he continued to insist that the contents would make the perfect gift for Liz.

The peddler pulled the quilt from the bag and continued telling the story as he opened it wide for Thomas to see.

"The captain's wife makes quilts," the round man continued as he yanked one out of the bag. "And she has them stacked up and folded neatly in a cabinet. She told how the Mailly women were so inspired by her quilts, in fact, that they could hardly think of anything else during their trip. Miss Mailly . . . er . . . Liz," the peddler stumbled over her name, "really wanted this one. She tried to buy it from her on that day, in fact, but the captain's wife wasn't ready to let it go just then. When she was ready, she traded it to me with strict instructions to only sell it to Miss Liz Mailly. So you see why I must be certain, Mr. Bratcher. Are you sure your bride is the right Mailly lady? I wouldn't want to disappoint the captain's wife by mistaking one Liz for another one. Ah, if your Elizabeth Bromont is the Liz Mailly as you claim, then you are a lucky man! Yes indeed, the luck o' the Irish is upon you today, Mr. Bratcher!"

When the peddler finally stopped talking, Thomas wasn't entirely sure he'd followed all the way through. But as he peered down at the quilt in the peddler's stubby arms, he instinctively knew Liz would love such a gift. The pattern—a circle, like a ring . . . like a wedding ring—combined many beautiful colors and prints.

"It's perfect," he told the peddler, and the little man cackled with excitement. "I will take it, and one more thing. Do you have a gold wedding ring?" Thomas asked, hoping that the Irish luck the man had spoken about still smiled down on him.

"No, but I do have a sterling silver one I think you will like. It's a very unique design," the peddler said as he retrieved a small box that held the ring and a few other pieces of jewelry.

Amazed at the inventory the man had tucked away and hanging in every nook and cranny of his wagon, Thomas's heart thumped out the seconds while Skelly plucked out the ring and placed it in his palm.

When he displayed it dramatically in his outstretched hand, Thomas pondered its intricate design. It wasn't quite what he had in mind, but the ring was very pretty and Thomas thought it would fit Liz's small finger. He took it from the peddler cautiously and placed it on his own pinkie finger for a closer look.

"Looks like I owe you some money, Mr. Skelly. How much am I in for?" Thomas asked as he admired the ring.

"Are you trading or buying today?"

Thomas placed the ring into his vest pocket and pulled out a shiny gold coin. "Will this be fair?" he asked as the sun glinted off the piece of gold.

"More than fair, Mr. Bratcher. It has been an honor to do business with you."

"Load up and I will take you into town to meet the women where you can deliver the letter personally. I bet they might even invite you to stay for supper," Thomas told the old Irishman. "And remember . . . what I bought today is a secret . . . no telling."

The man, happy as a leprechaun—and looking a little like one too in that odd green suit—climbed up to his wagon and placed his finger over his mouth to let Thomas know that he wouldn't tell the secret.

Thomas folded the quilt carefully and put it back inside the bag, tying it to the horn of his saddle. After securing the horse's reins, he climbed up to the wagon and sat beside Skelly. With the quilt secure and the ring tucked inside his pocket, they were ready to go. Thomas gave a quick pat to the pocket that hid the ring.

It was hard to talk to the peddler as they traveled together into town because the wagon made so much noise from all the clamor and clanging of all the items suspended from pegs and nails inside. It wasn't far though, and soon they approached the edge of the community.

"This way," Thomas said, and soon they stopped at the foot of the steps to the Mailly mercantile.

Liz came to the doorway to see what the noise all about, a dust cloth in her hand and a thick braid loosely dangling down her back. She wore an earthy brown calico dress with small flowers and random dots scattered across the cloth, and the apron she donned over it boasted a dark tan checkered pattern with little flower branches. Thomas thought she looked very pretty with tendrils of blonde hair springing from her braid and framing her flushed checks.

"Hello there!" she greeted him with a smile. "Who's your friend?"

"I think he will be your friend too, after you see what he brought you," Thomas answered. "He has a letter for you!"

Liz grinned and bounded across the threshold of the store.

Thomas made the introductions and, as predicted, Liz invited Skelly to stay for supper. After accepting her invitation, Megan and her cousins appeared out of nowhere and looked over Liz's shoulder as she opened the letter.

"Thank you, Mr. Skelly. It is an unexpected pleasure to have a letter from friends. Will you be going back that way?" Liz asked. "We'll write one for you to take back to her when your travels take you that way."

"Sooner or later, I always make it back to Fort Polk. I'll be happy to take her your letter." The peddler pulled his watch from the tight pocket at his waist.

"Why don't you rest for a while and we'll find you when supper is ready. Emma will finish up soon. Do you pass our way often?" Liz quizzed the peddler.

Thomas thought Liz had as many questions as the peddler did!

"No, not really, but if the place becomes stable and settled, I'll return as often as you'd like, m'lady." He paused and looked at her storefront. "Looks like you could use some glass windows for your new business."

"Yes, I hope to have some sent our way with the first load of freight." Liz looked at the empty door and window frames that needed glass.

"If you like small windowpanes, I have them on my wagon now. I think I have enough windows and doors." The peddler turned to retrieve the windows from the back of his traveling store.

Liz tucked her towel into the waist of her apron and scampered down the steps to the wagon to see what Mr. Skelly had inside.

This man has everything in that wagon of his, Thomas thought as he peered into the back again. He wanted to inspect the window panes himself since he knew that he would be the one installing them.

Liz looked them over and Thomas nodded his approval.

"Yes, we will take them all. What do I owe you, Mr. Skelly?"

CHAPTER 18

The sun came up that Sunday sending a message of hope and peace to Liz's new world. She and the others had had a good night's sleep and felt well rested for the first time since they'd left Lecompte.

Liz needed to adjust to one of her new dresses, as well as to her new relationship with Thomas. She felt much better about things that morning, and had decided overnight that it was a good choice to marry Thomas. He was her friend as well as a good man who had loved her for a long time. She'd awoken with a new resolve, she was even looking forward to settling into her new relationship as Thomas's soon-to-be wife. And seeing Thomas's excitement about it endeared him even more to her heart.

The other Mailly women wore dresses that had been packed away for months. Her sister and both of her cousins behaved as if they'd just purchased them that morning. The day had finally arrived when the family would attend church together and enjoy a whole day of festivities afterward. It was a short stroll to the church and the ladies chatted with anticipation as they walked part of the way on the wood sidewalk and then crossed the dirt street. They stepped along a patted-down trail created by many others before them on their way to church or the pastor's home.

"I can't stop thinking of all the school children who will be taking this same path to our classroom," Abby told them.

"You'll probably meet a lot of them today," Emma pointed out.

"I hope I make a good impression," she replied, suddenly pensive.

"Of course you will," Liz reassured her. "You look lovely in that dress."

"Do I?" Abby asked, and all three of them confirmed Liz's encouragement. "You don't think we dressed up too much, do you?" Megan asked Liz in a hushed voice.

Liz shook her head and smiled. "I think most will just have on their best cotton dresses and newest bonnets."

Liz didn't tell them that she'd already noticed that their bonnets seemed nicer than most she'd seen, but Megan seemed to sense her reluctance.

"I just don't want to seem unapproachable," she whispered.

"You think we're unapproachable?" Abby exclaimed.

"Not at all," Liz said as they reached the curve in the path leading to the church.

"I just don't want to appear uppity," Megan said, "but I want everyone to be sure to see what lovely dresses I can make for them or teach them how to make on their own." She stopped and planted her feet. "Maybe we can go back and take our layers of petticoats off so that our dresses appear less fancy."

"The good book said to wear our best to worship the King," Liz pointed out. "And that's what we're here to do, above anything else. Now let's lift our heads up and walk into the church together, remembering why we came."

"Good morning, don't you all look lovely," Anna complimented the women as they filed up the path toward her. "Come and meet some of the others."

"We were about to turn around and go back home," Megan said to Anna, and Liz shushed her with a soft jab to the arm.

"Why? Is something wrong?" Anna asked.

"We're afraid that we're overdressed and want to make the proper first impression with the townspeople and Abby's students," Megan told her anyway.

"You look very nice. Don't worry. I think they're expecting you to be a little more cultured than we are. Word has spread like a wildfire that you're here and that all of you are exactly what Fort Worth needed."

Liz smiled at Anna for having soothed their worries as the woman took Liz by the hand, moving them in the direction of the church. "Most everyone has already arrived and is over by the shady side of the church visiting."

As Anna led the women along, voices and laughter rang out like a lovely song. Two children ran around the corner and stopped in their tracks as they saw the ladies coming toward them.

"Look, Sissy . . . they are so pretty," the youngest of them said.

Anna bent down to the girl's level and said, "I want you to meet my new friends, and your new schoolteacher." Anna motioned to each one as she introduced them. "And this is Miss Wilkes, your new teacher."

Abby reached out to take their little hands. "Lillie, Daisy, it is so nice to meet you. I can't wait to have you in my classroom. Do you know how to read yet?"

"A little, Miss Wilkes," the older one spoke proudly. "Mama went to school back east before she married Pa and she has taught us a little. I can get some of the words in the primer and Sissy knows most of her letters."

The younger one was so excited to talk to her new and very pretty teacher that she started reciting her numbers for Abby right there on the spot. Abby chuckled over the little one's mistakes.

"That's very good, Daisy! We'd better meet the others now." Anna encouraged Daisy toward the shade where the crowd had gathered.

"Good morning!" Anna called out in her sweetest attention-getting voice. "Earlier this morning you met the men from Louisiana, and now I would like for you to welcome the women who have come with them."

Before Anna could get all four names out, small groups gathered around each one with outstretched hands and ready smiles. As the church bells rang, the people of Fort Worth began making their way up the steps to hear the sermon Pastor Parker had prepared for them on this Sunday morning.

Liz and her family sat on the left side of the church, a few rows from the front. Behind them were all the others who had traveled with them, but Thomas sat down to Liz's right, with Anna at the aisle. A few of the ladies went to the front to sing along with two men who played instruments to accompany them. Liz didn't know the men and couldn't recall the names of the women, but they sounded lovely. She enjoyed the lively sound of the harmonica played by youngest man. The familiar hymns had never sounded so good!

Her attention diverted to the pew benches across the aisle. A large white dog stood there with the rest of the congregation, and howled as if he knew the song quite well. Liz glanced around to see if anyone else was amused by the singing dog, but no one seemed to pay any real attention to the dog.

Pastor Parker prayed, and the dog bowed his head. He welcomed the new guests, and the dog looked around as if he wanted to see who they were. Liz was almost sure the dog winked when Pastor Parker welcomed her, and when Pastor Parker asked the congregation to be seated, the congregation's furry member took his seat on the pew also.

Liz smiled and lifted her hand to hide her amusement. She was afraid she would laugh out loud any minute. She could feel it bubbling up inside of her, threatening to spill out. Thomas looked down at her and she pressed her lips together to hide her giggle. She didn't dare look at Megan. If their eyes met and she had seen the dog too, then there would really be trouble! The more she watched the dog participate in the worship service, the more her control wavered, and soon her shoulders started to shake.

"What is wrong with you?" Thomas whispered, but Liz held her hand tight to her mouth and waved at him with the other. Her eyes welled with tears in the effort to stifle her laughter.

Liz hoped she would not have to discuss the sermon after church. She had not heard a word the pastor said! When the service finally ended, Liz turned to Megan in amused disbelief, and Megan burst into cackling laughter. "You saw it, too?" Liz cried.

Anna joined in the conversation with a giggle of her own and explained. "Angel is the dog's name, and she belongs to Parker. He always practices his sermons with her during the week. Everyone knows Angel. I'm sorry, we should have warned you about her earlier."

Megan held her stomach. "I have never behaved like this in church before. It is just so funny." She laughed again. "Angel knew just what to do and when to do it." Liz held her Bible in her hand and reached inside the cover for a hanky. All the joking had brought the tears in her eyes to burst free.

A loud scream sounded suddenly from somewhere outside. Liz and the other women quickly followed Anna out the side door where a small girl squeezed her doll to her chest and stood facing a fallen tree trunk, paralyzed with fear as a large prairie rattler coiled defensively within inches of her and appeared ready to strike. The ominous sound of the snake's tail rattled out a warning.

Without thinking it through, Liz was guided by instinct and rapidly retrieved the small pistol from the church handbag she had around her wrist. After taking careful aim, she squeezed the trigger gently. The shot rang out and the bullet ripped the head clean off the deadly snake. Its writhing, scaly body fell over the small leg of the child and she screamed loud enough for the entire state of Texas to hear her. In seconds, her mother sprinted to the horrified child and folded her protectively into her arms of reassurance. The little girl wept against her mother's shoulder.

As everyone gawked at Liz in shocked silence, the little girl's mother mouthed, "Thank you." Huge, grateful tears glided down her face.

It seemed to Liz that the child's scream had brought everyone running toward them just in time to catch her sharpshooting. The father of the child stepped up to Liz and put his hand on her gun to lower it. He took her by the shoulders and looked into her face. "Mrs. Bromont, I don't know how to thank you. You just saved my little girl's life."

Liz blinked to clear her head and answered, "Is your daughter hurt?"

"She's fine, thanks to your quick thinking and good aim."

Tex let out a snort as he joined them.

"These dainty-looking city ladies didn't need any of us men to accompany them." He took his hat and brushed it against his leg, shaking his head. "I'll know who to call the next time I get in a jam. You Mailly women, in your fancy city dresses ... I think you've earned the respect of everyone in your new town."

Liz hadn't noticed that Thomas had come a-running at the sound of the gunshot until he said, "I always marvel at your hidden talents." Liz leaned against him and chuckled. "Very impressive, Elizabeth Bromont."

Parker called out, "Let us give praise to our God, for He is good. Now let's get these tables set up so the women can get our lunch baskets laid out for everyone to share."

When everyone had enjoyed their Sunday dinner and all the children had settled down in safe places for a nap, the women excitedly set up the two quilt frames. Anna's backyard was the perfect spot. A cool, light breeze made this Sunday afternoon very pleasant.

"Emma, have you named your quilt yet? It's a nine-patch something, isn't it?" Anna asked as she threaded her needle to start on the red squares.

Emma stood back for a moment, admiring the top stretched in the frame. The setting gave it a two-block interaction. She commented, "Maybe it should be EMMA'S FOLLY!"

"I like it," Megan said. "And I'm going to call mine, MEGAN'S FEATHERED STAR."

Liz admired Megan's twelve beautifully pieced feathered stars. Each center was a different star block with intricately pieced triangles. Black star points with red feathered points continuously flowed through the quilt top.

There was a nice turnout of women to work on the two framed quilts and the afternoon went by quickly. Liz concentrated on learning all of the names and who belonged to which family. She thought that was important and would help Abby with the school children as well.

Three women were pregnant and a lot of the talk centered around babies. Emma picked up her thimble and scissors and moved over to the feathered star quilt. "Megan, do you have room for me at your frame? I really want to quilt some on your pretty star."

"Sure. I'll trade spots with you so I can quilt some on yours. I see it's almost finished, so I'd better hurry."

As they passed each other, Liz touched Emma's arm and whispered in her ear, "Too much baby birthin' talk?"

"How did you know?" Emma asked with a smile.

The day had grown long and Liz was pleased with the friendships that her little band of women had made. The quilt frame had always been the perfect place for women to learn more about each other. With caring families around each corner and scattered along the countryside, life would be happy and rich in Fort Worth. She wished she could let her grandfather know how lovely she found their new home, and how well they were settling in.

Liz stood to stretch and go to the pump for fresh water, and she found Pastor Parker there as well.

"Having a good time?" Pastor Parker asked. "How is our new town heroine?"

Liz chuckled. "I really am enjoying myself. I didn't know what to expect. I feel like this is home already," she added as she took a drink of cool water.

"I talked with Thomas some today. We talked about your wedding plans, and some about Caleb. If you need to discuss anything at all, Anna and I are always here for you. And remember that it stays with us. We care about you along with all of our flock. Thomas is a good man and he sure seems smitten with you."

Liz listened to what her new friend and pastor had to say and decided to confide in him. It seemed that he could see straight through her anyway.

"Yes, I know, and I care about Thomas. He has been a close family friend. It seems that he has had a long time to think about his feelings for me and I'm only discovering mine for him. He is ready to jump ahead and . . ." She hesitated before adding, "I still feel connected to the one I loved. I don't know if Thomas can give me the time I need—" she paused, collecting her thoughts—"to learn to depend on him."

"I understand how you both feel. I think, given some time, it will work itself out. Both of you are good, sound people. Thomas will give you the time you need, I feel convicted of that. Just be honest with him, Liz."

She nodded thoughtfully, and the pastor switched topics.

"By the way, great shooting today! That poor family has already lost one child and another death would have devastated them."

Pastor Parker smiled at Liz before heading toward the men at the fire pit where wonderful smells of roasting meat circled the air.

As the afternoon turned to evening, Abby decided to look for the school committee to discuss her decision and turn in her signed contract, and she asked Liz to go with her.

Samuel and Smithy looked over the contract presented to them with perfect penmanship and a signature at the bottom. They seemed very pleased with their new schoolmarm, Abigail Victoria Wilkes, and Liz beamed proudly.

"When would you like school to start?" Abby asked.

"What do you think?" Smithy asked her. "We could start with the younger ones and then add the older boys after harvest."

"That sounds good. We can pick a date in a few days," Abby said to the board members as she shook their hands to seal the deal.

A few moments later, Pastor Parker joined the group and called out, "I have an announcement to make and then we can get ready to eat again." The citizens of Fort Worth gathered around once again in anticipation of what would be said. Pastor Parker cleared his throat so that he could be heard well. "We are waiting on final word for the permanent location of the county records. We have reason to believe that the location will be here."

Cheers went up from the crowd.

"We also have a signed contract for our teaching position. Miss Abigail Wilkes has accepted the assignment."

Parker held the contract up for all to see. Whoops and hollers came from parents and children alike, while Abby blushed over the attention.

"I don't think anyone has ever been so welcomed into a teaching position before," she told Liz.

The pastor held his hands in the air to calm the crowd. "We will announce the first day of school soon. We plan to let the harvest hands start at a later date, so let us know what suits you and we'll take that into consideration."

This time, the older boys sent out a cheer of excitement, and members of the congregation chuckled.

"May I introduce to you our new teacher, Miss Abigail Wilkes?"

Liz watched the color bloom to Abby's cheeks again as Parker made the announcement. She felt so happy to see her cousin welcomed, privileged to be teaching in this community. Their children really wanted to learn, from what she had assessed, and she looked on as Abby approached the front where the pastor stood and faced the expectant crowd.

The sun had started its descent in the west and a warm yellow glow surrounded the town. Abby looked out over the crowd, lingering on her sister and cousins with big loving smiles, clapping and cheering for her. Liz's heart beat fast inside her.

"I want to thank you," Abby announced to them, "for the opportunity you have awarded me to give knowledge to your children. I take this privilege seriously and I hope you will help me by encouraging them to keep up with their assignments."

The parents laughed in unison as some of the children groaned.

Abby began to walk away, but Pastor Parker stopped her. "One more thing." He paused. "Mrs. Longmont and the others have a welcome gift for you."

Katie Longmont came to the front with a large fabric bundle. With the help of another lady, they opened a beautiful schoolhouse block quilt.

"We want to welcome you and give you this quilt in appreciation," Katie spoke softly but with confidence. "Each family made a block for each child that you will teach. We quilted each of those names into the block. I would like for each student to step forward when I read your name."

She called her own three children last. "Daisy, Lillie, and Daniel

Longmont. Daniel will start next year, but he really wanted to have a block in the quilt."

Katie smiled as her children acknowledged the new teacher.

Daisy spoke out. "The setting stars in the quilt are for good luck and good marks on our assignments." She smiled shyly and twisted at the waist.

Liz's heart squeezed as she observed Abby's reaction, obviously overwhelmed as she looked into the faces of her pupils. The quilt was more eloquent than any speech could ever have been. Thomas moved beside Liz and touched her hand with his as Abby thanked them.

"Thank you so very much." Abby beamed. "I will treasure this beautiful quilt always."

"Well, this certainly is the night for surprises." Thomas said, nudging Liz toward the east. "Look who's riding in as we speak."

CHAPTER 19

A chestnut mare stirred up the dust as it galloped closer to the festivities at the church. The rider turned the horse toward the congregation and pulled back on the reins to slow down. Even in the dusky darkness, Liz knew it was her grandfather. The other three granddaughters along with Liz picked up their skirts and ran to greet Lucas Mailly.

Liz reached him first as he dismounted, and she threw her arms around his neck "I didn't expect you so soon, but I was just thinking about you."

"You didn't think that I would let you have all the fun, did you?" Lucas gave her a firm hug and turned to the others who had now reached him.

"You look well," Megan said as she hugged him.

"As do you," Lucas replied as he kissed her cheek.

"We didn't expect you so soon," Abby said as he put a large arm around her and Emma and pulled them to their toes in a big bear hug.

"Sir, it's good to see you." Thomas shook hands with Lucas. "Looks like the trip went well for you." Looking around, Thomas asked, "Did you come alone?"

"Yes, I traveled alone. I figured I'd make better time that way. The timber contracts didn't take as long as I thought and I didn't want the girls to have all the fun without me."

Thomas slapped him on the back and laughed.

Lucas Mailly and his kin walked closer to the group who had been watching the reunion. Liz realized that the people of their new town now saw a family unit that was complete, knitted together in love and respect. This gentle giant of a man had big ideas and was not afraid to live them and share them with the people he loved and cared about. This man would not allow the women in his life to be weak or dependent. He gave them strength, courage, and the desire to take life by the reins and direct it in the direction they wanted.

Liz felt stronger with his presence. She could feel it in her bones. When she'd been a little girl, Liz and Megan had come to live with their grandfather. Lucas Mailly, a kind and loving man, had calloused hands and wise eyes. He'd been gentle with them and instilled strong values of character and wisdom. He encouraged his granddaughters and they grew to be well-educated women of strength and perseverance.

She grew nostalgic as she watched Lucas move about the crowd, making introductions and shaking hands. She remembered how he used to read books to them and discuss politics from the prominent newspapers of the day. Their grandfather always found time for them no matter how busy he was at the timber mill. Grandpa Lucas always knew just how hard to push to get the best out of them. He never restricted them just because they were women, and Liz loved that most about him. Just being around him made her a better person, and she didn't think she'd been fully aware of how much her grandfather strengthened her until now.

She'd never been apart from him before. She'd been able to make the trip without him largely because he expected her to and believed she could do it. She looked at him now as he walked across the church yard, placing his arm around Megan as she scurried along with him.

When Liz joined them, her grandfather gazed down at her as one lone tear crept out of the far corner of her eye. He reached over with his rough lumberjack thumb and gently took the tear from her.

"I'm here now, Liz. None of that."

"Luke!" Liz called out, and Luke stopped playing catch to look over at a group gathering around a tall, stately gentleman that he realized was his great-grandpa. He dropped the ball and ran to greet his namesake.

Liz thought for a moment that Luke might knock him down. Grandpa Lucas messed his hair and gave him a good-natured shove.

"You should have seen what Mom just did. She saved a little girl's life by shooting the head of a snake clean off!"

"You must be the famous Lucas Mailly," Pastor Parker greeted him with an outstretched hand. "It's good to finally meet the man that raised the fastest gun in Fort Worth."

"Someone tell me about this snake. It sounds like I just missed all the excitement!" Lucas said.

The men were all gathered to make acquaintances with Mr. Mailly and the story of the snake was told. Lucas smiled with pride as he heard how Liz had saved the child.

"It doesn't surprise me much. Liz has always been a woman of action!" Lucas smiled. "Where can a man get something to eat around here? It sure smells better than what I've eaten on the trail."

✳   ✳   ✳

As the sun began to sink on the edge of the Texas plains, the barbecue was in full swing with an abundance of good food and music. The tables were spread with tasty dishes brought by the townspeople to welcome the new Mailly family, and a bubble of pure joy lifted inside of Thomas at the realization that Lucas had arrived just in time to join in on the fun and fill his belly.

The same man from the morning's church choir played the harmonica along with several other men with fiddles, guitars, and a banjo. He couldn't help tapping his toe, and he looked around for Liz in hope that she might want a dance companion. He noticed Luke filling his plate again as others around him grabbed the hands of their partners and hurried out to the makeshift dance floor.

Megan especially loved meeting all of the single men of Fort Worth and swirling around the floor with them. One particular man, twice her age, kept coming back for dances. Finally, when Megan had danced enough, Thomas watched her head off for a break and to pour a cool glass of water. He got his first glimpse of Liz, standing there next to Megan.

"Megan, you're spending a lot of time on the floor with that older man," Thomas observed as he joined them.

"Well," she tried to catch her breath and take a drink, "he is a really good dancer and I can let my guard down with him. He's very nice."

Liz shook her head at her impish sister just as another cowboy approached and wheeled Megan off to be his partner as the Virginia Reel started.

Thomas bent down close to Liz's ear and said, "Would you mind if we stepped away from the music for a while?"

He placed his hand on her elbow and steered her over to the steps of the church where they could still hear the distant music.

"Are you having a nice time?" Liz asked, still tapping her boot to the song and looking over at the dancing couples. "This has been a wonderful day, hasn't it, meeting everyone and Grandpa Lucas arriving? I'm relieved that he arrived safe."

Her head bobbed with the music that danced on the night air. Thomas wanted and needed a little of her attention, and he touched her arm lightly. She looked up into his eyes and smiled. Instinctively, he bent down and gently brushed her lips with his. He just needed a moment to reconnect and be reassured of her feelings for him.

"I'm sorry, you wanted to tell me something and I'm just going on."

"I talked with Lucas and told him of our plans to marry." Thomas rested one arm behind her on the porch railing as he stared into her eyes. "He gave us his blessing."

"Did you expect him to say no?" Liz inquired. "I think he stayed behind and planned this trip intentionally so we could discover and talk about our feelings for one another."

Thomas thought that one over. "Well!" he reflected. "Maybe he did. I guess it worked."

"I guess it did," Liz stated, still in the euphoric mood of the festivities.

They listened to the music and laughter for a few minutes while Thomas screwed up his courage. When he couldn't wait another minute longer, he reached under the steps and pulled out the special gift he had purchased earlier from the peddler and had hidden there to await just the right moment.

"I have something for you," he said, and he handed her the large bundle.

Liz untied the end, her eyes glimmering as she asked him, "What is this?"

She pulled out the familiar circling wreath quilt that she had seen several months ago, and Thomas could see that she recognized it at once. Her mouth couldn't form the necessary words, but her questioning eyes inquired how he'd come by such a perfect gift.

"I bought it from the peddler. He told me Mrs. Sewell passed on the information that you seemed to be drawn to it when you saw it at Fort Polk."

She was speechless as she ran her hand over the tiny quilting stitches. She placed her hand affectionately on Thomas's smooth cheek.

"I can't believe my eyes. What a perfect coincidence that you would come across him and make this happen. But Grandpa Lucas always says there's no such thing as coincidences."

Thomas was delighted that she was so touched by the gift. The peddler was right. Liz did indeed love the quilt.

"Mr. Skelly told me Mrs. Sewell only sold it to him after he told her that he was coming this way. She sent the letter to deliver to you, and it was just luck that I met him first and discovered the quilt before he found you to deliver the letter."

"Thomas, I don't know what to say. This gift means so much to me. I'll always treasure it, especially since it came from you. Thank you."

Thomas was encouraged enough to boldly ask, "Liz, will you accept this bridal wreath quilt as your engagement gift?"

"Oh! Thomas! It's a beautiful and perfect gift, but I don't have a gift for you."

"Don't worry about that. The best gift you could give me is if you'll agree to marry me without waiting any longer. I've already waited so long. Now that Lucas is here, we could marry right away."

He saw the conflict in Liz's beautiful eyes. He imagined that her heart tugged at her from two very different directions, the past and the future. Could she really walk forward into Thomas's life without looking back?

He repeated, "So, Liz, what do you think? Do we have to wait any longer?"

"I . . . I just thought I would have a little time is all. Thomas, you are so special to me, and your gift has touched me so. I don't want to hurt you, but it's only been a few days. I'm sorry that you planned this moment to be so special and now I have ruined it. I'm so sorry." A tear slid down her cheek.

Thomas didn't know what to do. What was Liz saying to him? She pushed away just as he thought things were moving in the right direction. He had made her cry just by loving her. He felt confused and turned to step away. If he was pushing her, then he would step back.

She turned away, and Thomas placed his hands on her shoulders. Her back to him, he leaned into her hair and whispered, "Liz, I love you and I want to marry you right now. I don't want to wait anymore. I don't see the need to court you. You have known me longer than you knew Caleb. You know me, the man that I am. I told you that I could live with the memory of Caleb. All you have to do is try to love me half as much. But you have to decide if my love is enough. I have already waited a lifetime to love you and I don't think I can wait any longer. I'm sorry, but I think you need to make a choice."

"Oh, Thomas . . ."

"In the morning at dawn, put the engagement quilt in the chair at the back door where I can see it and we will move forward with our plans to marry. If I don't see the quilt, I'll know your decision. I love you, Liz. My heart is yours if you want it."

Thomas kissed her hair where it remained warm from his words. Without another moment of delay, he turned and walked away.

If she turned back to look after him, she didn't call out to stop him, a fact which just about broke Thomas's heart. He stopped to speak to the pastor and made every effort not to look Liz's way again before heading home.

He sat in the rocker by the upstairs window above the mercantile with a perfect view of the house where Liz now lived. He watched as she came home moments after he settled into his spot. Abby and Emma arrived next, chatting as they went inside. Last came Megan, walking home with the tall cowboy who had kept her on the dance floor most of the night. She thanked him for walking her home and turned to go inside. He took her by the arm and said something close to her face. She frowned and tried to wiggle free from his grip.

Thomas saw the exchange and could only guess what the cowboy had said. He decided the cowboy might need a little schoolin' on the proper way to walk a lady home. He jumped up and took the steps three at a time down to the back door. He caught the man by surprise as he bolted from the door and crossed the yard. The cowboy immediately turned Megan loose.

"It's time for you to go home, Cowboy, and tell your friends to stay home with you!" Thomas said firmly.

"I didn't mean any harm," the cowboy said. "Just making the lady feel welcome is all." He tipped his hat to Megan. "Thanks for the dancin', ma'am."

He backed away and turned to walk across the yard.

"Megan, don't be a flirt. The men will get the wrong idea," Thomas chided her more firmly than he guessed Megan had ever heard from him before.

"Thank you, but I can handle myself fine," Megan bristled back.

"Megan, you don't weigh more than his leg. You are going to get caught in some trouble. Why didn't you walk home with Jackson or the others?"

Thomas began to settle down, but he could see that Megan had only begun to get fired up.

"I was," she snapped, "but they left without me, and Tex took Jackson and Colt back to the bunks because they are riding out early. Thomas, what's wrong? Did that cowboy really make you that upset?"

Thomas turned to leave then hesitated. "Just be careful and watch out for the others. You're like a sister to me and I don't want to hear of anyone hurting you."

"Thomas, you talk like you're leaving. Are you going somewhere?"

Thomas took his hat off and held it in both hands, twisting it a little. He looked back toward the distant sound of the music where the festivities were coming to an end. "Just watch yourself and take care of everyone."

He nodded goodnight and went to the back door of the mercantile.

Thomas returned to his chair by the window, watching the chair where he hoped a quilt might appear by dawn. As night pushed its way in, Thomas swung his leg over his mare and rode north from Fort Worth.

⋇　⋇　⋇

Liz rubbed her eyes as the morning sun peeked in between the gray clouds. Normally, the warmth of the sun would wake her at daybreak, but not today. The cloudiness and the late night had caused her to oversleep. She stretched and tugged back the quilt to swing her legs free, and she pulled herself upright. As she ran her fingers through her loose hair, she saw the circle quilt still laying where she'd left it. Liz bounced out of bed to the window.

How long has the sun been up? she wondered.

The gloomy morning had tricked her. Liz gathered the gift from Thomas and scurried barefooted without her wrapper to the back door. She passed Megan in the kitchen, already dressed and cooking breakfast, singing to herself as she flipped the bacon sizzling in the cast iron skillet.

"What time is it?" Liz asked as she stepped outside and spread the quilt across the chair near the back door. She wanted to make sure it was easy to see from Thomas's window. She stood in her nightwear and looked to the back of the mercantile. She saw no sign of him. It was breezy and cool for late summer, and gray clouds loomed overhead. Liz folded her arms across her chest for warmth and modesty. She looked into each direction but saw no one.

Where is Thomas? she wondered.

She had to find him right away.

Why did I have to oversleep, today of all days with Thomas waiting for a sign of my commitment?

Liz spun around and ran to her bedroom. She needed to find Thomas before it was too late.

She nearly knocked Emma down in her wake, and she heard Emma ask Megan, "What did she say? And where's the fire?"

"Watch the bacon and I will go see what all this is about."

Megan followed her into their room just as Liz frantically buttoned the bodice of her green calico dress. Liz tugged a brush through her hair in hurried strokes.

"How did I let things get like this?" she asked Megan. "What is wrong with me?"

Liz willed the comb through her sleep-tousled hair as tears stung her eyes.

"Liz, what is it?" Megan asked her.

"Megan, have you seen Thomas this morning?" she asked urgently.

"No. Why, what happened?" Megan asked, drying her hands on her apron and stepping aside to get out of Liz's way as she approached the doorway at a full run.

"If you see him, hold him until I return. I need to find him. I'll explain later. Oh! And don't bring in the quilt that's on the chair outside the back door."

Liz passed the corner of the mercantile, walking hurriedly along the dirt road. She couldn't take the time to use the wooden walkway in front of the store. She peered into both directions but saw nothing. She decided to ask at the pastor's house to see if they had seen Thomas this morning and, lifting the edge of her skirt slightly off the ground, she moved quickly. Calming herself some and with the scant tear wiped away, she knocked on the door.

"Good morning, Anna," Liz quickly said to the pastor's wife, "I'm sorry to bother you so early, but have you seen Thomas this morning?"

"No, I haven't," Anna replied sweetly. Liz looked up at the intimidating sky growing darker, and another tear escaped her eye. "Do you need help with something? Parker just went down to Smithy's to get his horse. He's leaving town to meet up with the Rangers. It sure looks like rain is in store for us today."

"Thank you," she called out as she waved goodbye and rushed over to the livery where she hoped to find all the men, including Thomas. Surely they would still be there. She had all but forgotten about the missing county records from the neighboring Birdville community.

The wind picked up as she silently wished she had grabbed her shawl on the way out.

As she approached, she saw many men, but not the one for whom she'd come looking. She reached the corrals and Samuel saw her first. He sent a smile her way just as she looked into his eyes.

"What brings you out so early this stormy morning?" he asked as he pulled the strap under the belly of his black mare. Samuel was dressed in his long riding coat, and he paused to study her and gave his cowboy hat a firm tug against the wind.

Pastor Parker had finished saddling his horse when he looked up and saw Liz. He tucked his Bible into his saddlebag and came to the fence where she stood. "Liz, do you need some help?" he asked as he buttoned his rain slicker that flapped in the wind.

Liz looked past him at the men, hoping one more would appear. The gust rearranged her hair and the comb fell out and into the corrals. A pony, skittish with the storm, pranced on it and cracked the comb in one step.

"I was hoping to find Thomas with you," Liz stated, holding her hair with one hand, trying to keep it from her face as she spoke.

"Thomas told me last night at the church social that he may leave early this morning and go north to look at some ranch land," the pastor told her. "I assumed he had discussed his plans with you."

Samuel had finished securing his bedroll and canteen to his saddle.

As he came closer, he picked up the broken comb and handed it to Liz. "Sorry," he said, and he shrugged as he handed her the broken comb.

"Me, too," she sighed.

"Smithy said Thomas was here at sun-up to get his pony saddled up and wasn't much on conversation, but he did say that we were not to wait on him to come back."

Samuel's father now joined the group and added his two cents' worth. "I think he planned on being gone for a while. He had a good-sized pack with him."

Liz nodded her head in understanding. "Thank you. How long will you all be gone?"

Samuel spoke up. "We are meeting up with the Rangers south of here. Not sure if there will be trouble bringing the records back, but Tex thought it would be good to have backup and some town authorities with us, just in case. Parker, being a preacher, should help keep everyone calm."

The pastor chuckled. "We live in hope."

Grandpa Lucas appeared at the livery with Luke mounted and ready to ride. He seemed quite surprised to see his oldest granddaughter standing at the stables.

"Liz," he called out, "you better get out of the weather. We have to ride out this storm if we are going to leave on time. Thomas will be back soon."

Her son gave her a smile and prodded his horse in step with the others.

Liz wasn't sure how her grandfather could be so confident about Thomas's return. Had he spoken to him?

The wet wind swirled about her, enforcing her state of mind. She felt so confused and out of control about everything. With the change in living conditions, she wasn't even aware of what Luke was up to or had been doing. He had grown up so much over the time they'd spent traveling west. Thomas had taken Luke completely under his wing in the last few weeks. Luke loved the freedom of riding with the Rangers to Fort

Worth and bunking with the men in the barracks of the fort.

The group of Fort Worth men mounted their horses and rode out of the stables. They all touched or tipped their hats as they passed Liz standing in the street. The rain had started and was cold as it hit her face. Instead of running home, she paused and gazed at the mercantile for a moment. It boasted new window panes and two new red doors made to order. It looked just as she had always imagined. Thomas had worked hard to grant her every wish, and now she had a storefront to be proud of.

Liz went up the steps to the mercantile and pulled open the door. Her wet hair puddled on the shoulders of her damp dress as she looked after the group of riders again, silently hoping to see one more added to the company. She only saw Pastor Parker give Anna a goodbye kiss in front of the church, and she heard him pray over the band of men for protection. His hearty "Amen!" traveled on the wind as she stepped inside the building. A gust of wind blew the door ajar behind her and she turned to bolt it.

His room, she thought. *I haven't checked his room.*

Liz climbed the stairs to the living quarters above the mercantile, not yet ready to accept the fact that he had gone.

"Thomas, are you here?" she inquired, before she entered.

Only the whistle of the wind disturbing a window answered her. The loft looked much as she had left it days ago. Some of his clothes had been removed from the pegs.

He packed them, she thought. *He really is gone?*

His worn family Bible lay open to Romans 8:28, and she slumped into the chair to read it.

"And we know that all things work together for good to them that love God, to them who are the called according to his purpose," she read aloud.

A sterling silver wedding band had been placed on the open page. Liz could imagine Thomas seeking Scripture to comfort and guide him. She knew that she had hurt him and she ached with sadness at the thought. Thomas had already purchased a wedding ring by the time she had rejected him.

Liz shook her head and clamped her eyes shut to hold back the tears. Thomas had such a quiet determination, so different than Caleb.

Why does he have to push me so?

She dropped her head into her hands as she leaned back against the chair and began to sob.

What have I done?

She'd played a sad, self-indulgent game and lost. She didn't mean to hurt Thomas or force him to leave. She had not meant to sleep so late and lose her future in this careless way. She didn't like how things had turned out. She didn't like playing the fool, being wrong, or losing control of her life.

"How can this be fixed?" she cried as the storm intensified outside the window.

The rain came down in steady streams until the street out front began to look like a muddy river.

Ting-ting came the sound of the wind as it whipped the rain into little metal needles that crashed against the glass. Thunder boomed and rattled the newly installed windows in the red door of the mercantile.

Liz wrapped herself in the log cabin quilt made by Thomas's mother. She could smell Thomas on it. She looked to the open Bible from which all of her strength, faith, and courage had always come. She whispered a prayer for her family and all of the men on horseback, asking for wisdom, direction, and a second chance, from the God of second chances. Liz wiped her eyes as the passage of Scripture she'd read echoed through her mind and a sudden prompting spoke to her heart.

My daughter, you don't have control over your life. I do, and all things do work together in My plan and My timing.

Liz looked around but knew that she would find no one. She recognized the familiar voice; she'd heard it before and it always comforted her and gave her strength. She smoothed out the quilt and lifted herself up, heading out to face the storm with restored confidence.

Chapter 20

Thomas inspected his clothing and the bedroll that hung drying in the tree. It had rained for three long days and nights. He spent the next two days rotating his belongings on the branches of a big oak tree. His things weren't dirty, just soaked. He even had to take valuable time off so his horse could dry out as well. The rainy weather had been good for him though; it afforded him thinking time about his future and what he wanted to do at this point.

The land was rich and beautiful with small hills, scattered trees, and good open pastures for grazing livestock. This was just what he hoped to find. Thomas looked down upon the perfect spot to build a big white ranch house with white corrals full of good horses, for breeding or to sell. Cattle would roam the outstretched hills around the ranch.

He envisioned the front of the house, and suddenly there was Liz standing on the porch. He shook his head to make the picture fade, but she was tenacious, that Liz. Always there, looking just like the first time he saw her as a young woman. She always stood like that . . . on the outskirts of his life, never really allowing him to step in.

Thomas poured the last of the coffee from the enamel coffee pot simmering on his campfire. He hoped the strong, hot drink might clear his head. To extinguish his small fire, he kicked dirt over the red hot coals as he came to the final decision that this was the piece of land for him. Despite all that seemed to have gone wrong, this decision just felt right.

He would purchase the land around him; Denton County land, close to the Trinity River where it drained into the Elm Fork.

Thomas saddled his horse and packed up his dry things, ready to move on, rather excited to file on the perfect piece of land. He would keep his plan moving forward, with or without Elizabeth Bromont.

This place would be close enough to monitor his responsibilities in town. He would most likely place his good friend Chet as foreman on the ranch, and designate Blue to oversee the freight line. Thomas placed his boot in the stirrup and mounted up. He turned his horse to a small settlement called Medlin, Texas.

As he rode into the community of settlers, just where Tex told him it would be, he found a small supply store with grain stacked along a table made from barrels. It really wasn't a building, just a roof without walls and a dirt floor. A rooster strutted between the barrels, making the hens cluck and move along in the powdery dust of the floor. Thomas reined in his horse and let them hang loose as he dismounted.

A big man working over a blacksmith's iron next to the supply store looked up. Wiping the sweat from his brow with a red bandana, he studied Thomas and stood to greet him.

Thomas took a few steps toward the big man with soot on his face. "I'm Thomas Bratcher," he stated, nodding his head. "I'm looking for Big Moe. I was told I could find him here."

"Who told you that Big Moe would be here?" the man replied in a deep voice as he wiped his hands on his heavy apron.

Thomas replied, "My friend Tex, a Ranger. He said to talk to Moe about some land I want to buy."

Thomas waited and watched until the blacksmith finally smiled, and all six and a half feet of the man came toward him.

"I'm Big Moe, and any friend of Tex's is a friend of mine."

The now-friendly giant shook Thomas's hand vigorously as he asked, "Which piece of heaven do you have your eye on?" Big Moe blocked the sunlight from view when he stood and the earth shook a little as he stepped.

His voice was deep and thunderous, and he even made the Ranger Jackson seem small by comparison. Thomas was glad he knew Tex and was able to use him as a reference.

Moe showed him around the corner to a shady spot with a table, and he motioned for him to take a seat. Moe continued standing and called out toward an open cabin door where it sat nestled in the grove of trees. A young girl, maybe ten years old, pretty and petite, came to the opening.

"Yes, Papa?"

"Bring a plate for our friend, and a drink from the well, too."

Moe sat on a tree stump on the other side of the table while Thomas watched the little girl go and do as her papa asked. She brought a chunk of beef and two slices of dark bread, heavy with fresh churned butter. Thomas didn't realize how hungry he was until he smelled the meal placed before him.

Moe smiled at her and asked, "Didn't I smell a peach pie cooking earlier?"

"Papa, it's almost ready. The crust just needs to brown a little more."

Thomas saw her smile at her papa as she served the food prepared with her small hands. Her slender body did a small curtsey and she headed back to the opening from which she'd first appeared.

"She's been cookin' for a few years now, ever since her ma passed. As you can see, she has a big job cookin' for me." Moe patted his stomach and gave a nod to Thomas.

Thomas had not had a meal since the Sunday welcoming party, and he was famished. He had left before dawn, just as a storm was moving in. Jerky was all he had in his saddlebag, plus some fruit he found along the way. Game was hard to find in the rain.

He finished off the last bit of bread and licked some of the butter off his hand. Moe continued talking about the small settlement he called home; Medlin had been named after Louis and Charles Medlin. About twenty families had settled there eight years back. Moe let Thomas eat without asking any questions. He obviously respected a man's meal time.

Thomas had barely swallowed his last bite when the blonde girl appeared with a hot peach pie and a crock of milk. Thomas smiled in amazement as she cut one third of the pie and placed it on his plate. She smiled shyly at him and giggled as she moved the rest of the pie in front of her papa.

Thomas placed his hands on his tight stomach and laughed as she turned and skipped toward a puppy that had wandered over in hopes of a tasty treat. She sat in the grass and played with the puppy, tossing a rag ball.

"Your daughter is delightful and a really good cook for someone so young," Thomas said over a forkful of the sweet pie.

Moe looked over to the child and nodded his head in agreement. "Bethany is good in many ways and I will hate the day I have to part with my only daughter. He will have to be a good man or he will have to deal with me and her five brothers."

Thomas chuckled at the image of a young suitor and the six giant men who would have to approve of the relationship with their much-loved Bethany.

"She reminds me of her mother, sweet as a honeycomb, floats around happy as a butterfly. It was a sad day when she passed. Do you have a missus and children?"

Thomas's thoughts went to Liz. "No, not married." He paused.

"But you have a sweetheart," Moe interrupted. "Will she not come west with ya? Are ya gonna send for her soon as you get the land?"

Thomas wasn't sure where he stood with Liz at the moment. He had waited all night for the quilt to appear on the back porch. When it didn't, he knew he had to leave.

"Yes, I do have a sweetheart." Thomas smiled, thinking of Liz and how excited she was when he surprised her with the quilt. "Our relationship has taken a bump in the road, you might say." Thomas looked at Moe and even though they had just met, he felt comfortable enough to share his dilemma. "I'm not sure she wants to continue with our plans to marry. She is in Fort Worth, widowed with a half-grown son and very independent."

Moe sat quietly with his arms folded across his chest listening to

Thomas. "Is she a good woman?" Moe asked.

"Yes," Thomas replied.

"Are you over being mad at her?" he asked intuitively.

Thomas smiled sheepishly as he looked at this man who already seemed to know him better than most. "How did you know?"

Moe sat up and leaned across the table, which groaned under his pressure. "You said she was independent. Means stubborn. You two locked horns means you left mad."

Thomas listened as Moe summed it up so simply.

"Let me tell you how to keep your woman happy," he continued seriously. "I was a big clumsy man, no looks, no money. But my Mary was a looker and had many to pick from. I just loved her and made her believe in herself, said, 'yes ma'am' to most everything. The sweet woman died birthin' my last son. If you love her, let her know, and give her a second chance. I'm sure she's worried sick over you bein' gone and I'd bet you didn't even tell her you were leavin'."

"I'll give it some thought."

"Don't wait too long. Life has a way of givin' and takin' and it don't ask our opinion on the matter." Moe looked Thomas in the eye as he spoke the wise words.

"Thanks, Moe. For the food *and* the advice. I have some riding miles to think on it."

Thomas folded up the paperwork for the title to his land and neatly pushed it into his inside vest pocket. Thomas had gotten more than he planned on; a good meal, advice, and an honest new friend. Even one of those was hardly easy to come by.

"We can file your land patent with the Texas Land Office when they send the traveling agent our way, if you don't want to travel all the way to Houston," Moe stated. "It's a long way and the agent will be by here in a few weeks."

"Thanks again, Moe, but I'll feel better filing the patent in person. Please tell Bethany the meal was as good as any I've had," Thomas said, and he let his horse get one more drink at the trough.

Bethany and her puppy ran up to Moe, and he scooped up the little dog and pushed him down into his apron bib with one giant hand. The fluffy pup poked his head out of the pocket as Moe lifted his pint-sized little girl and a planted a kiss on her forehead. Her little arm tried to wrap around her papa's huge neck as she sat neatly in the crook of his elbow. They both waved and the pup barked as Thomas mounted his horse and began his journey south to the Texas Land Office.

It would take him at least two weeks to make it there and back if he rode hard and had no trouble. But already, he heard the still small voice prompting him to get back home to Liz.

Chapter 21

Liz shook the quilt that had been left in place on the back porch ever since Thomas left. She worried that it might become faded and weathered after staying in the sun on that chair for the last two weeks. Once she'd shaken the dust free and carefully laid it out, Liz smoothed her hand over the circle wreaths and thought of the man who had given it to her.

How could I have been so stupid and stubborn?

Liz shook her head in disbelief. She scanned the dirt road as she'd done so many dozens of times in the hope of some sign of his return. Like always, she saw nothing more than a dust devil dancing down the road toward the livery.

Megan came to the doorway to retrieve her sister. "Liz, don't worry. I know you must be thinking of Thomas. I'm sure he'll be home soon. Come inside and let's get started on our sewing. Anna has just arrived and she brought her wonderful molasses cookies. Let's make this a good afternoon with friends, hmm?"

Megan gave her sister a shoulder hug with one arm, and Liz went inside with her to help pour the tea into Granny Claire's china tea cups. Small red wildflowers with five petals and long thin leaves adorned each cup, saucer and plate. Megan filled the large serving platter with warm brown spice cookies. The smell of freshly baked cookies hit Liz hard, and she went straight to the cookie plate and took two.

"I'm anxious to get to work on my cracker box quilt," Megan said as she replenished the cookie platter. "Did I tell you the peddler, Skelly, had noticed it at supper when he was there and asked to purchase it from me?" When Liz didn't reply, her sister continued. "I only have to complete the binding. I'm just about to finish sewing the first edge of the quilt. The peddler said he would return in a few weeks and trade me for some silks and sateen."

They joined the other women and Megan went straight to work pinning the fabric strips neatly to the trimmed edges of the quilt. Liz noticed that the mitered corners were neat and precise as Megan's needle moved easily in and out the five thick layers of cotton.

"Anna, I keep forgetting to ask you about the two quilts you had on the tables at our first meal together," Megan said. "Did you make them?"

Anna sat stitching on a beautiful blue and cream two-tone quilt that looked like a bear paw block except that the triangles for the claws were longer than usual.

"No, my mother did. The blue one is mine. She called hers LICKETY SPLIT because it went together so quickly, and blue is my favorite color. Mama had a secret for making all of those triangles so quick and easy. She would put them in almost all of her quilts. She even did it for my brother's quilt that was on the other table that day. She named it MONKEY TAILS."

"How funny! How did it get that name?" Emma asked.

"When he was a little boy, Samuel saw a monkey on a wagon train passing through and was so intrigued with the impish creature. So Mama named his quilt MONKEY TAILS. After that, he pestered our father for a monkey. He wanted one so terribly bad." Anna smiled and shook her head as she remembered.

"Samuel?" Megan piped up. "Is Samuel Smith your brother?"

"Yes, he is."

Emma turned to Anna again and asked, "And what do you call the bear paw quilt?"

"This one has the long claws like the legend down on Bear Creek. Story has it that there is an old bear that lives there with claws like knives and he hunts big game that he never eats, just kills for fun."

"Oh," Emma exclaimed and backed away from the blue bear paw quilt.

Liz chuckled.

"It won't bite you, Emma."

She had previously decided to call her new nine-patch project EMMA'S CROSSROADS, and she told Liz that she felt like she stood at the crossroads of her life and would soon need to make some decisions about what she wanted for herself. She felt that her life was as boring as the nine-patch quilts she always seemed to make. The black represented the somber mood she was in. Emma desperately wanted to break away and find out who she really was.

Liz reached for the teapot to refill her cup and Megan's. "Am I the only one who didn't know that Samuel is Anna's brother?"

Anna smiled at Liz and said, "Yes, Samuel is my older brother and Smithy is our father. Papa has always been the cavalry's blacksmith, but he didn't want to go on west with them at this age and we all like it here, so we stayed. Since we were married, Parker and I have followed Papa as he travelled with the cavalry. Seems like the men needed a minister. As for Samuel, he never felt compelled to join after he finished his education back east, so he just returned home and helped where he was needed. Samuel is a lawyer but he isn't much for sitting in an office, said he liked to practice on the open range."

Abby listened attentively to Anna's family history. "That explains a lot," she commented.

"Oh?" Anna said.

"I . . . I was just thinking of the detailed teaching contract he drew up."

Emma asked, "What about your mother?"

"The west is a hard life for anyone. She was a strong, good woman and followed Papa anywhere, always making a home from nothing. She passed on shortly after we arrived at this post. She was bitten by a copperhead in her garden, and she's buried in the church cemetery. Mama was one of the people responsible for getting this church built and having a real place of final rest, our little cemetery. At the time, the only other church graveyard was way over in Grapevine. You all would have enjoyed her company. I miss her so much. That's one of the many reasons I'm so glad you all came along. I'm so happy for your company."

Liz made a mental note to be more cautious in the garden.

Megan looked at her over the edge of her binding, which was coming along nicely. "You have been a bit preoccupied the last few days."

"Yes, I guess I have."

When Liz heard horses on the dirt road, she rushed to the window.

"Liz, you will never get that multiple triangle quilt started if you jump up every time you hear a wagon or horse on the road," Megan stated.

Abby got up and went to stand at Liz's side as she peered out the window. "You poor thing, Thomas will come back to you eventually."

Liz took a deep breath and let the curtain fall back into place. "It's my own fault he's gone. I wouldn't blame him if he never returned."

Abby squeezed Liz's shoulder before they both returned to their seats. Liz resumed working on the red triangle units. It seemed like she needed a million of them. She could feel Abby's pity for her as she looked at her with her entire mouth curved downward in a pout.

"I wish I knew what that quilt was going to look like, Liz. I'm sure it will be beautiful. The brown and black stars surrounded by all of those red triangle blocks are really nice."

Megan looked over at the quilt that Liz had barely started. "I thought you were going to make it indigo blue, like Mrs. Sewell's."

"I thought about it, but then I saw these dark reds and I just couldn't keep my hands off them. These scraps are from one of Granny Claire's scrap collections." Liz admired the fabric as she said, "We really don't have too many of her things left."

"Did you get any blocks completed at the mercantile this week?" Anna asked.

"Yes, I did. I wasn't that busy during the day, so I managed some piecing," Liz replied.

"The mercantile looks nice," Megan stated, "but we do need more inventory. John and Chet have been gone for over a week. Grandpa said it wouldn't be any too soon for them to return either. They're organizing more drivers along the way so that they don't have to make the whole trip. In fact, they will be picking up the wagons of freight at the Texas border, close to Marshall."

Emma asked, "Will they bring the rest of the canning supplies? Our garden is bursting at the seams and Mrs. Longmont asked for them today at church."

"I wish she could have stayed in town today and stitched with us. She is such pleasant company," Abby said. "She did such lovely work on the schoolhouse quilt. It really has helped me learn the names of the children and their families. Knowing everyone's name will make the first day of school much easier for me."

"The canning supplies are on their way, as well as many sizes of nails. I've never seen such excitement over nails before. These men think of them like school children do candy. I'm sure the first shipment is spoken for already. Word that multiple-sized nails were on the way spread through town this week like a wildfire." Liz laughed. "I surely didn't get any extra star blocks made that day!"

"Do you know yet when school will start?" Megan asked.

"I'm just waiting for them to tell me," Abby replied. "We decided to let the little ones start first and then the older boys will join us after the crops are in. It will be much easier for their fathers to let them go then." Abby's voice bubbled with excitement. "I also want to start visiting the families that don't live near town to invite them personally."

"This week has already gotten busy," Megan started. "Looks like Emma and I will be the only ones in the garden and working over that hot stove canning."

Liz was about to finish another set of red triangles. "Abby, will you start the first visits right away?" she asked.

"Most likely toward the end of the week. I want to get the classroom ready first. I would like to start the older girls with some arithmetic without the young men around."

Abby leaned forward for another cookie and brushed a crumb from her lap.

"Will you use a quilt as you did before?" her younger sister asked. "It went so well when you used your basket sampler quilt. If you need any help, I'm available."

"Thank you, Emma, I'll let you know." Abby placed her sewing in the basket by her chair and let out a sigh. "I have so much to attend to. It would be nice to find someone who would make some donations for the school. There are so many things we need."

"Have you thought about writing back east for some help?" Liz asked.

"Yes, I just need to write the letter."

Anna finished gathering up her piecing work into her woven basket. "I'll be able to help you with most all of that this week, and I can give you a map of the homes you need to call on. Maybe Parker can even help you later this week."

Liz sighed. Anna was proving to be a good friend to the Mailly women. The time spent together with friends sewing and chatting was a treasure.

"Before I go," Anna said with a serious expression, "I must tell you that I'm very concerned about the county records. It's such a very touchy issue and it's not over yet. Parker and Tex have spoken a great deal about it lately. One man from Birdville was badly injured. Parker has told me to be aware of my surroundings and to be very careful. It could be a while before all this is settled. For the time being, the records are hidden away in case someone tries to steal them again."

Liz added to the story. "Luke went with the men when they left a few days ago. I had no idea just how dangerous the circumstances actually were or I might never have let him go along. Thomas left that morning and I wasn't thinking about any trouble other than my own. As you know, it was several days before they all returned safely and Luke said there were a lot of fighting words exchanged, some fists, and even gunfire." Liz nodded her head at Anna. "Tex and Samuel have gone to Austin to try to settle things legally. Thank goodness we have Samuel's expertise on our side. Jackson and Colt have stayed in the Birdville area to keep an eye on things until Tex returns, hopefully with good news that will settle things once and for all. With most of the men away we need to be on our toes and stay alert. It's a scary situation that won't be solved in a day."

Liz made a mental tally of the men who were left in town. Only four were still around to defend the town. Smithy and Grandpa Lucas were older men, and that only left Luke—not even a grown man himself—and Pastor Parker, a man of the cloth. The rest were gone or lived on the edges of town with their families. Farmers and cowboys came and went in and out of town every day, but they wouldn't necessarily be aware if the women were in danger.

This new information seemed to concern them all, and they ended their gathering on such a serious note.

※　※　※

Thomas had ridden tirelessly for days to get to the land office. He only had one thing on his mind: Making the land officially his—and hopefully Mrs. Bromont's, too. He thought of a number of ways to approach her upon his return, but none of them satisfied him.

What if she had placed the quilt on the porch and he had somehow missed it? It was still dark with another storm brewing when he rode out of town. What must she be thinking if she had put out the quilt, only to find him already gone?

Thomas gave the flanks of his horse a squeeze and urged her on to Fort Worth. He had ridden the pony pretty hard, and reluctantly decided to stop at the next creek to give her a drink and some needed rest. It wouldn't do him any good to lose his horse this close to the end of his journey.

He hoped that Liz had come to her senses over the weeks and that she felt just as anxious to see him as he was to see her. His mind flipped back and forth, never coming to a rest. How could one woman confuse him so? This definitely was not as easy as he thought it would be. In fact, if love was always this hard, he didn't figure he'd missed a thing by not tying the knot sooner.

Thomas had never been in this part of Texas and it reminded him a lot of his home in Louisiana. He enjoyed riding among the trees that hung heavy with vines, moss dripping from the branches.

This was the legendary Sam Houston territory. Houston was instrumental in creating the government of this state, already rich in history and pride. The settlers retained tremendous spirit and guts, and Thomas reveled in the gratification that oozed from the pores of the Texans. This unusual state had flown flags under Spain, France, Mexico, and at one time was a nation of its own. Since 1845, it had flown the American flag, and the brave and loyal people of Texas called it the Lone Star State. Thomas felt proud to be a part of it, and excited that he could officially call it home now that his land title had been filed.

As he rode over the ridge, he spotted some unexpected riders. From a distance, he felt certain he recognized Tex and Samuel watering their horses and filling canteens in the shade of a few live oaks. His horse neighed at the sight of the others and their tails swished at the random fly that buzzed their hide.

Tex lifted his head as he heard the animals and appeared happily surprised to see Thomas coming toward the watering hole. Samuel came around the far side of his horse to look toward the approaching rider. He moved his hand away from his gun belt when he recognized Thomas.

"What brings you this far south, Mr. Bratcher?" Samuel asked. "Looks like you are headed north to Fort Worth."

Thomas threw his leg over the back of his horse and stepped down. He shook the hands of his friends and let his animal drink from the creek with the others.

"Yeah, I'm on my way home. I've been to Houston to the land office to file the papers on some land I just purchased." Thomas patted the vest pocket on his left side. "It's a great piece just north and east of Fort Worth."

"Did you have any problems?" Tex, being a lawman, wanted to know.

"No, and by the way, thanks for referring me to Big Moe." Thomas slapped Tex on the back and smiled. It was good to be among men he knew. "Big Moe was just as his name suggested. Big!"

Tex chuckled and shook his head in agreement. His horse stamped his front hoof in the dirt a few times.

"How are things with you?"

Tex answered, "Good. We are on our way back to Fort Worth as well. Samuel and I went to Austin to see if we could settle the county record issue. But I'm afraid we didn't make any progress. The authorities told us that it has to be settled among the counties. I'm concerned that there will be a tussle. Someone could get hurt before this is eventually settled."

Samuel took one more drink from the canteen and then reached down into the cool stream for a refill. "I can try to defuse the situation by drawing up a legal document, but if Birdville won't sign it, well, we'll just have to wait it out."

Thomas had completely let it slip his mind. Fort Worth could be in a battle and the Mailly women were smack-dab in the middle. He assumed that there were others there if the need arose.

"How long do you think?" Thomas asked, not caring which one answered. He looked from the old Ranger to the lawyer.

"Could take years to settle," Tex answered as he checked the hoof of his painted mare. "How far are we from home?" Thomas asked.

"With hard riding, maybe by late afternoon tomorrow," Tex said, ready to saddle up.

Thomas filled his canteen, went behind a bush to relieve himself, and was up on his horse before Samuel.

"I have been away for two weeks. Which men are left at the fort?" Thomas asked as the three began to ride.

"I'm not sure, but I would guess Pastor Parker, Smithy, and our two newcomers, Lucas and Luke," Tex replied. "I think your men went for more freight, and Jackson is with Colt close to Birdville keeping an eye on the situation."

Samuel remarked, "Two old men, a preacher, and a young boy still wet behind the ears. The county seat resides with whoever has the records. As far as we know, Pastor Parker has them hidden in a safe, public place in Fort Worth."

Samuel had just given information that could get the women killed. Thomas wondered where the safe place mentioned was and just who knew about it.

Thomas looked at Tex and asked, "Are you concerned about the welfare of the fort?"

"I could be."

CHAPTER 22

Liz woke early that next morning, dressed quickly, and went across the yard to the store. She felt somewhat revived, ready to accomplish some things on her list. Hard work and staying busy were the best way to keep her mind and emotions in order. She might just work herself to the bone by the time Thomas returned. If he ever did.

Liz proceeded briskly up the back steps and unlocked the door, returning the key to her dress pocket. The store apron she wore hung on a peg near the back door where she'd left it the day before. She shut the door and pulled the frock over her head in one swift motion then stood tying it in the back before walking out to the front where she planned to rearrange the display of yard goods and sewing notions.

First, she poured the buttons into a crock and set them aside. Then she placed the spools of thread into a wooden box that had once held cheese. She pulled a note pad from her pocket to make a reminder to order more thread in tan and trouser brown. The women here were industrious and her thread supply was getting low.

She needed a table on which she could place supplies, and she thought of the perfect solution. Several barrels used by the cavalry had been left behind, and Liz used them to create a long table in the middle of the store. She pushed, pulled, and rolled the barrels into just the right spot before she added long boards to create a surface. She soon put together a nice display, just in time for the arrival of her first customers of the day.

Liz stood back admiring her work. Tall bolts of fabric lined the floor in between the barrels of the newly made table. Above, smaller flat folds of fabric were attractively displayed on one end of the shelf. She arranged needles and other notions temptingly. Finally, the finished sewing collection was complete.

The sun hovered above the front window, indicating that the time had come to open for the day. Liz felt satisfied being a merchant, and she took pride in her work. She enjoyed the bookkeeping, ordering the inventory, and she especially liked the conversation with her customers.

Keeping the store clean and neat was also to her liking. There simply was not enough work at the house with four grown women on hand to attend to the chores. She loved to sew, but she couldn't do it all day like her sister, Megan. Someday, she hoped Megan would open her millinery and dress shop right next door. Liz's thoughts strayed for a moment as she imagined the hats and dresses.

Maybe even a door placed between them would be nice so that they could move back and forth without going outside to do it. She would ask Thomas about it, she thought, and then remembered that Thomas was not around to ask anything of, and she wondered if he ever would be again.

Suddenly, she heard footsteps approaching on the boards outside the front door of the mercantile. Liz squared her shoulders and chased away her thoughts of Thomas. She unlocked the red doors and welcomed her first customer of the day. She stole a peek down the road but only saw the sun settling in for another warm Texas day. Liz ran her hand across the top of her damp lip and scolded herself for forgetting her hanky.

"Good morning, I'm Mrs. Perkins. It's a fine day today. You must be Mrs. Bromont."

The round, older woman seemed energetic and very friendly. Once the introductions and pleasantries were exchanged, Liz got busy filling a long list of supplies for her new customer. Some of the items she didn't have but knew they were coming on the next wagon, and Liz promised to have Luke bring them out to her.

Before she knew it, the morning was gone and her stomach began to growl. She had been in such a hurry that morning when she left the house, she didn't even grab a piece of bread. Customers had come and gone all morning, keeping her busy filling list after list. She sat for a moment recording the transactions in her ledger and organizing the items to be sent on the next freight wagon.

Mr. Wilton wanted a new stove for his wife right away. She wondered how his wife had prepared such appetizing dishes at the church gathering without one. Mr. Wilton had assured her that this was her first after ten years of marriage, and he wanted to surprise her with the thoughtful gift. Liz thought it would have been more thoughtful if he had done it several years back, although she was grateful for the business and excited that Fanny would soon have a new stove.

Luke burst through the back door. "Where are the nails, Maw? We need more nails. Grandpa is putting on those extra rooms."

Luke's hair was ruffled and sawdust stuck to the sweaty areas of his face. He was handsome and looked like his father, Liz noted. Looking closely at him, she realized again how much he had grown. Since their arrival, he'd been sleeping at the barracks with the men and working with them each day. Liz stood in amazement at the boy-turned-man standing in front of her.

"Nails, Maw, where did you stock the nails?" he asked again, looking at the shelves.

Liz went to the correct location and took down a box. "How many do you need?" she asked with another box in her hand.

"That's good. Thanks, Maw." He took the boxes from her and smiled, heading out the back door in a flash.

Liz followed him to the back door to have a look at the addition being added to the house they now called home. Grandpa placed a board across a tree stump. He motioned for Luke to hold the end as he began to saw. Liz enjoyed watching her two favorite men working together. Her only son was almost grown; in another year, he would be as tall as his father had been. Luke's hair was even lighter now, as the sun had bleached it. His face was Texas tanned, and his pant legs were growing short over his boots. He certainly did look like his father, but he acted just like his Grandpa and Thomas.

He's turning into such a fine man, she thought. *I hope we can get him to complete at least two more years of school.*

Liz looked up and saw Megan coming to the mercantile carrying a basket. She stepped out the door to welcome her sister inside.

"Thank you for bringing me some lunch. I left this morning without a thing to eat for either meal. You are a dear!"

Liz took the basket from her sister and peered inside. The cloth was neatly tucked inside holding fried chicken, biscuits, garden vegetables, and a jar of sweet tea.

"Before I eat, I need to go out back. Can you watch the store for a quick minute?"

Megan nodded and turned to go up front as Liz quickly went down the back steps to the outhouse, leaving Megan standing there admiring the new sewing display. She heard the red door jingle as she left and turned back to spot a dusty, bearded man she had not met coming into the store.

"Good afternoon," she heard Megan greet him. "How can I help you?"

When Liz returned a few minutes later, she walked in to find the man looking Megan over as if she were a pig on a spit, and he glanced past her toward the back room.

"I need some bullets and some of that sweet stuff there," he said just as his unwashed stench drifted into Liz's nostrils.

She thought he pointed to the peppermint sticks setting on the counter by Megan's hand. He looked at her with a curl on his lips that made Liz think of a snake before it pounces on a mouse. A chill went between her shoulder blades.

Where is that gun? Liz thought, standing in the doorway completely undetected.

Another man stood out front with his back to the store window.

How do I handle two outlaws? Liz thought. *And how do I do it without Megan getting hurt?*

"What do you have in the back?" he asked in a rough tone.

Megan ignored his question, and the bearded man smiled and his teeth disgusted Liz. The revolting smell of him reached Liz as he leaned across the counter toward her sister.

"We could go in the back and have a little fun. My friend will keep anyone from bothering us. It won't take much time. You're a pretty little thing. Smell nice, too."

She forced her mind to stay calm while her heart thumped clear out of her chest.

Think, how do I get us out of this?

She remembered the boxes of ammunition in the storeroom, and pictured the shotgun Luke had hung on a rack on the wall beside them, and the two Colt revolvers in the metal cabinet under the counter.

In the most innocent voice Megan could muster, and with her best Southern accent, she lied. "Why, aren't you a charmer, but I do think my new husband, being a Texas Ranger and all, would look badly upon our new friendship. Just a few weeks ago at our church picnic, a cowboy offered me a chair and I thought Jackson would kill him right there on the spot. He beat him black and blue before the pastor and all God's people. I surely would hate for that fate to come upon you. I expect him any minute now."

Liz stood there, frozen, waiting for everything Megan had said to sink into that small brain he seemed to have. He glanced at the door and his eyes landed on Liz. She didn't know if he smiled at her, or smirked.

"Jackson, who works with Tex, is your husband?" he said with a different tone to his voice.

Liz wanted to lift her hands and praise Jesus right there and then. She hoped he quivered with fright and respect for the Rangers that he obviously knew rode these parts.

He grabbed a couple of peppermint sticks from the counter, threw down some coins without asking for the change, and turned to leave.

When he reached the door, he looked back at Liz. She felt positive that under that unruly beard he had snarled at her. The door swung shut and Megan's hand went up to her face in a prayerful stance as she sat down on a stool behind the counter. Her forehead was in her hand as she took a deep breath of fresh air. "Thank you, God!" she cried.

Liz rushed into the storeroom and returned with two loaded Colts. She placed one under the register, where it belonged, and the other under her apron.

"Megan, are you okay?" Liz placed her arm around Megan's shoulder. "You were wonderful. I'm so sorry the Colt wasn't where it should have been."

Megan raised her head and weakly smiled at her older sister. "When did you even come in? I didn't hear you."

"I came in when just before you played that monster like a fiddle. That was very quick thinking!" Liz started to chuckle as she thought back on Megan's acting. "Do you even know Jackson's last name?"

Megan laughed and released some tension. "No, I don't. I'm glad he wasn't quick-witted, or we would have been in some real trouble."

"That wasn't real trouble?" Liz picked up the coins lying by the ledger and flipped them in her hand. "Well, at least we made a profit from those bandits."

"Do we need to tell the others?"

"Maybe." Lowering her voice to a whisper, she added, "With Grandpa Lucas's gold hiding under the stairs and the county records hidden here, I guess we'll need to be on guard at all times."

"I don't think he will be back," Megan said. "But you never know."

Both women looked to the front of the store to see if anyone was on the sidewalk.

"I've been so busy today. Do you think they just happened to come into the store when no one else was here? Or do you suppose they've been watching the mercantile?" Liz wondered out loud.

"I'm going to tell Grandpa Lucas right now and see what he thinks. Be careful. I'll check back in a little while." With a grin, Megan added,

"Tomorrow, you bring your own lunch!"

Megan turned to leave and went out the back door as if nothing had happened.

Liz checked both revolvers again and walked to the front with her broom. She could scout out the street while she swept the boardwalk. Hopefully, the men had moved on. And while she was hoping, she hoped Thomas would come back soon.

Liz swept the boardwalk—as well as her mind, which buzzed with thoughts about Thomas—but her eyes remained steadfast on her sur-roundings. She made several passes, barely noticing that the walk had been spick-and-span since her first run at it.

When a pair of boots made a loud whack on the boardwalk, Liz jumped, clearly anxious.

"Grandpa! You about scared the life out of me," she exclaimed, hold-ing the broom handle like a weapon.

Grandpa Lucas raised his hands in surrender. "I'm sorry," he said. "Didn't mean to frighten you. Heard you two had a scare this morning!" Lucas placed a hand on his granddaughter's shoulder and looked into her eyes. "When you leave tonight, I'll come over and help you lock up. We don't need to be taking any chances. The others will be around soon and we'll see what Tex has to say. Seems they already had the acquaintance of the Rangers. Tex will know if they're trouble or not. Think I'll talk to Parker about some sort of nightly guard duty until we iron a few things out."

Liz listened and understood, nodding her head in agreement. She started to sweep the top step, thinking that her grandfather was finished.

Lucas paused. "Heard I got one granddaughter married off today."

Liz stopped sweeping, remembering what Megan had said earlier about Jackson.

"How does it look for the other one?"

Liz sat on the step and released a bewildered sigh. "I don't know. I seem to have a problem communicating with Thomas. I don't mean to cause him so much pain. He just always expects me to do things his way.

He's so good to me, sweet and kind, Grandpa. But he just has an opinion about *everything.* Sometimes I think the only way we can get along is for me to keep my mouth shut."

Her grandfather plunked down to the step beside her. "That must be rough, him having an opinion on everything that way."

She glared at him, understanding the unspoken jab beneath what he'd said.

"I'm not supposed to have my own opinions then?"

"Liz, you're both adults, you will find a way. Marry Thomas and have fun figuring it out. Don't waste precious time. Every day is a gift from God. You know that. I wish I had one more day with your grandmother." He was quiet for a moment. "Do you think you can grow to love Thomas?"

"Yes, I do. Grandpa, he asked me to put the quilt he gave me as a gift out on the chair on the back porch if I wanted to marry him. But I overslept. And when I realized he rode away and didn't see the quilt, I . . . I knew then how much I care for him."

"Then, for goodness sakes, marry the man as soon as he returns."

Lucas gave her a quick hug as he stood to go. "See you at closing time."

Liz silently thanked the Lord for such a loving relationship with her grandfather. Her best memories involved figuring life out with him. She would never forget all the advice he gave her while sitting out on the steps of the old porch back in Lecompte.

Liz's afternoon didn't ease up after the frightening incident. Thankfully though, the busy day helped push away thoughts of Thomas and the quilt, the men being away, and how afraid she had been. Each time the bell on the door jingled with a customer's arrival, Liz gladly looked up to see who it was. Before she knew it, the time had arrived to close the store. She pulled the wooden stool up to the register counter and went through the day's transactions, entering them into the ledger.

She drew a line at the bottom of the sheet as she completed the final bookkeeping and suppressed a squeal. It had been their most prosperous day so far! The order book had three pages of necessary supplies. A smile formed on her lips as she thought back to Fanny's new stove and how proud her husband had been to order it for his wife. Liz enjoyed being part of the secret. It made her feel closer to the people of Fort Worth somehow. Liz looked to the door, wondering when her grandfather would return. She wanted to tell him about the sales for the day and to find out about the next freight wagon. She flipped the pencil back and forth in her slender fingers.

The sun sinking beyond the side window signaled that the workday had officially ended. She closed her accounting ledger and placed it below the shelf next to her pistol. A copper-colored bag with a drawstring at the top would hold the day's profits. She thought to herself how Lucas really needed to build them a vault soon, since Fort Worth didn't have a bank and the closest one was quite a distance away.

As she tossed the bag full of coins and bills next to the ledger and the gun, she realized that the front door still remained unlocked. The clock chimed, and Liz expected her grandfather at any moment. Her view of the house out back was obstructed from where she stood; if her grandfather was coming across the way, she didn't see him.

Just as she reached out to turn the lock on the red doors, the two filthy men from earlier pushed their way in and pressed a long gun barrel into her ribs. Liz fell backward and landed on a pickle barrel. The skinny man who had stood out front grabbed her by the chin with one hand and squeezed her face so hard that her teeth cut into her cheek. She could barely breathe.

CHAPTER 23

W here's the money?" the man growled at Liz as he leaned down, applying more pressure. His foul breath assailed her nostrils, but she couldn't turn away. The tall, thin man squeezed harder and shook her head as if the answer would tumble out of her open mouth. The larger one kicked the door shut and moved closer.

"This one's different," he said, bearing down upon her with his bloodshot eyes.

The way he looked at Liz made her feel as if she had nothing on. It repulsed her and at the same time truly frightened her. He waved his gun at Liz with one hand and ripped her dress sleeve to reveal a bare shoulder with the other.

Liz smelled his filthy stench and realized that the skinny one had released her face. She rubbed her numb cheek and tried to breathe, but it didn't come easily. Willing the pain to go away, she tasted fresh blood in her mouth. She tried to inch backwards without being noticed, away from the men. Within seconds, though, the big one had his hands around her neck, picking her off the ground, the toes of her black boots barely touching the wood floor.

He growled at her as he held her against a support post. "You can give us what we want, or we can have some real fun and just do it our way."

His dirty calloused hand held her firmly around the neck, blocking her air. It became harder and harder to focus, but the fleeting thought that this had nothing to do with the county records fluttered through her humming mind. *God, please help me!* she prayed.

The big man loosened his grip slightly and she instantly grabbed a gulp of much-needed air. The oxygen allowed her brain to clear enough that she thought to reach for the gun under her apron. He stood just a step away from her and didn't notice her movements.

The skinny man looked to the red doors and reached to turn the lock. He came closer to her and repeated, "Where's the money?"

Liz thought he looked more evil than anything she had ever seen before. Clearly, they would kill her without a thought. Her fingers found the gun under the apron and she pointed it at the big man's gut and squeezed the trigger. The Colt went off and both men looked at her, not knowing from where the shot had come. The big, stinking man loosened his grip completely and fell to the floor, pinning Liz under him as he fell.

A hole had burned through Liz's apron, and the man's blood had splattered across her. She knew she had to get up and pull the trigger once again, and his blood on her was of no consequence at all, nor was the dead man lying across her. The only thought she had was to stop the skinny man from moving toward the back of the store and absconding with her money.

She knew he would try to get the bag holding the day's proceeds, and that he wouldn't think a thing about killing her afterward. As he moved, he knocked over the display she had made earlier that day, and buttons flew across the floor like ants scurrying from an ant hill that had been kicked. Just as he reached the register, two gunshots blasted through the store. Liz scrambled to her knees as the smoke cleared.

Horror struck her heart as she saw that two more men had sprawled across the wooden floor of the mercantile, both of them covered in blood. One of those men . . . was her grandfather.

Liz scrambled across the floor toward her Grandpa Lucas, looking for either of the robbers' guns as she crawled. Liz stayed low until she finally spotted the gun of the skinny man and slid it under the denim display.

He's not moving. She continued across the floor on her knees until she reached Lucas. "Grandpa," she cried. "Are you all right? Tell me you're all right, please."

Dear Lord, this is too much blood, she prayed.

Tears streaming down her face, she took hold of his hand as he struggled to get a breath. She wanted to embrace and comfort him but didn't know where to touch him safely.

"What . . . should I do?"

Lucas fluttered his eyes and then squeezed them shut as he winced in pain. He lifted his head a little, taking in the quiet mercantile after so much calamity only moments earlier.

"Are they dead?" he asked before letting his head drop down again.

Liz looked back at the two men and said, "I think so." She could barely make out their bodies through her tears.

She tore a section of her petticoat with her teeth and quickly folded it, looking for the source of so much blood loss. His thick crimson blood pooled around her, making it hard to find where it originated. Lucas moaned when she applied pressure to the left side of his chest.

"Don't you dare leave me, Grandpa!" Liz begged as she tore at the edge of her petticoat again. "We'll get you some help! It'll just be a minute. Just stay with me."

Liz tried to gain a little control, but the flow of blood continued to saturate the petticoat bandage.

Lucas's voice was weak as he spoke. "Liz, take care of the others. Remember where your strength comes from."

"No!" she sobbed. "Grandpa, noooo! Please, please don't go. We need you here with us."

Liz whimpered and leaned down to him, her dress soaking up his life blood. She wrapped her arms around his thick neck and draped her body across his chest.

"You can't leave me," she cried. "Don't leave me, Grandpa."

He stuttered out his last words. "Liz, the death angel is here for me. I see him in his white robe and the pearly gates are behind him." He coughed, more blood coming from his mouth, his words slurred, "Marry Thomas, child. You need each other." His eyes began to shut and he whispered, "Don't worry, Elizabeth. I hear music. My Claire is waiting there for me."

Liz fell completely limp across him. She heard the emptiness echo as his heartbeat slowed and then stopped, and she felt his last breath leave his body.

Her own cries howled as if they had been thrown into a barrel in some distant location.

⁂ ⁂ ⁂

The sun hung low in the sky as riders anxiously approached home, at last. Thomas, Tex, and Samuel had ridden together for two days. They didn't talk much, but Thomas had begun to appreciate Samuel a little more as he got to know him better over the course of their ride. It turned out that Samuel owned land for a ranch not too far from where Thomas planned to build his own.

The motion of the horses as they galloped hypnotized Thomas and took him deep into his own thoughts, which placed him back in the land office in Houston.

The door had jingled as he entered, and the man with round glasses peered up at him from his desk. "Be right with you, mister," he said, adjusting the bill of his hat. Thomas watched the little man as he continued with the work in front of him and dipped his pen into the inkwell three more times before looking up at Thomas again. "Welcome to the Texas Land Office. What county are you filing in?"

The man's spectacles sat perched on the end of his long, pointed nose, and he looked at Thomas over them. He couldn't help thinking that the man resembled a rat. "Denton County," Thomas had responded.

The man pulled out a new form and dipped his pen. He held it firmly and began to fill in the lines. Within the hour, Thomas had filed on his land.

"I need to send a letter. Can I borrow a paper and pen?" Thomas asked the clerk. The man reached into his desk and pulled out a clean sheet and pen with an inkwell. "You can write over there." He motioned to a counter by a window.

Thomas looked out to a busy city. Horses and people, all in a hurry to go somewhere. He knew the quiet ranchland he had purchased was exactly what he wanted. He couldn't imagine ever longing for the hum of city life. He looked forward to sharing his excitement with Liz, Lucas, and the rest of the family. The time he was away made him forget his anger of days ago.

Thomas had picked up his pen and began to write:

Found land to purchase in Denton County. It is north of Fort Worth, where we are now. Ready for the total amount of my belongings. Send it with the next freight wagon leaving Saint Louis. Also please arrange for my inheritance and all items to be shipped as soon as possible. Thanks. Your nephew, Thomas W. Bratcher.

Thomas read the letter over again and folded it into the envelope. He addressed the outside and sealed it shut.

"Where can I post this letter?" he asked, and the clerk motioned with an ink-stained finger.

"Down the street a ways." He rubbed his nose, and now it had ink on it. Thomas smiled as he tipped his hat to bid goodbye.

Samuel asked Tex a question, bringing Thomas back from his daydream.

"We'll be in Fort Worth within the hour," Tex answered.

Thomas began to recognize the countryside, and he enjoyed the landscape as much as he had the first time. His own land looked much like this, and he could hardly wait to begin construction on a homestead there. He felt like a real Texan-in-the-making as he mulled over his plans of breeding fine horses and cattle and thought about where exactly he would place their house. Did he want it to face the west or east? He even pondered where Liz might want to put the henhouse.

It was easy to think on the back of a horse.

Tex yanked the reins and exclaimed, "Hey, men! I think that's gunfire!"

The three riders jabbed their spurs at the flanks of their mounts, leaned close to their mares, and took off. They rode hard over the last hill toward Fort Worth.

Suddenly, Thomas realized shots had indeed been fired.

※　※　※

As Thomas, Tex, and Samuel rode into the dirt streets of Fort Worth, they saw a commotion in front of the mercantile. Immediately, Thomas's heart lurched. Horses stood silently without riders, and people that Thomas didn't recognize turned to look at them. Thomas instinctively knew something bad had happened. He could feel it hanging about the crowd and over his gut like a steel beam. Everyone in the street watched as the three rode up, and Thomas leapt from his horse first.

Tex pulled his gun and cautiously looked around. Gunpowder hung in the air, and Thomas drew his weapon as well. The red doors swung open and Pastor Parker came out with a stunned look of disbelief. He scanned the crowd, noticing that Tex, Samuel, and Thomas had returned.

Thomas took the steps of the mercantile three at a time and stood there facing the pastor. When instinct propelled him toward the front door, Pastor Parker placed his hand on Thomas's shoulder.

"Liz is inside and she needs you, Thomas. Lucas was killed, along with two strangers."

Thomas shoved through the doors and searched for Liz. He stepped over a dead man and found her crumpled in the back corner of the room beside Lucas's still and motionless body. She rocked back and forth, weeping with no sound. Only the occasional gasp of breath on her lips betrayed her, and her shoulders convulsed.

Blood covered his beautiful Liz. He couldn't tell if it was hers or not, and Thomas fell to his knees beside her.

Megan was on her knees at her grandfather's head, with one arm on Liz's shoulder and the other arm under Lucas's neck, weeping quietly. Abby and Emma stood by the back door of the mercantile, quietly in shock, tears streaming down their faces. Abby held the edge of her apron and used it to stop the tears at her chin. A thick trail of blood trickled past them on the wood floor and dripped down the back step. Thomas knew they had never witnessed anything like this in their young lives.

Luke stood like a fence post just beyond Abby and Emma with his hands jammed down in his pockets, his face ashen in color. When his gaze met Thomas's, he kicked at a rock and took off running to the woods by the cavalry barracks.

Thomas saw his mentor, a man he loved and respected, lying on the crimson-stained wooden floor. He looked to his left at the register and saw another dead man he didn't know with the copper-colored register bag lying open on the floor next to him. A few coins had spilled out. After surveying what he saw, it didn't take him long to figure out that the men had tried to rob the mercantile. Thomas looked back to Liz and saw that her dress had been torn. He prayed to God that the men hadn't done anything to her, and anger began to swell inside him.

Thomas helped her stand and she became limp in his arms. She had no words, and he couldn't blame her. She buried her face in his chest and whimpered.

Thomas stepped back for a moment and looked her over. Covered in blood, from her face to dress, she looked as if she'd been painting that red door of hers. She looked small and broken, almost unrecognizable, and Thomas wrapped her up in his arms and held her close to him, rocking her from one side to the other.

"Thomas—oh, Thomas—" she croaked, and the pain in her voice was enough to break Thomas too. He worked hard to hold back his own tears as she continued to repeat his name again and again. "Thomas—oh, Thomas—"

When she started to trail off to silence, he reached one arm out to comfort Megan, and the two Wilkes cousins who hovered at the back entry moved toward him as well.

"Come here," he reassured them. "Come to me."

He unexpectedly found that his arms were long enough to encircle all four women, with Liz at the center of the circle pressed against his pounding heart. The women felt wilted in his embrace, and Thomas felt slightly wilted himself. Shocked by the scene in front of him, he made a conscious decision to stuff his own personal grief deep down inside in order to help this family survive this tragedy. He was now responsible for them. They were in shock and would feel the loss of Lucas Mailly for the rest of their lives. Thomas knew he would feel the loss almost as horribly.

Tex timidly approached the group and offered his sympathy to the Mailly family.

Thomas looked to Tex and asked, "Will you go after Luke? He ran off in the direction of the old barracks. Make sure he's all right and bring him here to me?"

"I'll see if I can find him and make sure he's okay." Tex nodded his head and walked to the door and spoke to the pastor and Samuel before the three of them headed off with conviction in their eyes. Thomas spoke softly to his group of women. He knew they needed to get to the house and out of the mercantile.

"What can I do?" Anna blurted, and Thomas sighed out of sheer relief.

"Do you think you can help me get the women out of here? And Liz will need a hot bath and a change of clothing. Megan, too."

Anna nodded, and she looked more than ready to take on a task in the name of helping her new friends.

"Abby, Emma," she said with her arms outstretched toward them. "Come with me, darlings."

"I want to leave this place and never come back," Abby wailed, and she wriggled into Anna's embrace.

"Let's get you and your sister over to the house," Anna said, and Thomas marveled at her ability to remain calm in the midst of such a horrendous storm. "Liz, Megan? Can you come with me?"

Megan followed silently, her eyes wide, and Thomas realized how shocked she was. When Anna tried to nudge Liz along with them, she whined and tightened her grip on Thomas.

"Go ahead," he told her. "I'll bring Liz along."

Megan took one last look over to her grandfather and asked, "Thomas, can we go out the front?"

Thomas nodded and wrapped his arm around her shoulder before leading both of the sisters through the front door. Anna led Abby and Emma ahead of them, and Abby reached for her sister's hand as they passed the first dead intruder. Emma stopped for a moment and angrily spat on him before she continued.

A group of people gathered on the street as the evening sun faded to twilight. The night sounds began their somber prairie symphony. Women dabbed their eyes and men held their hats in their hands. One small boy hid in his mother's skirt. Thomas observed all of this in slow motion as he led Liz and Megan home.

At the back door of the small porch, Thomas stopped in his tracks as he saw the quilt spread out across the chair. Abby saw him as he noticed it and she managed a weary, fragmented smile. His mind went back to the morning that he had saddled up and left Fort Worth, and his heart heaved under the heavy weight of the memory.

"It's been there the whole time," Abby told him, and Megan lifted her head and looked him in the eyes, simply nodding her agreement.

Inside, Emma started the teakettle while Anna went with Liz and Megan to help them begin the arduous task of removing the last living traces of a man so deeply imbedded in their lives from their clothes and skin.

Anna turned back to him at the door. "Thomas, I will see about things here. I'm prepared to stay the night. Parker and Tex could probably use your help back at the store." She leaned toward him and touched his arm. "There was nothing you could do, even if you had been here. God is good, and He will get us through this tragedy."

Thomas stood on the back porch in the new darkness. His chest felt close and heavy. He had let this family down with his own stubborn foolishness. He hung his head and took a deep, shaky breath. As he started to the mercantile, he stopped at the quilt and ran his hand over the catalyst, the reminder of the chain of events that led to such disaster.

If it had been on the porch, would he have been here to save Lucas? The thought made him sick and full of misgivings.

CHAPTER 24

The group around the breakfast table remained silent when Tex and Samuel tapped lightly at the door. Liz flooded with relief when Anna opened it to let them inside. She poured steaming cups of coffee and offered them a chair.

Thomas walked in just as they cautiously took their first sips. He leaned on the cupboard behind Tex.

"We know of those two outlaws, suspect them in two other robberies and three murders. Never thought that they would be put down by a woman and her grandfather."

Tex paused for a moment before he continued. He looked away, and Liz saw that he held back his own emotion. He tapped his boot and twisted his mouth around the words of loss that followed.

"I'm real sorry about your grandfather, ladies. I enjoyed working with him. He thought highly of all of you." Tex smiled. "I thought for the longest time that he had all grandsons. I would have never known from the way he spoke that you would be women."

Samuel spoke next. "Parker and Smithy have Lucas at the church." He swallowed and cleared his throat. "He looks real peaceful."

Liz swiped at the unyielding rivulet of tears that washed her face. Abby handed her a fresh, embroidered hanky with an "A" on the corner.

"Pastor Parker is planning to have a prayer service at the church before the burial. Will that be fine?" Samuel asked soberly.

"Thank you, Samuel," Megan replied. "Just let me know the time and we'll be there."

⁂ ⁂ ⁂

A few gray clouds lumbered across the sky as Lucas Mailly's friends and family stood by the open grave. Lucas had not been in Texas long, but the local folks had already come to care about this new family. Pastor Parker opened with words of praise that pinched Liz's heart.

"Blessed by God, even the Father of our Lord Jesus Christ, the Father of mercies, and the God of al comfort; who comforteth us in all our tribulation, that we may be able to comfort them which are in any trouble. Blessed are they that mourn for they shall be comforted. God shall wipe away all sorrow, crying, and pain." Parker paused for a moment and cleared the huskiness from his throat. "If you have a relationship with Jesus, you will see Lucas again. We can rejoice in that. If you do not, you have a real reason to mourn, for you will never see Lucas Mailly again."

Liz looked at the closed wooden box that held her beloved grandfather, wrapped in the last quilt his beloved Claire had made for him. Even from her grave, she comforted her husband with the warm brown and green hues of the timber trail quilt. Megan had suggested it as his burial cloth.

Sweet Anna Parker began to sing, and the crowd looked at her as she sang the inspirational song. Liz felt numb again to the world around her, but she somehow managed to bow her head to pray.

"God, I can't do this again. I don't want to put a wall around my heart. Please, sweep me away in Your love and comfort. I can't do this alone."

Liz's prayer fell silent with her head lowered when she heard the answer dropped into her soul, clear as a bell.

You are not alone. I am here in your sadness. I will carry you and comfort you. I am as close as your breath and I love you.

Liz knew that voice so well. She always felt amazed at the way God could talk to her so personally.

"Thank you, Father God," she whispered. "I love You, too."

She raised her head and took a small step closer to Thomas. Her gloved hand found his hand and she entwined her fingers with his.

Thomas looked down at her and she smiled weakly.

Liz looked at the crowd of people. Some of them she did not know at all, but they were there for her family. She began a silent prayer of thanksgiving for them all, and Liz could feel the strength coming back to her. She inhaled a deep breath of hope. She would be strong and comfort her family through this tragedy. She knew how to live through it, after all. She had done it before.

After all, she thought, *the Mailly family is a family woven together with threads of hope.*

A Word of Thanks

I want to thank God from whom all blessings flow. God had a plan for my life and he has a plan for yours. He states it over and over again in the book of Ephesians. When Jesus Christ walked the earth, He showed us how to live that life. Then the Holy Spirit helps you as you walk it out each day. He continues to pour out His promises and fulfill His Scripture. Thank You, Jesus. I'm so very grateful for Your storehouse of blessings!

ABOUT THE AUTHOR

J odi Barrows is an author, speaker, and quilting revolutionary. She speaks to quilting audiences throughout the United States and around the world, weaving in the story of the Mailly cousins as she goes. Her unique teaching method includes her Square in a Square quilting technique. Jodi has produced dozens of teaching tools and developed several fabric lines. Commissioned to compose quilts for state and national organizations, Jodi also worked with the Kansas Historical Society. She enjoys spending time with her family and her husband, Steve, her high school sweetheart. For more about Jodi, her novels, and the Square in Square method of quilting, go to her website at: www.squareinasquare. com.

FICTION FROM MOODY PUBLISHERS

River North Fiction is here to provide quality fiction that will refresh and encourage you in your daily walk with God. We want to help readers know, love, and serve JESUS through the power of story.

Connect with us at www.rivernorthfiction.com

- ✔ Blog
- ✔ Newsletter
- ✔ Free Giveaways

- ✔ Behind the scenes look at writing fiction and publishing
- ✔ Book Club

www.MoodyPublishers.com